'All right, skinny-gal!' Calamity said truculently. 'Happen you're so god-damned fancy footing, let's see how good *you* can dance.'

'Certainly,' Belle replied, raising her arms and putting her hands behind her head.

Moving with graceful dancing steps, the slender girl brought first her left and then the right elbow around sharply to land on the red head's cheeks. Letting out a yell of well simulated anger, Calamity swung her right fist to connect with Belle's jaw. Following the staggering Rebel Spy, she tore off and flung aside the togue to sink both hands into the short 'blonde' hair. Being treated in the same fashion, she pushed Belle backwards to fall on to a table and, while its occupants vacated it hurriedly, was brought down on top of her.

Screeching, tugging at hair, scattering bottles and glasses, the girls rolled across and caused the table to tip over. Still entangled, they were deposited on the floor. Churning over and over, putting considerable vigour into a far less skilful kind of brawling than either would generally have employed, they made the customers and employees who were gathering around yelling encouragement move out of the way and they disappeared under a chuck-a-luck table.

'Well, we've got us a fight going!' Calamity said quietly, between shrieked out curses. 'There's only one thing, though.'

'What's that?' Belle inquired *sotto voce*, employing similar tactics to avoid being overheard.

'Which of us's going to *win*?' the red head wanted to know.

Revised list of J. T. Edson titles in chronological order:

* *Awaiting Publication*

J T EDSON

THE WHIP AND THE WAR LANCE

CORGI BOOKS
A DIVISION OF TRANSWORLD PUBLISHERS LTD

THE WHIP AND THE WAR LANCE
A CORGI BOOK 0 552 10964 9

First publication in Great Britain

PRINTING HISTORY
Corgi edition published 1979

Copyright © J. T. Edson 1979

This book is set in 10/11pt Monotype Plantin

Corgi Books are published by Transworld Publishers Ltd.,
Century House, 61–63 Uxbridge Road,
Ealing, London, W.5.
Made and printed in Great Britain by
Hunt Barnard Printing Ltd., Aylesbury, Bucks.

For Nicola Gibbon, a 'orrible infant and the evil spirit of my 'spiritual home', the White Lion Hotel, Melton Mowbray, who assures me that she hates me more than she hates anybody else.

While complete in itself, the events recorded in this work continue from those which take place in THE REMITTANCE KID.
As usual, for the benefit of all new readers, but to save our 'regulars' from repetition, we have given the histories and special qualifications of Belle 'the Rebel Spy' Boyd and Martha 'Calamity' Jane Canary in the form of Appendices.

J. T. Edson,
Active Member, Western Writers of America
MELTON MOWBRAY,
Leics. England.

CHAPTER ONE

MAYBE RECKONS SHE'S *JAN-DARK*

'They're down in the valley, like I told you they'd be,' Roland Boniface announced, returning to where his two companions were sitting their horses. Gathering up the dangling reins which had served to ground hitch his own mount, he slipped his right foot into the stirrup iron and swung astride the saddle. 'But are you *sure* that you want to go through with this?'

'Of course I'm sure!' retorted Irène Beauville, at whom the question had been directed, without a moment's hesitation. 'Why do you think I told you to bring me here?'

'It's not wise!' Jacques Lacomb protested dolefully. '*M'sieur* Cavallier won't be pleased if anything goes wrong.'

'Let *me* worry about what will, or won't, please *le Loup-Garou, Vieux Malheureux,*' Irène commanded in an imperious fashion, although she conceded to herself that – in addition to living up to his nickname 'Old Miserable' – the elder of her companions was making a considerable understatement in his reference to how Arnaud 'the Werewolf' Cavallier would react should her intentions end in disaster. Thrusting the thought aside, as she had never been one to worry about what *might* happen when she had put her mind to something, she shook the weapon grasped in her right hand and continued, 'I'm the one who is going to have to use *this* when the time comes. So I want to be sure I'm able to.'

Although the trio on the ridge about ten miles north of the junction of the Red Deer and South Saskatchewan Rivers were speaking French, the side of the horse from which Boniface had mounted, and their appearances were more suggestive of Indian than Gallic origins. The sheaths of the knives, their belts, moccasins, and other items of attire were of Indian manufacture. 'Medicine' patterns made of brass tacks decorated the woodwork of the old Henry rifle resting across the crook of Lacomb's left arm.

All three sat their wiry, smallish horses with the relaxed, effortless-seeming grace of highly competent riders. Single cinched, with high, sharply curved cantles and pommels, the saddles were almost skeletal in design and had wooden trees to which rawhide had been shrunk. The animals were controlled and guided by hackamores. With a head-piece something like a bridle, a wide browband which could be slid down to act as a blindfold and a rawhide loop – known as a *bosal* – around the head immediately above the mouth serving in place of a bit, these resembled an ordinary halter except for having one piece reins instead of a lead rope. Such equipment was indicative of Indian rather than European equestrianism.

That there should be suggestions of two different racial cultures was not surprising. The trio were *Metis*; members of the race which had evolved in Canada – the name being a corruption of the French word, *metissage*, meaning miscegenation – as a result of marriages between *voyageurs*[1] and women belonging to the various Indian nations with whom they had come into contact.

Eldest of the three by a good twenty years, Jacques Lacomb also gave the clearest indications of possessing Indian blood as he slouched on the back of his kettle-bellied dun gelding. Short in stature, stocky of build, bareheaded, he had shoulder long straight black hair. Never pleasant or amiable, his features were aquiline, but also somewhat Mongoloid in appearance and of a deep coppery bronze pigmentation. At that moment, they were registering resentment over the disrespect shown to him by one who was only a mere woman in spite of the responsible function she had been selected to fulfil and which she was about to endanger needlessly. He wore plain, grease blackened buckskins. Only the scarlet Hudson's Bay 'Three Point' blanket draped over his shoulders, the rifle and the J. Russell and Co.

---

[1] 'Voyageur': *a boatman, or fur trader, generally of French-Canadian origin. J.T.E.*

'Green River' knife[2] in his Assiniboine Indian-made sheath were the products of the white side of his upbringing.

Tall, slender, yet wiry, Roland Boniface had light brown hair. It was just as long and straight as Lacomb's, but emerged from beneath a round topped black bearskin cap with flaps which could be lowered to protect the ears in cold weather. Although almost as deeply tanned, his fairly handsome face had blue eyes and a moustache to make it seem more Gallic than Indian. He had on a fairly clean elkskin shirt emblazoned by red, white and blue medicine symbols, but his nether garments, ending in the calf high leggings of his Blackfoot-style moccasins, were a pair of dark blue British Army riding breeches. In addition to his 'Green River' knife, he carried a Colt 1860 Army revolver butt forward in a cavalry holster, from which the flap had been cut, at the right side of his belt. The Winchester Model of 1866 carbine he was drawing from the boot of his leggy roan stallion's saddle was unadorned.

By the standards of either race, Irène Beauville could be regarded as an exceptionally fine example of feminine pulchritude. Close to five foot eight inches in height, she was in her mid-twenties. Unlike her companions, she had her tawny almost blonde hair cut short. Less deeply tanned than either of the men, she had grey eyes and her features, while warning of her arrogant nature, had an aquiline beauty. She wore a dyed horse-hair shirt which clung to the twin mounds of her imposing bosom and slender waist in a way which showed it alone covered them. Curvaceous hips and well muscled thighs filled the fringed buckskin trousers just as adequately. There was a Plains Cree Indian bear-claw necklace about her throat and each wrist was graced by a wide Navajo silver and turquoise bracelet. The eight inch bladed, Alfred Hunter 'Bowie' knife had a fancy bone handle and German silver mountings. Although it had been made in Sheffield, England, it was no less

[2] *This very popular kind of all purpose knife was first manufactured at Greenfield, Massachusetts – on the banks of the Green River – in 1834. The maker's name, 'J. Russell & Co./Green River Works' was inscribed along the blade just below the guard of the hilt. This gave rise to the expression 'give him it up to the Green River', meaning to kill, as any knife driven so deeply into a human adversary was likely to prove fatal whether the inscription was there or not. J.T.E.*

an efficient weapon than those carried by the two men.

All in all, Irène's appearance was striking as she sat straight backed and proud on the small, well built paint gelding. However, the men of her people having strong views on the proprieties and the status of a woman in their society, her attire was to say the least unconventional. She had never been unduly troubled by the possibility of offending masculine suscep- tibilities and, being so well regarded by *le Loup-Garou*, she no longer needed to concern herself over whether they approved of her dress and behaviour or not.

The knife was not the girl's only armament. However, despite being decorated by a clump of eagle feathers and painted in the traditional fashion, the lance held vertically in her right hand was not the usual kind carried by Indian warriors. The diamond-section steel head was twelve inches in length and two and a half inches at its widest, tapering to an acute point. It was fastened to the sturdy nine foot ash handle by a pair of steel languets, each thirty-six inches long and secured with five screws. Passing around her wrist, a rawhide loop was attached to the shaft at its point of balance. On the bottom of the pole was a rounded metal 'shoe' and, as an aid to being carried, it rested in a metal cap attached to the saddle's off side stirrup iron.

Setting the horses moving at a slow walk, the trio rode in the direction from which Boniface had returned. After covering about half a mile, first down and then up a gentle slope, they drew rein and scanned the terrain ahead of them from the concealment of a clump of bushes. At the bottom of a flat and fairly open U-shaped valley some three hundred acres in extent was a herd of about thirty buffalo.

'Well, there you are,' the taller man said. 'But going after them will be very dangerous.'

'I've run buffalo before,' Irène answered, yet her tone was just a trifle less arrogant and certain.

'You was using a rifle and on a full village hunt,' Boniface pointed out. 'Setting after one alone and with only a lance is a *very* different kettle of fish, particularly when it'll be one from a bunch of "settlers" like that lot. Their big boss bull won't be frightened off by a single rider.'

'From what I've heard, you've done it,' Irène replied, knowing that the lanky man was an accomplished hunter and, despite her imperious nature, being sufficiently cognisant of the danger to be willing to listen to his advice. 'So what's the best way to go about it?'

As the girl was aware, even before the wholesale slaughter of the once enormous herds, small groups of buffalo – particularly those of the 'wood', *Bison Bison Athabaseae*, sub-species rather than the 'plains' variety, *B.B.* would forsake the completely migratory habits which the sheer volume of numbers caused the majority of their kind to adopt in order to find sufficient food to support life. Known as 'settlers', such dissidents were invariably led by a bull of sufficient size, strength and aggressiveness to take over and defend a suitable location against all comers. Once this happened, the dominant male, whether the original or the successive leaders among his offspring developed strong territorial instincts and would not hesitate to attack on sight potential trespassers or enemies. What was more, as a full grown bull could measure twelve feet overall and stand six feet high at the humped shoulders, with a weight of between two and three thousand pounds, it was no mean adversary when charging.

'I don't know what *M'sieur* Cavallier's going to say when he hears about this,' Lacomb protested miserably. 'In fact, I shouldn't be letting you do it.'

'And I don't think it's up to *you* to say whether Irène can, or can't do anything,' Boniface answered. Although he had never seen France, the combination of his paternal Gascon and maternal Blackfoot bloodlines revolted against taking orders, or even accepting sound advice, from one born out of Provencal and Assiniboine stock. So, in spite of having no doubt what *le Loup-Garou* would say and might try to do if the girl should be rendered incapable of carrying out the task for which she had been training, he was goaded into supplying her with information. 'I know you're a damned good rider. That horse you're on's been trained for running buffalo with rifle, bow and lance. He's as agile as a cat. As long as you stick on his back, the buffalo hasn't been born that can get to you.'

'What happens if it falls?' the older man demanded.

'He never has and you couldn't knock him off his feet if you tried!' Boniface replied indignantly.

'And the horse hasn't been foaled that I can't stay on!' Irène supplemented boastfully, but she could not stop herself thinking of what she had seen happen during a village hunt when a rider was thrown while racing alongside a fast fleeing herd of buffalo. However, her pride and hot temper would not allow her to call off the attempt after having insisted upon being brought out of their way to make it. 'So, as *he* won't fall, I'll still be with him when he catches up to them.'

'That's something else,' Boniface went on, while *Vieux Malheureux* scowled his disapproval. 'If you go down there yelling as loud as you can, they'll take off along the valley bottom because that's the easiest going – '

'Fine,' Irène said eagerly. 'That will make it easier for me – '

'Not entirely,' Boniface contradicted, beginning to wish he had pretended he could not locate the 'settlers'. As it was, he knew the only hope was for him to alert the headstrong girl to all the dangers she would be likely to encounter. 'The rest will take off all right, but not the big boss bull. His kind don't scare one little damned bit and he'll be coming to meet you. That's when you'll really have to watch your riding. The paint knows what to do. He'll swerve around the bull at the last moment and keep on after the others. And that's what you do, keep going. Don't slow down, because he'll be round and chasing you as fast as he can when he sees you're running his herd. Pick the one you want and let the paint know which it is. He'll keep you by it. Then use the lance the way you've learned and then get the hell out of there even faster than you went in or the big boss will have you.'

For a few seconds, Irène sat committing all she had been told to memory. Then she sucked in a deep breath, grasped the reins more tightly with her left hand and set her feet securely in the stirrups. Having done so, sensing that her companions were studying every move she made and wanting to avoid letting them know her misgivings, she gave the signal for the paint to advance. As it did so and started to pass around the edge of the bushes, she lowered the lance to the horizontal and tucked the handle firmly between her right forearm and ribs. With that accomplished, she kicked her heels against the horse's sides.

Realising what was wanted from it, the little paint increased its speed even though it was approaching a slope which was fairly steep and covered in many places by patches of shale-like gravel. Instead of holding back, it continued thrusting with its hind legs and sending sprays of the small rock fragments flying to the rear.

Grazing about four hundred yards below, as yet the buffalo were unaware of the intruders. Watching them and concentrating upon remaining aboard the paint, Irène found her worries disintegrating and was filled with a growing sensation of wild exhilaration. Although she would be using a different, more impressive animal for the work that lay ahead, she had already formed a rapport with the little horse. Before they had gone many feet, she had sufficient confidence to let it have its head and found it needed no guiding, but headed straight for the herd.

'We should go after her!' Lacomb declared, gesturing with the Henri on his left arm. 'A lance isn't a fit weapon to use against buffalo.'

'Us Blackfoots do it regular,' Boniface answered, although much the same idea had occurred to him. 'And, like she said, when the time comes she's going to have to know how to use the lance. If she puts down one of them, there'll be no doubt she can.'

Wild with excitement, Irène still remembered the advice she was given prior to setting off. The screech she gave might lack the resonance of an Indian brave's war whoop, but it produced the desired effect. Almost too successfully, in fact. Hearing the cry, the paint clearly concluded it was made as a signal for extra speed and accelerated with such force that the girl was pressed against the saddle's high cantle.

Twice more Irène yelled. On each occasion, she felt the little horse quiver and increase the pace of the descent. Starting to rush across the level ground at the foot of the slope, she saw the herd was stampeding along the valley about a hundred yards away as Boniface had said they would. He had been just as accurate in his summation of how the dominant bull would respond to the invasion of its territory. Instead of fleeing with the others, it was already about halfway between them and the intruders, charging with every intention of pressing home the attack.

Despite her exhilaration, the girl felt a sense of awe as she watched the enormous beast rushing ever closer under the impetus of their combined speeds. She tightened her legs around the paint's body and grasped the reins until her knuckles showed white as she prepared to retain her seat through what she knew would be a sudden and violent change of direction.

Thirty yards separated Irène from the bull!

Twenty!

Ten!

For a terrifying moment, the girl thought the horse was acting in panic and meant to meet the gigantic approaching beast head on.

Uttering a whistling sound as loud and shrill as the noise made by high pressure steam bursting from a locomotive, the bull lowered his shaggy head and his short tail became as stiff as a poker, the very hairs of the tassel at its tip seeming to stand erect. He was preparing to drive home the stout, outward and upward curved horns which seemed to Irène to be of far greater size than their actual twenty-three inches of length and seventeen inches circumference around the base.

Timing the move perfectly, the paint gelding justified Boniface's confidence. As the bull prepared to launch the attack, it swerved to the left. Only slightly, but sufficient to avert the collision. Irène was carried by the huge beast so close that she could have kicked him in the ribs while passing.

Letting forth another Indian-like shriek, the girl went after and bore down upon the rest of the herd. Even though she had run buffalo before, it had always been in the company of other hunters and armed with a Winchester carbine capable of discharging up to twelve bullets extremely rapidly. So, aware that she must rely upon a much more primitive weapon, she found the pursuit far more thrilling.

Soon, such was the speed at which the paint was galloping, Irène found herself reaching the stragglers. As they were old cows, or young calves, she ignored them. So did her mount, swerving and veering to pass between them and awaiting

16

notification of which beast she had selected as her quarry.

Briefly the girl considered taking one of the younger females, but in her wildly exalted mood she rejected the idea. Instead, she picked a bull almost as large as the one she had avoided. For the first time since starting the descent of the slope, she used the reins and guided the paint towards the selected animal. Knowing what was wanted, it built up more speed until drawing alongside the bull and, satisfied that he was her choice, steadied until they were moving in time with one another.

Aware that the moment of truth was upon her, Irène prepared to strike and decided upon the best way to do so. Reasoning that impaling the lungs would bring death quicker than a blow to the heart in the bull's present heated condition, she aimed accordingly. Gripping the lance's handle with all her far from inconsiderable strength, she thrust as she had been taught. Made of the finest Sheffield steel, with a needle point and edges close to as sharp as a well-stropped razor, the head went home just behind the shoulder and sank deep into the chest cavity.

Although the bull seemed to buckle slightly under the impact of the blow, it did not fall or even slow down. Cursing and a little frightened by the apparent lack of effect, Irène tugged at the lance. For a moment, it stuck. Then, with the paint easing away in accordance to her signal, but keeping pace with the speeding beast, it began to slide free. An instant after it was liberated, its recipient faltered. The bull's front legs buckled and he went down end over end. Crashing to the ground, he slid to a stop in a cloud of churned up dust.

Delighted by what she had achieved, the girl forgot one very important part of Boniface's advice. Eager to take a closer look at her prize and to see *Vieux Malheureux's* face when he arrived, she tried to rein in the fast running horse. Hitherto completely obedient to her whims and wishes, it showed no sign of responding.

Then Irène remembered the herd bull!

Glancing over her shoulder, the girl felt as if she was being touched by an ice cold hand. Obviously the paint had been aware of their peril. The huge beast was thundering along in hot pursuit and not more than half a dozen yards behind them. Startled by the discovery, Irène gave vent to an ear-splitting screech and kicked sharply against the horse's heaving flanks. As she did so, realising that they had covered close to a mile at a full gallop, she wondered if her mount had anything left in reserve. There was, she discovered, no cause for alarm. Having been given the signal it anticipated, it started to go even faster and, without requiring guidance, swung away from the rest of the herd. After following a short distance, the bull veered towards his departing companions and accompanied them in their flight from the valley.

Pulling the lathered paint to a halt, the girl threw back her head and filled her aching lungs with deep breaths. She was shaking with excitement and triumph, but controlled her impulse to scream joyfully. Instead, she patted the paint's neck with her left hand and praised it verbally. As soon as they had both got back their breath, she turned it towards her trophy and saw her companions were already galloping into the valley.

*   *   *

'Now I wouldn't be knowing what you reckon, Jerry,' remarked the taller of a pair of spectators whose presence in the vicinity was unsuspected by Irène and her companions. He was speaking English, but his voice had the dry yet somehow lilting accent of the Scottish Highlands. 'But that's as quick, clean and neat as I've ever seen a buffalo killed. Yon grey-eyed klooch[3] of *le Loup-Garou*'s has learned how to use a lance real well.'

Topping six foot in height, the speaker was a rawboned man of indeterminate age. His moderately short hair was white, but his blue eyes – seeming out of place in such a dour-looking and tanned set of leathery features – were bright and keen. Although he was clad in a buckskin skirt and moccasins of Cree manufacture, he also had on a pair of 'trews' and a sash about his waist bearing the tartan of the Clan Mackintosh. Perched at a jaunty angle on his head was the kind of knitted woollen cap with a tight headband and full flat top surmounted by a fluffy pompon known as a tam-o'-shanter. A long Scottish dirk was sheathed on the left side instead of at the front of his belt as

[3] '*Klooch*' : *derogatory name for a young woman of mixed blood and dubious morals. Mainly Canadian Northwest and Alaskan usage. J.T.E.*

18

tradition dictated and the matching, if smaller, thistle-shaped hilt of a *sgian dubh* peeped almost coyly from the top of his right moccasin's calf-high legging. A leather ammunition pouch was suspended over his left shoulder and rested on his right hip. In his right hand, he grasped the foregrip of a well worn, but spotlessly clean Winchester Model of 1866 rifle.

Lacking some six inches of his companion's lanky height, the second man made up for it with a stocky and exceptionally muscular physique set upon powerful, if somewhat bowed legs. As dark as that of Lacomb, his ruggedly good looking face was equally and justifiably suggestive of mixed blood. His coal black hair was cut short, but he sported a sizeable and luxuriant moustache. He wore a low crowned, wide brimmed black J.B. Stetson hat, a waist-long fringed buckskin jacket over a dark blue and green check shirt and Levi's pants tucked into the leggings of Blood Indian moccasins. A well designed and made weapon belt of the kind developed by gun fighters south of the international boundary with the United States of America carried a walnut handled Colt Artillery Model Peacemaker revolver in the open topped, contoured holster tied to his right thigh by the pigging thongs attached to its bottom. Balancing the firearm on the left of the belt was a sizeable, Sheffield-made W. F. Jackson 'bowie' knife. Resting along his bent left forearm, the dull black colour of the Winchester rifle's frame, as opposed to the brass which had produced the sobriquet 'Old Yellowboy' for the type carried by his companion, indicated it was one of the later Model of 1873 variety.

Of all the people in Canada, out of consideration for why Irène had been taught to use the lance, the pair of observers were among the last she and her escort would have been willing to let witness her exploit. Even before they had become scouts for the recently formed and already very efficient Northwest Mounted Police,[4] they had displayed a complete lack of sym-

---

[4] *According to the legend, when formed in May 1873, the force was to have been called the Northwest Mounted Rifles. However, when the Government of the United States of America registered protests over the presence of a military body operating so close to its border with Canada, wishing to maintain the spirit of co-operation he had established with various law enforcement agencies there – an example of which is given in Footnote 2, Chapter Seventeen of* THE REMITTANCE KID –

pathy for the kind of enterprise which Arnaud Cavallier was engaged upon. However, individually or together, each possessed a rugged spirit and ability for self protection, with weapons or bare handed, which rendered them superior to criticism or physical objections to their dissent. What was more, such was their skill in their present line of work, they had successfully avoided their presence being detected all through the five days they had been following and keeping the *Metis* under practically constant surveillance.

That his comment elicited no more response than a single grunt from the other man came as no surprise to Sandy Mackintosh. Jerry Potts had a well deserved reputation for brevity of speech. Born of a Scottish father and a Blood Indian mother, he was fluent in French, several tribal dialects and, to a less extent, English. However, he had small use for words in any language and employed them as sparingly as possible.[5]

'Aye,' Mackintosh went on. Not usually a frivolous or extensive chatterer, he invariably found himself talking far more when in the younger scout's company than he might on other occasions. 'She handles yon lance mighty well for a wee lassie who's no better than she should be other ways. But for the life of me, what's left of it at my age, I can't think why they've been taking so much time and trouble to teach her. Or why she'd be wanting to learn comes to that.'

'Maybe reckons she's *Jan-Dark*,' Potts suggested, in what amounted to a burst of loquacity for him.

'Maybe she does at that,' the lanky Highlander admitted. 'Except with that yellowish hair, light skin and grey eyes, for all her mother being a Plains Cree, there's not many would be

---

Colonel George A. French, the first commanding officer, substituted the word 'Police' for 'Rifles' and this was accepted as a satisfactory compromise by both countries. J.T.E.

[5] *Two legendary examples of Jerry Potts' economy of words are as follows :*
While on a long march, being impatient to reach his destination and having grown tired of the endless vista of rolling prairie stretching ahead, an officer of the Northwest Mounted Police demanded, 'What do you think we'll find on the other side of this hill?'
Potts replied, 'Another hill.'
At the conclusion of a lengthy speech, during which – with Potts acting

willing to share her belief was she to announce it.'

'*Nobody* believe,' Potts agreed, watching the trio gathering around the dead buffalo.

'Mind you though, Jerry lad,' Mackintosh continued. 'Seeing as all of a sudden just recently there's started to be all that talk about the *Jan-Dark* going around, we both know what might happen if *somebody* did manage to make out she's come at long last.'

'Be plenty trouble,' Potts stated.

'Aye, that there would,' Mackintosh seconded, deciding – although a fancy talking politician might have replied at greater length – his companion's three words hit the mark more than adequately. 'So I reckon, taken with all we've been hearing here and there these past few weeks, Colonel French'd be wanting us to keep our eyes on them for a wee while longer.'

Despite being in complete agreement with his companion's summation, Potts made no verbal reply. Nor, for all his antipathy where such waste was concerned, did he comment when – having removed the tongue – the *Metis* left the remainder of the buffalo's carcase where it had fallen and rode away. Instead, he accompanied Mackintosh from their place of concealment and returned to where they had left their horses. Yet he was aware that, if the suspicions they both harboured should prove correct, there was a danger of Canada being plunged into a bloody conflict which would cost hundreds of people their lives.

---

as interpreter – the chief of a hungry band of Indians explained their predicament, having received no explanation of what was being said from the beginning to the end, Assistant Commissioner James Macleod requested a translation. Potts obliged with, 'Him want grub.' J.T.E.

CHAPTER TWO

I'LL *STRIKE* YOU

Arnaud Cavallier was bored and, seeking more convivial society than that of the man and woman whose assistance was – for the time being anyway – essential to the enterprise upon which he was engaged, he had come to the Fair Lady Saloon in search of it. He would not have been in such a relaxed and amiable mood if he had known how, at that moment, Irène Beauville was putting his endeavour in jeopardy something over a thousand miles to the north-west by running a buffalo armed with only the lance.

Hoping to receive important news at any time and, in consequence, having told his associates where he could be found if it arrived, Cavallier was not looking for feminine companionship and sexual stimulation. Nor, although there were only female staff in sight – the sole male employees being a trio of elderly swampers who appeared during the hours of business – was the Fair Lady a place in which to seek it. The owner, Miss Freddie Woods, did not permit other than friendly sociability between her girls and the customers while they were on the premises. As she was the town's well liked and respected mayor, in addition to running what was acknowledged as the best saloon in Mulrooney, Kansas, her wishes were generally accepted. When they were not, despite the lack of masculine assistance, her all female staff were capable of making the transgressors wish they had been.

Sweeping his gaze around the tasteful elegance of the main barroom as he passed through the open double doors, Cavallier concluded that he had arrived too early in the day to find relaxation in high stakes gambling. There were a number of customers present, but as yet only one game of chance was taking place. Half a dozen men, a cross-section of any Kansas trail end-railroad town's transient population, were seated around a table playing blackjack. Although he would have preferred the game to be poker, noticing there were two empty chairs, he strolled over.

'Do you mind if I sit in, gentlemen?' Cavallier inquired formally, speaking excellent English with only a suggestion of a French accent.

Six pairs of eyes examined the speaker. They saw a man close to six foot in height and who looked somewhat younger than his thirty-five years of age. Clean shaven, with short light brownish hair, he had a good – if not exceptional – width to his shoulders, a slender waist and conveyed the impression of being able to move with rapidity when necessary. Deeply tanned though they were, his handsome aquiline features were only marginally indicative of his quarter Assiniboine blood. Nor did they suggest how he had acquired the sobriquet, *le Loup-Garou*.

A round topped, broad brimmed brown 'plainsman' hat, well suited for wear upon the windswept open prairies of Canada, was dangling on Cavallier's shoulders by its fancy *barbiquejo* chin strap. He had on an open necked dark blue shirt, a fringed buckskin jacket and a pair of yellowish-brown nankeen trousers tucked into brown Wellington-leg riding boots.[1] Around his waist, a gunbelt had an ivory hilted 'Green River' knife sheathed at its left and a Colt Civilian Model Peacemaker, which also had an ivory handle, rode butt forward for a low cavalry-twist draw in the tied down holster at the right.

For his part, *le Loup-Garou* was studying his potential opponents just as carefully. In order of dealing from the chair at which he meant to sit,[2] they were: a tall Texas cowhand, tanned and as lean as a steer raised in greasewood country; a

---

[1] *In this context, not the modern, waterproof variety. Instead, they had legs covering as high as the knee in front and cut away behind, after the style made popular in the Napoleonic Wars by Arthur Wellesley, Duke of Wellington (1769–1852). J.T.E.*

[2] *The convention in most card games is that the deal goes in a right hand direction, with the man at the dealer's left cutting the deck. J.T.E.*

plump, middle-aged man in town dweller's clothes, whose means of employment was not obvious; a big and burly railroad brakeman identifiable by his official peaked hat and uniform; an as yet unclaimed seat; an attractive, not too daringly dressed blonde girl, with a white basin emblazoned by the name of the establishment and holding money, mainly nickels,[3] in front of her; and two young cavalry troopers, one tall, burly and Germanic, the other shorter, slim and Latin in looks, wearing such new uniforms that they were almost certainly but recently enlisted.

'Feel free, sir,' the girl replied, in a pleasant mid-West voice. 'The house rules are – ' She paused and, glancing past Cavallier, inquired, 'Do *you* wish to join us, sir?'

Glancing over his shoulder, the *Metis* had no difficulty in deciding to whom the question was directed. In fact, he had been aware that somebody was following him as he was crossing to the table and, although he would not have expected a game like blackjack would have interested such a person, he had had an idea who it might be.

Perhaps an inch taller than Cavallier, the man addressed by the girl was in his middle thirties. He had curly blond hair and a ruggedly good looking face which bore an expression of what seemed to be languid boredom. For all his well made physique, he moved in a lethargic fashion and yet conveyed the impression that he could burst into sudden and possibly violent motion. His attire was that of a successful professional gambler. A white, low crowned and wide brimmed J.B. Stetson hat was thrust to the back of his head. His frilly bosomed white shirt, with a perfectly knotted black string bow-tie, could only be silk and his black satin vest set it off perfectly. Equally faultless in cut, only the rosewood grips of what appeared to be a handgun of some kind peeking from beneath the left side detracted from the elegant appearance of his grey cutaway coat. High heeled, sharp toed tan boots of cowhand style – although the usually mandatory spurs were absent – emerged from the legs of his black trousers.

'I say, that's *awfully* decent of you,' responded the man behind Cavallier, removing his hat with a flourish. In spite of

[3] *'Nickel' a coin valued five cents. J.T.E.*

his clothing – with the exception of the boots – suggesting he had just come ashore from a top class Mississippi River paddle-wheel steamboat, his voice had the clipped yet drawling intonation of the English upper classes. Ignoring a snigger and nudge to the other trooper's ribs given by the Germanic-looking soldier, he drew out the second vacant chair with such a languid gesture that he might have been about to fall asleep and sat down, continuing, 'I think I will wait until there is a game of – poker, don't you colonials call it – is started. What were you about to say, dear girl?'

'Miss Freddie's house rules are in force,' the young woman answered briskly and in the manner of one who was following a well learned ritual, amused by the Englishman's expansive way of speaking and apparent languor. 'Except when you are holding the bank, you put a nickel in the pot for every hand you win. The limit is five cents to five dollars a *hand*, not per card. Any player may call for and shuffle the deck before a deal, but the banker has the right to shuffle last and every player who wishes has the right to cut the cards. With the exception of a "natural", which is paid off by the banker at two to one, all bets laid are at even money. No "insurance", or "double down" bets are allowed and there are *no* house "propositions" what-soever. All pairs may be split, provided the player duplicates the amount already bet. A player may only draw cards on his legal turn of play. If a player receives only one, or three cards on the deal, his hand is void. If the banker deals himself three cards, of which two are face down, he must take the one on top and burn the second; but if he has two up cards, the hand is void. *All* ties stand off. Each player holds the bank for ten successive deals, regardless of any "naturals" which may be dealt, and it passes to the player on his right on the eleventh. Lastly, in the event of a dispute on *any* matter concerning the game, *my* decision is final. Is all that agreeable?'[4]

'It is with me,' Cavallier stated, knowing the rules were not only fair but also removed the most common causes of dis-sension which arose among players used to local variations of the game.

[4] *An explanation of the game of blackjack is given in APPENDIX THREE. J.T.E.*

'Most assuredly, dear girl,' the Englishman seconded, drawing another snigger from the blond-haired soldier. 'But suppose one disputes *your* decision?'

'I suggest that, as he is dissatisfied, he leaves the game,' the girl replied, darting a frown at the soldier.

'And if he isn't disposed to do so?' the Englishman queried.

'I call over one of the barmaids to persuade him to go,' the girl explained, still in the same polite and friendly tone, directing the words to the soldier as much as at her questioner. 'And she's got a sawed-off ten gauge scattergun on hand to help her do it.'

'And a most persuasive argument one is, too, by all accounts,' the Englishman drawled contemplatively. 'But I didn't know you colonials used the word "barmaid".'

'Miss Freddie says we should,' the girl answered, as if that made the name not only satisfactory but mandatory. Then, seeing the two soldiers were showing impatience over the delay although the other three did not, she went on, 'I'm your hostess, Arlene and my friends are Tex, Roger, Sam, Dutchy and Tony.'

'Call me "Wolf",' Cavallier requested, as the other players looked at him, following the long established Western convention that a person was allowed to chose whatever name he wished to supply.

'My name is Patrick St John[5]-Haythornthwaite, dear girl, gentlemen,' the Englishman introduced. 'But that is something of a mouthful and, as my jolly old family are kind enough to keep sending me money to make sure I don't go back home, most people prefer to call me "the Remittance Kid".'

'I say, *dear boy*,' the Germanic-looking soldier put in, trying not too successfully to mimic the Englishman's way of speaking. 'All this is jolly old interesting, but how about letting us get on with the game?'

'Good lord, old chap,' the Kid answered mildly. 'I didn't realise *you* were British.'

'Like hell I am!' Dutchy ejaculated indignantly. 'I'm a one hundred percent American and we licked you Limeys back in "Seventy-Six".'

[5] *Pronounced 'Sinjun'. J.T.E.*

'Good heavens!' the Kid countered, hanging his hat on the back of the chair with his left hand while the right disappeared below the level of the table. 'I hadn't realised *you* were *that* old.'

'What in hell's *that* supposed to mean?' Dutchy demanded, scowling menacingly.

Watching the interplay between the two men, Arlene could not decide what would be her best line of action. Well trained in all aspects of her work, she had already grown irritated by the two soldiers' attitudes and sensed they could become troublesome. Newly arrived from big cities in the East, they were filled with notions of supremacy over the 'hicks' they met west of the Big Muddy.[6] Furthermore, conscious of being only raw recruits, they had adopted a demeanour of blustering arrogance in the hope of passing themselves off as hardened and seasoned campaigners. So they might react to any interference on her part by increasing their belligerence. On the other hand, for all his apparent languor, she had formed the impression that the Englishman was well able to take care of himself. Which raised the point of whether she could rely upon him to do so in a way that did not bring the other soldiers who were in the barroom into the affair.

'Only that the "licking" happened almost a hundred years ago, old boy,' the Kid elaborated, still showing no sign of noticing the blond soldier's growing truculence. 'And you strike me as being somewhat too young to – '

'I'll *strike* you, you Limey son-of-a – !' Dutchy began, in a louder voice, making as if to rise.

'Don't get up, old sport,' the Kid requested, without moving, but there was something in his manner which made the words more a combination of an order and a threat. 'It really wouldn't be *advisable*.'

'Easy, Dutchy!' Tony warned, being positioned so he was able to see as far as the Englishman's waist. 'That gun's not sticking out from under his coat any more.'

'True, dear boy, true,' the Kid admitted. 'And the *gun*, as your friend calls it, is pointing in such a manner that you could develop a somewhat squeaky tone of voice if I was compelled to use it.'

[6] '*Big Muddy*' : *colloquial name for the Mississippi River. J.T.E.*

'Well now, me boyoes,' called a voice with a heavy Irish brogue, accompanied by the sound of a chair scraping back. 'And what seems to be wrong, I'm asking?'

Swivelling his head around, as did everybody else at the table with the exception of the Kid, Dutchy felt a mixture of relief and alarm as he looked at the big, burly, red-faced red-haired non-commissioned officer belonging to his regiment who was approaching. He was aware of Sergeant Magoon's ability in a fight, but also remembered the instructions he and Tony had been given with regard to their conduct. However, he also saw that – one way or another – he was being offered an opportunity to avoid carrying the affair any further. While he had not wanted to back down, neither had he been able to see how he could do otherwise without putting himself into considerable danger.

'Just a little disagreement, Paddy,' Arlene supplied, having no doubt that the intervention would be beneficial. Not only was the sergeant fair and sensible, he had the greatest respect for Freddie Woods and would be disinclined to permit his men to become involved in trouble on her premises. 'Dutchy likes to make jokes about people, but isn't so willing to take them about himself.'

'Damn it, serge!' the blond recruit protested, feeling decidedly uncomfortable as Magoon's cold gaze swung his way. 'That tinhorn's pulled a gun on me!'

'A gun, old thing?' the Kid inquired mildly. 'Noisy, oily things which make most unsightly bulges under one's clothes and completely spoil the hang of a jacket. I never use one.'

'Then what've you got hid under the table?' Dutchy challenged, feeling sure the sergeant would support him against a proven liar.

'A *badik*,' the Kid replied, bringing his right hand into view and laying the unusual looking device he was holding on the table. It had an eight inch long blade like that of a pocketknife, but the hilt was shaped after the fashion of a pistol's butt. 'I took it off a Bugi pirate who was waving it around rather dangerously one night on a ship out of Singapore. I assure you, it wouldn't shoot any – '

'Why you sneaky – !' Dutchy began, furious at the deception and starting to thrust back his chair.

'That's right, me bucko,' Magoon growled, having been keeping an eye upon the two recruits and knowing the Englishman had just arrived, so the dispute had not arisen over the game. 'I reckon it is time you were quitting.'

'But – !' Dutchy commenced, watching the Kid return the *badik* to its sheath.

'Sure and you wouldn't be wanting to go squandering all your money gambling before you've had the courtesy to be buying your lovable old sergeant a drink,' Magoon interrupted. 'Now would you?'

'I reckon it wouldn't be right,' Tony stated, guessing that to do otherwise would result in repercussions at a later date. Although they might have, it would not have been for the purposes he envisaged. Magoon's motive was to prevent trouble which would have reflected badly upon his regiment's behaviour. 'Let's go and get them.'

'Perhaps you gentlemen will allow me to buy?' the Kid suggested. 'And all of my fellow players, of course, in apology for having wasted so much of your time?'

'That's good of you, sir,' Magoon declared, then favoured his recruits with a baleful glare. 'Which doesn't let you two spalpeens out of doing your duty to me.'

Once the drinks had been purchased by the Kid, and Magoon had escorted the two soldiers to the bar, the game was recommenced. Although pleased by the way the situation had developed, Arlene watched the Englishman and Cavallier with, if not noticeably, great care. Neither struck her as being the kind who would sit in on a game with such modest limits. However, because of the small sums of money involved, she considered it was unlikely they were partners working together to fleece the other players. Nor, as she had been given a thorough education in the ways cheating could be performed either by individuals or as a team, could she detect any suggestion that it was anything other than skill and good fortune, rather than some means of manipulating the run of the cards, that was responsible for their successes.

'Damn the luck, Kid!' groaned the Texas cowhand, at the

end of half an hour's play, folding his two cards and looking at the queen of diamonds and king of spades displayed by the Englishman. 'That's the fifth time you've had twenty against my sixteen, seventeen, or eighteen.'

'True, old boy,' the Kid admitted, the complaint having been made in friendly fashion. 'But, drawing such cards on the deal, mathematically your luck is better than mine.'

'Whee-doggie!' Tex drawled. 'You-all'd best drive that one by again, *amigo*, it went too fast for me to drop a rope on it.'

'As I said, mathematically, your luck in getting sixteen, seventeen, or eighteen is better than mine in drawing twenty,' the Kid obliged and the other players fell silent, but showed a puzzlement equal to that of the Texan.

'My luck's *better*?' the cowhand asked, frowning, as he was aware that a score of twenty beat one of sixteen, seventeen, or eighteen.

'*Mathematically* better,' the Kid supplemented.

'Would this here mathe – matics have to do with adding and taking away?' Tex asked.

'It would,' the Kid confirmed.

'Well what you said just can't be,' the cowhand declared. 'Because, after we-all'd added up what we was holding, you sure as sin's for sale in Cow-town[7] took away from me.'

'Ah yes, old boy,' the Kid answered. 'But you were still *mathematically* luckier than I was.'

'You prove *that* to me and I'll buy drinks for the house,' Tex stated.

'I'll settle for a five dollar bet against *me*,' the Kid suggested, then turned his gaze to Arlene. 'Unless that would be against the house rules, dear girl?'

'It isn't,' Arlene confessed, intrigued by the conversation. 'In fact, I'd be willing to take some of that bet myself.'

'How much, dear girl?' asked the Kid.

'Five dollars,' Arlene requested, unable to see how she could lose.

'Was you so minded, Kid,' the brakeman hinted, 'I'd take me five on it as well.'

[7] *For the benefit of new readers, 'Cow-Town' is the colloquial name for Fort Worth, Tarrant County, Texas. J.T.E.*

'You're both on,' consented the Englishman.

'Give me ten dollars?' the townsman inquired.

'With pleasure, old boy,' the Kid agreed.

'I'll take fifty dollars of it,' Cavallier put in.

'If you wish, dear boy,' the Kid assented and, after the money had been laid upon the table, he went on, 'First, though, we all agree that the more difficult a thing is to achieve, the more fortunate one is when it happens?'

'Sure,' Tex drawled, when the others had exchanged looks and nods of concurrence. 'But I still don't – '

'It's like this, old boy,' the Kid explained. 'There are one hundred and thirty-six combinations of two cards which total twenty in every deck of fifty-two. Count them, if you wish, but I already have. On the other hand, there are only one hundred and two combinations adding to sixteen, ninety-six adding to seventeen and eighty-six to eighteen. Therefore, it is more difficult to make sixteen, seventeen, or eighteen, than it is to make twenty. So, when you lose with one of them to a hand of twenty, you are mathematically *luckier*, but – because of the rules of the game – *financially* unluckier.'

For a moment, silence fell over the table. Leaning back in his chair, the Englishman watched as the others digested his words.

'Well I swan!' the cowhand whooped, slapping a hard hand on the top of the table. 'Took *that* way you're right as the Injun side of a hoss.' Pushing five dollars across the table, he went on, 'I don't reckon's how you'd be kind enough to write all them fancy figures down for me, now would you-all? That way, I'll be able to spout 'em when I get back home and everybody'll reckon I'm a man with real learning.'

'I'd like to have them as well,' the brakeman seconded, sharing the Texan's belief that he could use the Englishman's line of reasoning to win bets.

'I'd like to oblige, gentlemen,' the Kid declared. 'But I promised my aunt, the Dowager Duchess of Brockley, who presented the formula to me, that I wouldn't divulge it.'

'Shucks,' Tex protested, doubting that there was any such person. 'She'd never get to know about it if you did.'

'Writing always gives me cramp,' the Kid replied, waving a languid right hand.

'Maybe five simoleons would ease it?' Tex hinted.

'Ten per copy assuredly would,' the Kid stated and, as the two men each passed him the required sum, he took a pencil and notebook from his jacket's inside pocket.

Scowling a little at the thought of how he had been tricked out of fifty dollars, Cavallier was on the point of requesting a similar list when he glanced across the room and stiffened slightly. His male associate and another man were coming through the main entrance. Although they looked his way, they continued walking towards the bar.

'I'll see your turn through as the bank, Kid,' *le Loup-Garou* advised, counting out the money to pay his lost wager. 'But then I'll have to call it quits.'

'As you will, old thing,' the Kid replied cheerfully.

* * *

'And how did *you* enjoy yourself while *I've* been working?' demanded the occupant of the room the Kid was renting at the Railroad House Hotel, when he walked in about three-quarters of an hour after Cavallier had withdrawn from the game.

'I didn't do too badly,' the Englishman admitted. 'Won around a hundred and fifty of those dollar things you colonials use instead of sensible pounds, shillings and pence – and *le Loup-Garou*'s arms have turned up.'

'I *know*,' the person to whom the words were addressed replied. 'And I've found out how they're to be delivered.'

'Spoilsport!' the Kid complained, having made a similar discovery. 'Oh well, what do you say to taking a stroll to see if we can get an idea of when they're going to make the delivery – and try to decide how we're going to stop the arms getting there.'

CHAPTER THREE

SHE WON'T HURT *THEM* TOO BADLY

'No, dear girl,' the Remittance Kid declared with complete confidence, as he and his companion were strolling towards the southern front corner of the Fair Lady Saloon some thirty minutes after he had left to return to the Railroad House Hotel with his anticipated information. '*Le Loup-Garou* didn't recognise me any more than "Father Devlin" or his good lady "wife" recognised you and I. There's even less reason why he should. He didn't make such a close acquaintance with me as they with us and I neither look nor sound as I did the last time he had an opportunity to see me.[1] By the by, I saw Miss Freddie Woods, briefly as luck would have it, as I was leaving.'

'A most charming, if somewhat unusual, lady, from all I've heard,' remarked the young woman on the Englishman's arm.

'I know,' the Kid replied.

'Do you *know* her?' the young woman inquired, but with more curiosity than jealousy in her tone, considering the affectionate way in which she was behaving.

'Rather well,' the Kid admitted.

'Does she know *you*?' the young woman asked, sounding less concerned than might have been expected considering the nature of her and her companion's occupations and the business which had brought them to Mulrooney, Kansas.

Although the Englishman had introduced himself to the other blackjack players as Patrick St John-Haythornthwaite, only the christian name of the imposing title was strictly correct. Haythornthwaite had been his mother's maiden name. He had not lied when stating his nickname was 'the Remittance Kid',

[1] *How and when the meetings had taken place is told in :* THE RE-MITTANCE KID. *J.T.E.*

but he was far from being the waster paid by his family to stay out of England he claimed to be. He was Captain Patrick Reeder of the Rifle Brigade,[2] seconded to the British Secret Service and the assignment upon which he was currently engaged had brought him to the Kansas railroad town.

What was more, the young woman walking arm in arm with the Kid was not what she conveyed the impression of being. Five foot seven in height, she was very beautiful and, while slender in build, was neither flat-chested nor skinny. Her hair was completely concealed beneath a bluey-green, brimless and turban-like 'togue' cap from the front of which rose a small plume of white egret feathers. When in view, it proved to be blonde and cut boyishly short. High necked, her light blue walking-out costume had its jacket-type bodice extending to waist level on the front and sides and its three-tailed *basque* overskirt had the centre tail turned back and fastened low on the centre of its back. Two rows of white lace trimming on the 'sailor' collar gave the ensemble its name. Both jacket and *basque* were decorated by similar trimming and silver buttons. Close-fitting, the sleeves flared slightly at the wrists. Emphasising the hips in its snugness, the skirt had a tie-back fanned out in a short train and trimmed to simulate an over-skirt. From beneath it peeked the toes of dainty black shoes. An open parasol, which matched the costume, rested on her right shoulder and the left hand, tucked through the Kid's arm, held a dainty vanity bag.

Well dressed as she was, there were a few things about the young woman which suggested she was not exactly the class of person usually to be accommodated at the select and most expensive hotel in Mulrooney. She wore just a trifle more

[2] *The researches of fictionist-genealogist Philip José Farmer – author of, among numerous other works, the biographies* TARZAN ALIVE *and* DOC SAVAGE, His Apocolyptic Life – *have established that Captain (later Major General Sir) Patrick Reeder (K.C.B., V.C., D.S.O., M.C. and Bar) was the uncle of the celebrated detective, Mr Jeremiah Golden Reeder, whose career is recorded by his biographer, Edgar Wallace, in* ROOM 13, THE MIND OF MR J. G. REEDER, RED ACES, MR J. G. REEDER RETURNS *and* TERROR KEEP *and whose organisation played a major part in the events told by the author in :* 'CAP' FOG, TEXAS RANGER, MEET MR. J. G. REEDER. *J.T.E.*

make-up on her face than was deemed socially acceptable. In addition, costly as the jewellery which sparkled on her ears, wrists and around her neck appeared to be, it was slightly too ostentatious for good taste. Also, in spite of speaking with the accent of a well-educated Southron, it occasionally slipped and she would employ terms suggesting a less cultured background.

Having studied the Kid's companion with growing disapproval since her arrival, the chief desk clerk at the hotel believed her to be either a saloongirl or an actress. He also suspected, correctly that they were not married in spite of the wedding ring she frequently found ways of displaying. Shrewd as his deductions were, based upon the consummately skilful way she had given him the impression from which he had formed it, she was much more than the current mistress of a professional gambler. Her name was Belle Boyd.[3] During the War Between The States, she had earned the sobriquet, the Rebel Spy. However, she was now a member of the United States' Secret Service and working in co-operation with the British agent.

'She has done since we were children, old thing,' the Kid confessed. Then, glancing at the front doors of the saloon, he came to a stop. 'Drat! I hope those two young blighters aren't going to come this way. They may not have forgotten, or forgiven, our little contretemps earlier.'

Fortune favoured the Englishman before Belle could ask what had caused his comment. On emerging from the saloon, swaying slightly in a way which suggested they had taken a couple more drinks than was advisable, the two cavalry recruits found something to attract their attention in the opposite direction.

'Which do you reckon it is, Tony?' Dutchy inquired, his voice slurred although he tried to make it sound tough and commanding. 'Is it a man, or a gal?'

'I dunno, that's for sure,' the swarthily handsome young soldier replied, speaking in a similar fashion, as he started to swagger alongside his companion towards the subject of their loudly made comments. 'Those're men's clothes all right,

[3] *New readers can find details of Belle 'the Rebel Spy' Boyd's background and special qualifications in APPENDIX ONE. J.T.E.*

Dutchy-boy. But, unless my memory's going back on me, what's inside 'em sure looks like it's got all the right bits for a woman.'

'Now there are two young men who aren't showing what I would call real good sense,' Belle remarked, being close enough to hear what the pair where saying and feeling sure the remarks had also reached the ears of the person at whom they were directed. 'But we're in luck, Rem. There's a good chance we'll be able to learn more about that man who came to meet dear Vera, "Devlin", and Cavallier.'

Although puzzled by his companion's utterances, the Kid was more interested in watching the soldiers to ask what she had meant.

To be fair to Dutchy and Tony, even though – as Belle had intimated to the Englishman – she and anybody else with a similar extensive knowledge of the West could have warned them such remarks were extremely ill-advised, there was some justice in the context of the statements. The person they were discussing was dressed in a far from conventional fashion.

Matching the Rebel Spy in height, Miss Martha Jane Canary was a few years younger. While her tanned, freckled, good looking face, with its sparkling blue eyes, slightly snub nose and a full lipped mouth which had grin quirks at the corners, could not compete with Belle's beauty, she was even better endowed in the matter of physique. What was more, her attire was such as to display her magnificently contoured figure to its best advantage.

A battered U.S. cavalry képi was perched jauntily on the girl's mop of shortish, curly red hair. The fringed buckskin shirt – its sleeves rolled up to show strong brown arms – and trousers she wore looked to have been bought a size too small and had shrunk even further from being wet. Clinging like a second skin to her torso, the swell of her full and firm bosom caused the former garment's neck to spread open sufficiently to imply that she did not consider underclothing a necessity. Her waist slimmed down without the aid of a corset, then opened out to shapely hips and shapely, yet powerful legs which were emphasised rather than hidden by the trousers. Her ensemble was completed by the Pawnee moccasins on her feet. She wore no feminine adornment. Instead, a brown gunbelt slanted down from her left hip with an ivory handled Colt 1851 Navy revolver butt forward in its low cavalry twist draw holster. On the left side of her waistbelt, its handle thrust through a broad leather loop, was suspended a long lashed, coiled bull whip which looked far more functional than decorative.

'Those two silly young blighters mean mischief!' the Kid declared watching Dutchy and Tony come to a halt so they were taking up most of the sidewalk.

'I'd be inclined to say "yes" to that,' Belle replied calmly.

'Then hadn't one ought to do something about stopping them?' the Kid inquired, puzzled by his companion's attitude.

'I wouldn't trouble if I were you-all,' the Rebel Spy answered. '*She* won't hurt *them* too badly.'

'That wasn't *quite* what I'm concerned about, dear girl,' the Kid protested, although he realised there must be some sound reason for Belle's reaction. 'Rather the opposite, in fact.'

'Do you reckon she works in a circus, or a carnival, Dutchy?' Tony inquired, loudly enough to bring the couple's conversation to an end.

'She sure as hell doesn't look like she's come from no convent,' the Germanic trooper replied, running a lascivious gaze over the red head's figure rather than watching her face. 'I tell you, Tony, she puts me in mind of a gal I saw one time at Madame Lil's fancy cat-house in lil old New York. She used to wear pants and had a whip to whomp fellers who were took with such doings.'

'I wouldn't mind trying *that* myself,' the shorter soldier remarked, making the same error as his friend in studying the girl's body instead of her features. 'So long as it was done gentle and loving. Hey, Red, is that the sort of thing you do?'

'I've whomped one or two on occasion,' Miss Canary admitted, sounding mild and continuing to stroll onwards in an apparently unconcerned fashion. 'Thing right now, though, is whether you pair of prime specimens of the good old U.S. cavalry're expecting a poor, sweet, pretty lil gal like me to have to walk by you in the gutter. Because I'm going to be madder'n a hot-boiled screech-owl happen I have to.'

'You are, huh?' Dutchy growled, not too far gone in liquor to have failed to detect the cold sarcasm underlying the gentle tones. His attitude towards members of the opposite sex was what would in a later generation become known as that of a male chauvinist pig. So he found the girl's attitude irritating and considered she should be taught a lesson. Liquor always had the effect of increasing the tendency to be a bully which had been responsible for his enlistment in the cavalry.

'You'd better believe it,' Miss Canary confirmed, measuring the distance separating them with her eyes.

'She means it, Dutchy!' Tony ejaculated in tones of mock horror, moving until he was resting his rump against the hitching rail. Like his companion, he believed their conduct would be excused by the townspeople as they were members of the U.S. cavalry and the girl did not strike him as being of the kind regarded as 'good'. 'All right, *lady*, there's no need to get all *pushy*. Come on through.'

'Sure thing,' the larger soldier agreed, drawing a conclusion from the emphasis placed on the word '*pushy*' and stepping aside to stand with his back to the saloon's window. 'You do that, *lady*.'

For all the signs to the contrary she displayed, the red head might have considered the invitation to pass between the soldiers was genuine and harmless. However, if either had been more observant, he might have noticed that her left hand went in a casual seeming gesture towards the handle of the bull whip. In a similarly innocuous appearing fashion, as she was almost to them, she swung her torso so she was facing towards Dutchy and presented Tony with what was, on the surface at any rate, an ideal opportunity to carry out the hint he had given regarding his intentions.

Delighted by the way in which the situation was developing, Tony thrust himself from the hitching rail with the intention of shoving the young woman towards his waiting companion. Just as pleased and satisfied by the turn of events, Dutchy started to step forward and made ready to encircle her with his arms.

Even as the Kid was on the point of disregarding Belle's instructions, he discovered that her confidence was justifiable and there would be no need for him to intervene.

Slipping the whip free with a deft motion, Miss Canary did not attempt to uncoil its lash. Instead, she struck backwards with the handle so it met Tony's whiskey-filled belly. While she was just too late to prevent him from delivering the push, the blow was sufficiently hard to cause him to fold at the waist and retreat to the accompaniment of an agony-filled gurgle.

It was soon apparent that, in spite of being propelled forward, the red head had drawn a similar conclusion to Dutchy's with regard to the emphasis given to '*pushy*'. Nor was she being sent helplessly into his grasp. Instead, ducking her head, she delivered a butt to his stomach. Aided by the impetus of Tony's shove, her attack proved most successful. Its effect was increased by the impact coming while its recipient's right foot was raised to take a step. Caught unaware and off balance, he was knocked away from her. Having no control at all over his movements, due to the force with which he had been struck, he crashed backwards through the window, shattering the panes and sash, to disappear into the building.

Brought to a halt by the hitching rail, which also prevented him from toppling into the street, Tony spluttered out a breathlessly obscene suggestion as to his assailant's possible employment and the marital state, or lack of it, of her parents at the time of her birth. Having done so, he flung himself into the attack once more. Hearing what he said, despite the commotion arising in the saloon as a result of Dutchy's dramatic and unorthodox entrance, Miss Canary found it added to her annoyance over the earlier references made about her. She also deduced correctly that he would not restrict himself to just verbal abuse and had no qualms over the way in which she decided to respond. Turning fast, she caught his outstretched right wrist in both hands. Then, taking a rapid step to her right, she pivoted and gave a horizontal heave on the captured limb. It was powered by all the strength in her gorgeous, but firm muscled body. What little air remained in Tony's lungs was expended in a startled and alarmed wail as he realised what was happening and where he was going. Propelled across the sidewalk, he followed his companion through the window.

'There!' Belle remarked, with an air of smug condescension

and released the Kid's arm, having clung on to it to prevent him from going to the red head's rescue. 'I told you so.'

'So you did, dear girl, so you did,' the Englishman conceded, visibly impressed by what he had just witnessed. 'But if *that* is what *you* consider not hurting them *too* badly, I would hate to suffer what *you*'d regard as *rough* handling. You know her, of course?'

'I do,' Belle confirmed, seeing the people elsewhere along the street were looking at the cause of the commotion and that others were coming from the saloon to investigate.

'Who is she?' asked the Kid.

'Calamity Jane,' the Rebel Spy replied. 'Who else?'

CHAPTER FOUR

TALKED THEM OUT OF IT, SHE SAYS

'Who else, of course,' Captain Patrick Reeder drawled, showing none of the surprise he felt as he looked from Belle Boyd to the red head; who was just as much a legend in her own lifetime as the Rebel Spy.[1] 'I hardly needed to ask.'

Even as the Remittance Kid was speaking, the leading pair of customers who were coming to investigate the disturbance appeared through the front doors of the Fair Lady Saloon. They were closely followed by Sergeant Magoon. Neither had been present when the Englishman had left to collect Belle and one was the head of Mulrooney's municipal law enforcement agency.

Six foot tall, well made and ruggedly handsome, Marshal Kail Beauregard differed from the majority of Kansas trail-end towns' peace officers by being a Texan and scrupulously honest. He had on a wide brimmed, low crowned black J.B. Stetson hat and a neat brown suit, but the well worn Colt 1860 Army revolver he carried reposed in the fast draw holster of a well-designed and manufactured gunbelt.

Exceeding the marshal's height by a good three inches and weighing over two hundred pounds, none of it flabby fat, the second man out had a clean shaven face that seemed to express a benign innocence. Although he too had on a brown business-man's suit, his gunbelt had a James black bowie knife sheathed on the left side and a Colt Cavalry Model Peacemaker rode in its contoured holster. In spite of his attire, Belle recognised him as being Cecil 'Dobe' Killem. Not only did he operate a

[1] *For the benefit of new readers, details of Martha 'Calamity Jane' Canary's background and special qualifications are given in APPENDIX TWO. J.T.E.*

highly successful freighting business, he was Miss Martha Jane Canary's employer.

'God damn it, Calam!' Killem boomed, looking to where the red head was bending to retrieve the bull whip she had dropped when being pushed towards Dutchy. 'I just might've knowed it was you out here.'

'Well I'll swan if that just don't beat *all*!' Calamity Jane answered, exuding an aura of artlessness and mildly self-righteous indignation. 'If I'd've been in Chicago back to Seventy-one, Dobe Killem, I'll bet you'd've blamed me for that son-of-a-bitching fire they had.'[2]

'If you'd've been there,' the freighter countered, being all too aware of his unconventional employee's penchant for becoming involved in any trouble which occurred in her vicinity. 'I'd've known you'd *have* to be mixed in it somehow.'

'Excuse me, sir,' the Kid put in, walking forward, drawing the required conclusion from the dig in the ribs he was given by Belle's elbow. 'But I consider that in the interests of justice and fair play, I must state this charming young lady acted as she did under the most extreme and dire provocation.'

'Hot damn, Rem!' the Rebel Spy snorted, in louder tones than were necessary or tactful, following the Englishman with no sign of the delight she felt over the way in which he had interpreted her signal. 'Trust you-all to go billing in this way just because there's some over-stuffed, half-naked girl involved.'

Being aware that her far from orthodox way of life and mode of dress did not meet with the approval of many other members of her sex, Calamity swung a far from artless – if more genuinely indignant – look at the speaker. Recognition came almost immediately and, although for a moment the Rebel Spy thought she would express surprise over the meeting, her ability as a poker player prevented her from doing so. What was more,

[2] *Raging through an area of three and one-third miles of Chicago on the 8th and 9th of October, 1871, the great fire destroyed over 17,450 buildings valued at $196,000.00. Almost one hundred thousand people were rendered homeless and at least two hundred and fifty lost their lives. Of the $4,966,782.00 relief fund subscribed in the United States of America and overseas, half of the one million dollars' foreign contributions came from the British Isles. J.T.E.*

knowing how the slender girl earned her living, the words she had heard supplied a clue to the response that was required.

'Why thank you 'most to death, kind sir,' the red head responded, directing a smile apparently filled with gratitude and a suggestion of something even more personal at the good looking, well dressed Englishman. 'No matter what your *mother* reckons, it does a gal's heart good to find out there're a few for-real gentlemen left.'

'*Mother?*' Belle squealed, realising that the other girl's answer had been ideal for what she hoped to achieve at a more opportune moment. Furthermore, she felt confident that – provided the requisite co-operation could be obtained – there might be an even more useful solution to the problem which she and the Kid had been discussing on their way from the hotel. 'Rem-honey, did you hear what – ?'

'I heard, *dear girl*!' the Englishman confirmed, in tones which implied an exasperation that needed the exercise of considerable will power to keep under control. 'Now do keep quiet while the constable, or whatever this gentleman is called, asks us some questions.'

'Calam darlin'!' Magoon boomed out, advancing with out-stretched arms. 'Do you mean to tell me that them two Johnny Raws[3] had the "audacitariness" and stupidity to go picking on *you?*

'That they did, the heathen spalpeens,' the red head confirmed, throwing her arms around the burly sergeant's neck and giving him a smacking kiss on the lips. 'But I sort of talked them out of it.'

'*Talked* 'em out of it, she says,' Magoon ejaculated, extracting himself from the embrace with a surprisingly bashful grin. Then, remembering how the damage had been caused, he threw a glance at the ruined window and went on, 'Well, that's *one* way of putting it, darlin'. Sure and it's a fine wife you'd be making for me, as I think I've said before.'

'Sure you have, me broth of a boyo,' Calamity agreed, mimicking the sergeant's accent and, stepping away from him, returning the handle of the whip to its loop on her waistbelt.

---

[3] '*Johnny Raw*' : *derogatory name for a recruit, particularly one who is not too bright. J.T.E.*

'And as soon's I said "yes" the last time you proposed, you was up and headed for the high country as fast as a well greased jack rabbit with a weasel chomping on its butt.'

'That was *your* fault, darlin',' the sergeant protested. 'I was counting on you to say "no".'[4]

While the conversation was going on, the crowd of customers and girls which was blocking the doorway of the saloon parted to let a woman pass through. That they moved so quickly despite their interest in what was going on was indicative of the respect they had for her, both as the owner of the premises and as the person who more than any of the other citizens had caused Mulrooney not only to flourish but to have an unrivalled reputation for honesty and fair dealing exceeding that of any other Kansas trail end town.[5]

Although the same height as Belle and Calamity, the woman known in Mulrooney as 'Freddie Woods'[6] had such a regal bearing and carriage that she gave the impression of being taller. A few years older than the Rebel Spy, her figure was – if not so prominently displayed at that moment – even more curvaceous than the red head's and her contours were come by just as naturally. She had black hair, elegantly coiffured if somewhat shorter than the current fashion, framing a beautiful face with strength and intelligence in its lines. As she had been attending to her duties as mayor of the town, she was dressed soberly, if expensively, in a black two-piece costume and frilly bosomed white blouse of masculine line; but contrived to make it seem as sensual as the most daring ball gown.

'Hum!' Freddie said, having stepped through the doors and, looking around, bringing her gaze to a halt when it reached the red head. 'Some of *your* work, I presume, Calam?

'Oh no!' Calamity groaned, slapping the heel of her left hand

[4] *An earlier meeting between Martha 'Calamity Jane' Canary and Sergeant Patrick James 'Paddy' Magoon is described in :* TROUBLE TRAIL. *However, because of an error in the documents regarding the incident originally supplied to the author, he was mistakenly given the name 'Muldoon' in that work. J.T.E.*

[5] *How this came about is told in :* THE MAKING OF A LAWMAN *and* THE TROUBLE BUSTERS. *J.T.E.*

[6] *'Freddie Woods' real name was Lady Winifred Amelia Besgrove-Woodstole. J.T.E.*

against her forehead and raising her eyes as if searching the heavens for divine support. 'Like that jasper said in a play I once got took to by mistake, "Eat, you brute?". Whatever in hell *that* might mean.'

'Gracious me,' the lady mayor said, smiling, without offering to correct the red head's misquotation.[7] 'Has somebody else accused *you*?'

'Only about half the son-of-a-bit – gunning town so far!' Calamity exaggerated, changing the word 'bitch' for the more acceptable 'gun' out of deference for Freddie's presence. 'But I reckon the other half'll get 'round to it afore nightfall.'

'It's the penalty of fame,' the mayor pointed out, satisfied even without inquiring further that the red head must have had an excellent reason for causing the damage. Then a recollection of something she had seen while glancing around on her arrival, but which had failed to register fully at the time, struck her. Turning her head, she stared for a moment at the Kid and, such was her surprise on discovering she was correct in her identification, she could not prevent herself from ejaculating, 'Great day in the morning! It is *you*, Pat!'

'Hello, Freddie old thing,' the Englishman answered, amused to see such a strong reaction from a person who was normally so completely self-possessed. He waved his left hand languidly from Beauregard to Calamity as he continued, 'As I was telling the marshal, this young lady was not to blame for the contretemps.'

'Do you-all know this gent, Miss Woods?' the peace officer inquired, speaking formally as it was an official matter although he was on first-name terms with the mayor.

'Yes, marshal,' Freddie confirmed, but did not supply the Kid's name as – being aware of the duties to which he had been seconded from the Rifle Brigade – she realised he might not be employing it. 'We're friends of long standing. What happened?'

[7] *The actual quotation is*, 'Et tu, Brute?', '*And you also, Brutus?*' : *said to have been Gauis Julius Caesar's reproachful dying comment on discovering that Marcus Junius Brutus, who he had believed to be his loyal and devoted friend, was one of the assassins who attacked him at the foot of Pompey's statue in the Senate Building at Rome on the 15th (the Ides) of March, 44 B.C. and is quoted in Act Three, Scene One, of the play* JULIUS CAESAR, *by William Shakespeare (1564–1616). J.T.E.*

'I still haven't found out for sure,' Beauregard confessed. Glancing at the knot of customers and employees in the saloon's doorway, then to the other people who had been attracted by the commotion, he went on, 'You-all might's well get back to whatever you were doing, folks. It's all over and there'll be nothing more to be seen around here.'

It said much for the respect the Texas peace officer had built up since taking office that the onlookers obeyed immediately and without question. As they were dispersing, he suggested that all those involved accompanied him into the barroom so he could conduct an inquiry and decide upon what, if any, legal action was necessary. On entering, at the rear of the group, he glanced around. A short, stocky, white-haired and Gallic-featured corporal and three troopers were attending to the two recruits, neither of whom had as yet recovered consciousness. Leaving his companions, the non-com walked across to join the group at the counter.

'The boys are wondering what happened, serge,' the corporal stated and his long service in the U.S. Cavalry had not succeeded in removing his French accent.

'Would you be after believing it if I was to tell you both of the spalpeens slipped on a piece of orange peel, Henri?' Magoon inquired.

'I'd believe *anything* you told me, it's not wise to do anything else,' the corporal replied, then he noticed the red head for the first time. '*Bonjour*, Calamity. What did they do to annoy you?'

'There!' the girl wailed, glaring at Freddie. 'What did I god-damned tell you? I *allus* get the blame – '

'That's because *you* mostly deserve it,' Killem interrupted. 'How badly are those two hurt, Henri?'

'Not as badly as they could have been,' the corporal declared, duplicating Freddie's belief that Calamity had not provoked whatever trouble brought them to their condition. 'They're not cut up and 're recovering.'

'Whooee, that's a relief!' the red head gasped and told the small group about her all that had occurred outside, finishing, 'I'm right sorry about your window, Freddie. But everything happened so fast after that yahoo pushed me so's I didn't have

46

time to think about where the other one was standing when I rammed him. I'll pay for it to – .'

'That you will not, darlin'!' Magoon interrupted and the corporal nodded a vehement agreement. 'It's them two spalpeens's'll be making it good. Sure and they'll be able to afford it, not having time to spend any money for a fair while to come.'

'Naw, we'll go halves on it,' Calamity contradicted, showing another side of her nature. Hot-headed, reckless – though not to the point of imprudence – and quick to temper as she might be, she was too generous and kind hearted to let even two young men who had insulted and planned to do worse to her suffer so excessively. 'And don't you go picking on 'em when they get back to the Fort, Paddy Magoon.'

'Settle for a third each and I'll be kindness itself to the little darlin's,' the sergeant offered with what might have been considered an angelically forgiving smile.

'A third it is,' Calamity accepted and, knowing the burly Irishman, supplemented, 'But that goes for you and the rest of the non-coms, Henri.'

'You can trust me like you trust Paddy, Calamity,' the corporal declared.

'Yeah,' the red head said dryly. 'Which's why I'm telling you. Anyways, I'm getting thirsty. Is it all right if I set up a round of drinks, marshal?'

'Go ahead,' Beauregard offered. 'Unless you want to prefer charges against the soldiers, Miss Woods?'

'There's no need for it, I feel they've been punished enough,' Freddie replied. 'So, as Calam obviously doesn't, I think we can say it's over and let her buy the drinks.'

'Then over it is,' the marshal declared, knowing he could rely upon Magoon to prevent the recruits from trying to take revenge.

'I hope you and your friend will have time to come up and take a bite to eat with me, Pat,' Freddie remarked, after the red head had bought a round of drinks. She had been studying Belle with considerable interest and had drawn conclusions which were more accurate than those arrived at by the clerk at the Railroad House Hotel. 'We have a lot to talk about.'

'But of course we will, Freddie,' the Kid assented.

'By the way, Pat,' the mayor remarked, as she, Belle and the Englishman were making their way up the stairs leading to the first floor. 'How is your Aunt Caroline keeping?'

'Who?' the Rebel Spy put in, before the Kid could reply.

'Surely Pat's mentioned her to you,' Freddie asked. 'The Dowager Duchess of Brockley.'

'Oh he has,' Belle admitted. '*Frequently*. But I never really believed she existed until now.'

CHAPTER FIVE

I DON'T FEAR *ANY* EVIL

'Rather nice little place you've got here, old dear,' Captain Patrick Reeder remarked, looking around approvingly as Freddie Woods followed Belle Boyd and him into the sitting room of her tastefully and comfortably luxurious living quarters.

'It's my home now,' the lady mayor of Mulrooney, Kansas, replied with quiet pride. Then she turned her gaze to the Rebel Spy and went on, 'Pat's manners were always atrocious. He hasn't bothered to introduce us.'

'My name is Belle Boyd, Lady Winifred,' the slender girl replied, deducing correctly that her pose of being a gambler's mistress had not succeeded where the beautiful Englishwoman was concerned.

'I'm pleased to meet you at last, Belle,' Freddie declared, holding out her right hand. 'Dusty has often spoken of you. Have you seen him recently?'

'We were working together down on the Rio Grande a short while ago,' the Rebel Spy answered, shaking hands and impressed by Freddie's strong grip. She could hardly restrain a shudder as she remembered some of the weirder aspects of the latest assignment in which she had participated with the man mentioned by the mayor,[1] but controlled her emotions and continued, 'I hope you don't think this is an imposition,

---

[1] *For the benefit of new readers : the man in question was Captain Dustine Edward Marsden 'Dusty' Fog, details of whose career and previous meetings with Belle Boyd and Freddie Woods are given in the author's* Civil War *and* Floating Outfit *series. He later married Freddie and their grandson, Alvin Dustine 'Cap' Fog supplied the information upon which this work is based. What the assignment was is told in :* SET A-FOOT. *J.T.E.*

although it is, but would you invite Calam and Mr Killem to join us, please?'

'Of course,' Freddie declared, without a moment's hesitation, realising that a far more serious motive than a desire to renew an acquaintance with Calamity Jane lay behind the suggestion as she had noticed the Rebel Spy did not offer to do so in the barroom. 'I'll send word down and invite them. Do you want to speak with them in private?'

'There's no need for that,' Belle stated, knowing that she could trust her hostess's discretion.

'How serious is whatever you're working on?' Freddie inquired, after she had given instructions for the message to be delivered.

'*Very* serious, old thing,' the Kid replied and Belle nodded her agreement. 'But we may as well leave telling you until Miss Calamity and Mr Killem get here.'

'Have it your own way, you always did,' Freddie assented with a smile. 'Sit down, both of you. And, Pat, I wouldn't call Calam "Miss" if I were you. She's not so polite and formal as we British pride ourselves on being.'

'I'll bear it in mind, dear girl,' the Kid promised, drawing out a chair for Belle at the table. Having seated Freddie and taken a chair himself, he went on, 'I suppose you want to ask them about that chappie dear Vera, the good "Father" and *le Loup-Garou* have had come to meet them?'

'That's part of it,' answered the Rebel Spy, to whom the question had been directed. 'And, if we hear what I expect we will, I hope we can persuade Calam to help us.'

Instead of explaining what she had meant by the final comment, Belle sat chatting with Freddie until Calamity and Dobe Killem arrived. On the introductions being performed, she found that the red head had been discreet when telling the freighter about their previous meeting.[2] He had known they were acquainted, but not that she was now a member of the U.S. Secret Service.

In spite of the assignment upon which Belle and the Kid were engaged being of great importance, neither mentioned it while the party were enjoying an excellent meal. After it was finished,

[2] *The meeting is described in :* THE BAD BUNCH. *J.T.E.*

over their coffee, they began to explain what had brought them to Mulrooney. Killem showed no surprise on being informed of their official status. Instead, he sat as if half asleep yet was taking in everything they said. Just as interested, Calamity was more demonstrative and let out explosive exclamations of surprise, or anger, at various points of the narrative.

Led by an English actress, Vera Gorr-Kauphin, and a man who had murdered and taken the identity of a priest, Father Matthew Devlin,[3] a group of international anarchists had been in Chicago with the intention of organising an army of Irish Republican supporters for an invasion of Canada. Realising that if this happened it would not only lead to friction between Great Britain and the United States, but might also cause the former country to bring a legal action along the lines of the 'Alabama' Arbitration Tribunal to the detriment of the latter's finances,[4] Belle had been instructed by the head of the U.S. Secret Service, General Philo Handiman, to prevent it. With the help of the Kid – who had been requested by the British ambassador in Washington to follow and keep an eye on the anarchists when it was learned they were coming from Europe[5] – and Lieutenant Edward Ballinger of the Chicago Police Department's Detective Bureau,[6] she had carried out the

[3] *There is no mention of the true identity of the man who took the priest's place in either the records supplied to the author by Alvin Dustine 'Cap' Fog, q.v., or in* ON REMITTANCE, *Major General Sir Patrick Reeder's as yet unpublished autobiography, so we will continue to refer to him as 'Matthew Devlin'. J.T.E.*

[4] *For the benefit of new readers. In 1872, an international committee sitting in judgement on what became known as the* 'Alabama' *Arbitration Tribunal, over protests levelled by the United States of America at Great Britain's conduct during the War of Secession, ruled in favour of the complainants. For allowing vessels of the Confederate States' Navy, such as the cruisers* Alabama, Florida *and* Shenandoah *to not only be built in, but to operate from its ports – and being involved in blockade running and other activities detrimental to the Union's cause – the Government of Great Britain had been ordered to pay compensation to the sum of $15,500,000.00 J.T.E.*

[5] *Although Captain Patrick Reeder had been sent from Britain to observe the events recorded in* SET A-FOOT, *he did not have any active participation in them and so there is no reference to his presence in that narrative. J.T.E.*

[6] *For the benefit of new readers : The researches of Philip José Farmer,*

difficult assignment successfully and without letting it become known that her organisation was involved. Unfortunately, circumstances had allowed the actress and the bogus priest to evade arrest.

That Killem was paying far greater attention than was suggested by his attitude became apparent while Belle was explaining why it had been considered necessary for her to intervene. Politely and without giving offence, he had raised points similar to those made to the Kid by Ballinger on their first meeting. He had remarked that, particularly as there was not the slightest chance of the invasion being successful, the British Government might have preferred to let it take place in the hope of benefiting financially from a legal action against the United States. Like the detective, he had accepted the Englishman was completely sincere when declaring that – regardless of what any 'so and so political johnny' might think – he considered it was more important to prevent something which would result in pointless misery, suffering and killing than to be influenced by the possibility of monetary gains for his country.

In the course of their investigations, Belle and the Kid had discovered that the anarchists were involved with Arnaud Cavallier in what was almost certainly to be a plot to cause further unrest and strife in Canada. They had also suspected that, in addition to having collected money and purchased weapons to equip the Irish invasion, the actress and the impostor had also organised a supply of arms and ammunition to be delivered for use by *le Loup-Garou's Metis'* supporters.

On learning that the actress and 'Devlin' had escaped, suspecting that Cavallier's arms would be delivered to the Montana town of Stokeley, Belle and the Kid had come to Mulrooney with the intention of travelling there on a railroad spur line. It was fortunate that, prior to their arrival, they had settled upon the kind of identities with which to conceal their purpose. They had so changed their appearances that when they discovered their suppositions were correct and the anarchists had joined

---

q.v., suggest that Lieutenant Edward Ballinger's grandson, Frank, held a similar rank and appointment in the Chicago Police Department at a later date and his exploits formed the basis of the 1957 television series, M SQUAD, starring Lee Marvin. J.T.E.

le Loup-Garou – the discovery having been made when they went to the Railroad House Hotel for accommodation, found he had signed the register in his own name and was accompanied by a 'married' couple – they were able to stay under the same roof without being recognised.

'They haven't given up the idea,' Belle declared, at the conclusion of her narrative. 'And, if anything, what they're planning with the *Metis* could be even worse than the Irish invasion.'

'Wha're *Metis*?' Calamity inquired.

'Not what, dear girl, *who*,' the Kid corrected and, after explaining, went on, 'We, the Canadian authorities that is, had trouble with them a few years ago and they proved to be excellent fighting men over their own kind of terrain. But, while I'd be the last to argue that they haven't had cause for complaint, Cavallier's not like the Louis Riels, father or son. They were content merely to try and redress the *Metis*' grievances. I can't see Cavallier having no more than that in mind. It's rumoured he would like a nation of his own to rule and he's got a reputation for not being too particular how he goes after things he wants. They don't call him *le Loup-Garou*, the Werewolf, for nothing.'

'Seems to me like all you have to do is get 'em arrested and sent back to Chicago,' Killem remarked, scratching his jaw pensively. 'Only something tells me it's not as all-fired simple as *that*.'

'It isn't, for a number of reasons,' Belle conceded with a wry smile, thinking that at least one of her activities in Chicago would be better left unrevealed. 'In the first place, we can't have them arrested and brought to trial without the whole affair being made public. What's more, in spite of all we suspect, obtaining a conviction where the Gorr-Kauphin woman and Cavallier are concerned would be extremely difficult, if not impossible. We haven't any legally acceptable evidence against either of them. Although I doubt whether "Devlin", whoever he might be, would let her get away with it if he was being tried, she could even try to pretend she didn't know he was an imposter. Or at least claim she didn't know he had murdered the real "Father Devlin".'

'Even if we obtained convictions against both of them,' the

Kid went on, 'that would still leave Cavallier free. Although Marcel Tinville told us it was *le Loup-Garou* who killed him, I don't think our superiors would be any too pleased about our appearing in the witness box. They tend to be a bit snuffy about little things like that.'

'Looks like you'll have to figure out some other way of stopping them then,' Killem suggested, apparently sleepily.

'We will,' Belle confirmed, far from being taken in by the burly freighter's attitude.

'There's one thing I don't understand,' Freddie put in. 'You said that you believe they've arranged for a supply of arms to be used by the *Metis*?'

'We're not certain they did,' Belle admitted. 'But the evidence points that way.'

'Even if they did, they must have had to leave Chicago hurriedly,' Freddie went on. 'Would they have been able to fetch the consignment with them at such short notice?'

'They might not have needed to bring it,' Belle replied. 'There aren't too many sources capable of supplying such a large quantity of arms and ammunition. In fact, I only know of one man who could do it so quickly.'

'Why haven't you nailed his hide to the wall if you know him?' Calamity demanded.

'I should have said we know that he exists, but not who he is except by his nickname, *die Fliescher*,' Belle explained. 'That's German for "the Butcher". However, from what we learned in Chicago, I feel sure he lives there. So I intend to go and see if I can find him after we've dealt with Gorr-Kauphin and her friends.'[7]

'Would he be able to arrange for Cavallier's arms to be delivered to the *Metis*?' Freddie inquired.

'He's said to be able to deliver arms anywhere and at short notice,' Belle replied. 'And I'm sure he's done so this time. If he hasn't, there wouldn't have been any reason for Gorr-Kauphin and "Devlin" to come west after things went wrong in Chicago. Nor would Cavallier be helping them merely out of the good-

[7] *How Belle Boyd's search for Ernst* 'die Fliescher' *Kramer turned out is told in*: Part five, 'The Butcher's Fiery End' *of* J.T.'s Ladies. *J.T.E.*

ness of his heart. From what little I know and have seen of him, he doesn't have any goodness in it.'

'He's not noted for being overburdened with the milk of human kindness,' the Kid confirmed, looking and sounding as if the subject under discussion was more boring than important. 'And the arms may already be in Mulrooney, or are being brought here very shortly. A chappie called Lincoln has got in touch with them.'

'*Jebediah* Lincoln?' Calamity snapped, throwing a glance at her employer.

'That could be his name,' the Kid replied. 'At least, the charming young lady who was our hostess at blackjack said his name was Jeb Lincoln when I rather craftily brought the subject up in casual conversation. Do you know him?'

'Run across him a couple of times,' the red head answered. 'He's got a small freight outfit and rumour has it he's done him some selling guns to Injuns, but nothing's been proved or you wouldn't't've seen him today.'

'In that case, he may work for *die Fliescher*, or have been hired by him to deliver the guns to Cavallier,' Belle commented. 'Either way, it shouldn't be difficult for me to arrange to have his wagons searched.'

'Likely not,' Killem conceded. 'Only it's been tried afore now, more than once, but nothing's ever been found in them. And that includes twice when Injuns have sudden-like showed up with more than normal numbers of guns not long after.'

'Has he ever been searched properly?' Belle inquired.

'How do you mean, *properly*?' Killem challenged.

'Has it been done by an expert?' Belle queried.

'Like who?' Calamity put in, remembering how the Rebel Spy had acted and sensing what might be coming.

'By somebody who knows as much, or even more, than he does about wagons and freighting,' Belle elaborated.

'Somebody like Dobey here, maybe,' the red head guessed. 'Or better still, *me*.'

'Why you, Calam?' the burly freighter wanted to know.

'I don't reckon good ole Jebediah would take kind to the notion of you going over his wagons happen they were carrying guns,' Calamity replied. 'Or me either, comes to that, unless I was working for him.'

'*Working* for him!' Killem repeated. 'Why'd you be working for him?'

'Well now, was you to fire me 'cause of all the fuss I get into, I'd have to get took on by somebody else seeing's how driving a wagon's all I know,' Calamity pointed out, then became more serious. 'Damn it all, Dobe. You've heard what that actress and her bunch'll do to get what they want. Anybody who'd be willing to kill a priest, or let her own brother be made wolf-bait when he was bad hurt, to make sure he wouldn't talk out of turn when he came to in hospital, so's they can help start up a couple of shooting fusses's'll see a whole lot of innocent folks put under afore they're settled – well, I reckon they've just got to be stopped. And, hot damn, I'm willing to do *anything* I can to help stop them.'

'We'd appreciate having your help, dear girl,' the Englishman declared, admiring the red head for her spirited words. 'But giving it could put you in grave peril.'

'Is that the truth?' Calamity answered, grinning broadly and showing not the slightest perturbation over the prospect. 'Well, I figure I can go along with what it says in the Good Book. Hell, 'though I'm walking through the valley of the shadow of death, I don't fear *any* evil – 'cause I'm a whole heap meaner'n any son-of-a-bitch I'm likely to meet there.'

*   *   *

'Patrick St John-Haythornthwaite?' Vera Gorr-Kauphin said slowly, in answer to a question Arnaud Cavallier had put to her at the end of his description of the events in which he had participated at the Fair Lady Saloon. Almost two hours had elapsed since he left the blackjack game, but he and his associates had only just got rid of Jebediah Lincoln and he had not mentioned the matter while the freighter was present. 'No, I can't recollect having heard the name. Is there any reason why I should have?'

'I got the impression from his nickname, the Remittance Kid, that his family may have sent him from England because of some scandal, or to avoid one,' *le Loup-Garou* replied. 'At least, one or the other was the reason for every remittance man I've met so far being in Canada.'

'His name doesn't mean *anything* to me,' the actress stated. 'Of course, I didn't mingle with the upper classes to any great extent, or pay any attention to their gossip.'

Close to five foot nine inches tall, in her middle thirties, there was little sexually attractive about Vera. She had a thin face with prominent cheek bones, piercing dark eyes, a sharp nose and a chin that came to a point below thin, pallid lips. An expression of fanatical zeal which was repellant in its intensity, taken with a harsh and arrogant voice, prevented any chance of it being thought that her appearance masked a pleasant nature. She had covered her mousey brown hair with a more luxuriant blonde wig. Any poise, elegance, or charm her angular, almost boney figure might have had was effectively concealed by the severely plain brown taffeta dress she was wearing and from beneath which showed a pair of low-heeled, blunt-toed shoes. In spite of pretending to be 'Matthew Devlin's' wife, she wore no jewellery and prevented her lack of a wedding ring from being noticed by never appearing in public without gloves.

'What makes him so important?' the impostor asked.

Six foot in height, with a powerful physique, 'Devlin' was in his late forties. His voice was redolent of middle class Southern Irish origins. In addition to having changed his 'priest's' attire for clothing suitable to his new pose of being a wealthy business-man, he was covering his close-cropped iron-grey hair with a well made brown wig. He had an equally realistic matching false moustache and neat chin beard affixed to his hard, tanned face. They did nothing to relieve its bitter and unsmiling lines. Everything about him gave a warning that he was strong, authoritative and unforgiving of weakness in others.

'I would find any Englishman interesting after our troubles in Chicago,' Cavallier replied, showing no sign of being either impressed or concerned by the impostor's stern and forbidding demeanour. 'Particularly one who is staying in this hotel and, even without his name pointing to it, speaks in the manner of the British upper class.'

From the beginning of their association, there had been little love lost between *le Loup-Garou* and 'Devlin'.

In spite of his pretence of believing in equality, the anarchist had a tendency towards racial prejudice he could never entirely conceal. Furthermore, he assumed he had the right to command and believed everybody else should follow his orders without question. That Cavallier was not only born of mixed parentage, but was also rich and influential would have been sufficient to arouse his animosity. So did the *Metis'* refusal to accept subordinate status. The last thing he wanted was for there to be such a strong leader of the uprising he was helping to set into motion. Nor was the situation improved by 'Devlin' realising that his reputation for being tough and unscrupulous caused the equally ruthless *le Loup-Garou* not the slightest trepidation.

'Nobody's told *me* there was an Englishman staying here!' Vera said indignantly.

'He and his wife only arrived yesterday evening,' Cavallier explained, but did not mention that it was the actress's snobbish attitude which caused the hotel's staff to be so uncommunicative.

'His *wife*?' Vera repeated. 'Could they be the same couple you saw the night you killed Tinville?'

'I haven't seen the lady as yet, *mademoiselle*,' Cavallier answered, speaking more politely than when addressing 'Devlin'. 'They would be much of the same height. Although his hair is blond, it could have been dyed for the night, or done since, and he could easily have shaved off his moustache, but his nose is smaller and has not been broken. Also he does not have a Scottish accent and there is no scar on his face.'

Having well developed sexual desires and considering he was an invincible conqueror of female hearts, *le Loup-Garou* had looked forward to the meeting when he heard that the anarchists from Europe with whom he was allying himself were led by a woman. He had felt sure that he would be able to convert her to being a willing and unquestioning supporter of his aims and against 'Devlin'. Although he had not been impressed by Vera's appearance, he had not allowed it to deter him, but soon found that she refused to yield to his charm. However, in spite of realising that she was unlikely to regard him as a suitable leader for the *Metis* nation, he had continued to flatter and cultivate her so as to alienate her from the male anarchist.

'Then he *might* not be the same man, you're saying,' 'Devlin' suggested, with tinly veiled sarcasm.

'I'm merely pointing out the differences between them,' Cavallier corrected. 'Unless *you* left something behind, or said something to somebody which could have put them on our trail, there's no reason to believe the British Secret Service, or that of your country, know we're in Mulrooney. However, I don't believe in taking unnecessary risks. So I mean to go out and see if I can learn anything about him.'

CHAPTER SIX

CAUSE ANY TROUBLE AND YOU'RE THROUGH

'Hello!' Jebediah Lincoln remarked, looking at the young woman and the burly, older man who were entering the club car of the train upon which he, Vera Gorr-Kauphin, 'Matthew Devlin' and Arnaud Cavallier were travelling to Stokeley, Montana. 'I wonder what they're doing here?'

'Who are they?' 'Devlin' inquired, glancing over his shoulder.

'The feller's Dobe Killem, runs a freight outfit like me,' Lincoln replied and swung his gaze to the actress as he went on, 'The gal's Calamity Jane. I reckon you've likely heard of *her* even over in England, "Mrs Roxby"?'

'I can't say that I have,' Vera answered stiffly.

Like many of her kind and political persuasions, the actress was an arrant snob with delusions of grandeur and only used the pretence of believing in equality as a means of convincing the 'little people' of her deep concern over their welfare and betterment. So she had resented the familiarity with which Lincoln had treated her from their first meeting. Not only was he the type of man who believed his sex had an inborn and natural superiority over women, his thinly veiled disdain for everything English had failed to appeal to her when she had found herself to be included in it. In her opinion, as he was merely one of Ernst Kramer's hired hands and employed to transport her party's property, he should have displayed a vastly greater respect towards her.

The fact that neither 'Devlin' nor Cavallier had offered to intervene on her behalf and bring about a change in Lincoln's behaviour had done nothing to make her feel cordial to them.

What was more, she suspected that the male anarchist had invited him to join them in the club car knowing to do so would annoy her. Being compelled to accept his company, as an alternative to staying alone in the stateroom they had taken, robbed her of any satisfaction and pleasure in the thought that their affairs were running smoothly once more.

'Hey, Calam gal!' Killem boomed, sounding genuinely surprised by the discovery that another freight outfit operator was on the train, as he and the red head approached the conspirators' table. 'Will you just look at who's sat here as large as life and twice as well fed.'

'Well I'll be switched!' Calamity replied, in just as convincing a fashion. 'If it's not good old Jebediah Lincoln. Hey there, Jebediah. What's up, have all the wheels dropped off your son-of-a-bitching wagons?'

'Damned if I wasn't just going to ask you pair the same thing, Calam,' the freighter answered, coming to his feet. Although he had previously been on no more than nodding terms with Killem, he was far from averse to letting his customers assume he had a far closer social relationship with a young lady whose fame had spread across the United States even though it did not appear to have reached the circles in which the Englishwoman moved. 'Are you going all the way to Stokeley?'

Matching Killem in height, Lincoln's extra twenty or so pounds of weight was not attained by hard muscle. Rather he was corpulent in a fashion suggesting a love of good living and which implied his control of the freight outfit was dependent less upon manual skill than administrative ability. Balding – his fancy grey billycock hat lay on the table in front of him – with what was left of his light brown hair rendered almost black by a liberal application of bay rum, his florid features seemed jovial apart from his small and close set eyes. He spoke with a somewhat high pitched New England accent and, being patterned on the most recent fashion to have arrived from the East, his brown suit, white shirt and gaily coloured silk cravat gave no clue to the nature of his employment. Although there was no noticeable evidence of his being armed, he carried a short barrelled Merwin & Hulbert Army Pocket model revolver in what was known as a 'half breed' shoulder holster under his left arm.[1] For all his bulging paunch and bulk, Calamity and Killem, having seen him in action, knew he was competent in its use.

'All the way,' Killem answered. 'I'm heading up there to see if there's any work for us freighters who go where the railroad can't, or don't. You got the same in mind?'

'Nope, Mr Cavallier's guiding "Mr and Mrs Roxby" here on a hunting trip and I'm carrying their gear along,' Lincoln lied, but with an acceptable aura of veracity, indicating Vera, 'Devlin' and *le Loup-Garou* with a wave of his left hand. 'You know me, Dobe. I don't settle nowhere permanent.'

'There're some who might say you're wise not to,' Killem commented cryptically, knowing the second part of the explanation was intended to assure him that its maker was not proposing to become a rival for any business that might be going in the Stokeley area. 'Pleased to meet you folks and I surely wish you every luck in your hunting.'

'Our thanks for your kind wishes, *m'sieur*,' Cavallier responded, rising with his eyes drinking in Calamity's far from concealed feminine attributes. Despite being aware that Vera's scrutiny of the girl was disapproving, he was too eager to become better acquainted with the shapely newcomer to let it deter him. 'Would you care to join us?'

'Why that's right neighbourly of you, "mon-sewer",' Calamity assented, without giving her employer an opportunity to express his opinion. 'We'd admire to set 'n' talk a spell.'

'Do you speak French, *mademoiselle*?' Cavallier inquired, smiling a little at the girl's pronunciation.

'Not a whole heap more'n I just did,' Calamity confessed, also grinning. 'Only I heard fellers calling each other that when I was down to New Orleans a couple of years back.[2] You're sort

---

[1] *At the period in which this work is set, the withdrawal of a revolver from a shoulder holster was already being made easier by the use of clip springs to retain the weapon. If all the front leather was cut away, with the exception of a small cup to hold the revolver's muzzle, such a rig was known as a 'clip spring' shoulder holster. Leaving leather in place, except for an open seam through which the weapon is slid, turned it into a 'half breed' rig. A description of a modern version of the 'half breed' style of holster is given in the author's* Rockabye County *series dealing with the duties of a present day Texas sheriff's office. J.T.E.*

[2] *The story of the visit is told in :* THE BULL WHIP BREED. *J.T.E.*

of like a right nice feller I met there. Is that where you hail from?'

'Regrettably, I have never been there,' *le Loup-Garou* replied, his lascivious gaze continuing to roam over the girl's curvaceous body. 'But if that is *your* home, I will make every effort to pay a visit in the near future.'

'Blast if I don't wish that's where I lived then,' Calamity declared, studying the *Metis* with an intensity which appeared to be every bit as predatory as was his examination of her. She decided that, in spite of knowing he was a cold blooded killer whose morals where members of her sex were concerned left much to be desired – the latter information had been gleaned by Lieutenant Edward Ballinger from a man with whom he had quarrelled over the division of the profits and so broken off a scheme to supply Indian and *Metis* girls to be used as prostitutes – he looked as she put it, 'one tolerable hunk of a man'. 'Trouble being, there's no room at your table. So, much's I'd admire to, we can't sit and "sociable-ise" with you.'

'Then I'm sure my friends won't mind if I join you,' Cavallier countered, although he felt certain he was not expressing Vera's sentiments on the matter. 'As Mr Lincoln said, I am accompanying them as guide and would be pleased if you could give me any suggestions.'

'I surely hope you only mean about *hunting*,' Calamity grinned, but her manner implied that suggestions of a more personal nature would be far from unwelcome.

'But what else, *mon cherie*?' Cavallier clarified, finding the red head a most refreshing change after Vera's far from amiable society. 'And, while we are talking, why don't we take another table. Also, unless it will give offence, perhaps I might be allowed to order a drink for you – both.'

'Time comes when I get given offence by anybody, 'specially a handsome young feller like *you*, offering to set up the drinks, I'll know I'm getting old,' Calamity asserted, having intended to make a similar offer if it had not been forthcoming and realising Killem had only been included in the invitation as an after-thought. Nodding to the bar in the centre of the compartment, she went on, 'Only I'd sooner go and lean instead, happen that's all right with you. I'm not took with drinking when I'm sat, I don't know when I've had enough.'

'But how is it different when you are standing?' *le Loup-Garou* asked.

'Easy enough,' the red head explained. 'When I've had enough and I'm stood, I can fall down. Only it's never happened yet.[3] Are you coming or staying, boss-man?'

'I thought we were going to grab a bite to eat?' Killem protested, making it appear that he was not in favour of the girl drinking.

'Aw hell, there'll be plenty of time for us to do that after we've had a snort or three with the "mon-sewer" here,' the red head insisted, contriving to suggest she cared nothing for her employer's disapproval. 'Anyways, happen you don't want one, why'n't you stop and tell those good folks what you know about hunting while me 'n' him go belly up to the bar for a spell?'

'Do you mind if I buy the young lady a drink, m'sieur?' Cavallier went on, making the words sound close to a challenge.

'She's full grown and knows her mind,' Killem answered, in tones which lacked cordiality.

'I sure's hell's for sinners am!' Calamity confirmed, her attitude redolent of defiance. 'Let's go and bend an elbow, "mon-sewer".'

'That's Calam for you,' Lincoln commented with a broad grin, as – before Killem could say anything more on the subject – the girl and Cavallier walked towards the bar. 'Hey though, didn't I hear that she had a mite of trouble with a couple of Johnny Raws from Fort Connel outside the Fair Lady Saloon?'

'She did!' the burly freighter affirmed, his voice taking on an angry and disgusted timbre. 'They said something she didn't like and the damned hot-head threw the pair of them through a window. Miss Woods didn't cause any fuss, seeing as Paddy Magoon promised the Johnny Raws would pay for the damage, but I could tell she wasn't pleased it had happened.'

'She wouldn't be,' Lincoln commented. 'But isn't that Calam a pistol, things she gets up to?'

'It's not so all-fired, god-damned amusing when you're her boss,' Killem replied. 'And I hope she minds what I told her

---

[3] *As is told in* Part One, 'Better Than Calamity' *of* THE WILD-CATS, *Miss Canary's statement was not entirely accurate. J.T.E.*

about not getting drunk and causing a fuss up to Stokeley.'

'What was that?' Lincoln inquired, remembering the numerous other stories he had heard about the red head's penchant for becoming involved in disturbances and fracas.

'I didn't want to bring her, but she insisted on coming along,' Killem answered, noticing that the two anarchists were listening with as much interest as the other freighter. 'So, after all the money it's cost me to square things up after the fussing and fighting she's caused in other places and seeing as how I don't want anything spoiling my chances of picking up some business there, I've told her straight out, "You cause any trouble and you're through." And, by grab, I mean it!'

'You mean you'd fire *her*?' Lincoln asked, glancing to where Calamity was lounging against the bar with all the aplomb of a seasoned habituary of such establishments. 'But she's a damned good driver.'

'She's all of that, fact being I'd say there's not many better,' Killem conceded, sounding as if he begrudged having to make such a concession. 'But I'm getting sick to my guts over having to hand out *my* money to pay for the damage's gets caused when she starts a ruckus with another gal in a saloon and getting it damned near wrecked when everybody else joins in. And I don't take kind to it when a marshal tells me to keep my crew out of his bailiwick because they're trouble-makers, which's started to happen. No sir, Jebediah, I've had my fill of it. Good as she is, just one more god-damned bit of trouble and she's finished with my outfit.' Then he brought his tirade to an abrupt halt and, swinging his gaze to the anarchists, removed his hat hurriedly and continued apologetically, 'I'm right sorry for taking on that way, ma'am, sir. It's just that she gets me riled up. Anyways, trouble is I've not done any hunting this far north, so there's not a whole heap I can tell you.'

Having noticed how a wistful note had crept into Lincoln's voice when referring to Calamity's ability as a driver, the burly freighter felt certain that the plot hatched in Freddie Woods' sitting-room would succeed provided its other elements could be implemented. Because of the rumours about his clandestine and illegal cargoes, Lincoln had great difficulty in obtaining the services of skilful and conscientious employees. He was likely to leap at an opportunity to acquire one as capable as she had been taught to be since joining Killem.

Not only had Calamity and her employer already been meaning to visit Stokeley for the purpose he had given to Lincoln, appreciating how great would be the cost in human lives and suffering if the conspiracy was allowed to be accomplished, they had expressed their willingness to help circumvent it. Showing the reckless disregard for danger which had produced her sobriquet, the girl had expressed delight rather than apprehension over the part she would be expected to play. She was, although she had not mentioned it, looking forward to participating for a second time in a perilous assignment with the Rebel Spy.[4] It said much for Killem's faith in her ability to look after herself that, even knowing everything possible was to be done to lessen the danger she would be facing, he had raised no objections to her taking part in the scheme. What was more, he was playing his own role with considerable histrionic ability as befitted a man known for his skill at poker.

'That's all right,' Vera answered shortly. 'We were assured that Mr Cavallier is a competent guide, so he can take us to where we want to go.'

'We might's well go and take a drink with him and Calam then, Dobe,' Lincoln suggested, sharing *le Loup-Garou*'s wish to have a change of company from the unsociable 'Mr and Mrs Roxby'.

'We might at that,' Killem assented, nothing loth for all his earlier apparent reluctance. 'If I'm there, she ought to stay something like sober.'

'My name is Arnaud Cavallier, *mon cherie*,' *le Loup-Garou* was saying, in response to Calamity's request to be told what she might call him, as the two freighters arrived at the bar.

'Damned if I could get my tongue around anything's fancy as that,' the girl objected. 'So, happen it's all right with you, I'll just stick to "Mon-sewer".'

'But of course, *mon cherie*, whatever you wish,' Cavallier authorised. 'And what can I get for you?'

'I'll take me a snort of that fancy red-eye and a cigar, 'less you don't hold with smoking,' Calamity replied.

[4] *The previous occasion is told in* : THE BAD BUNCH. *J.T.E.*

'Your wish is my command,' Cavallier declared. 'May I order for you, gentlemen?'

'Well I'll swan if it's not getting to be just like old home week,' Calamity ejaculated, swinging her gaze to a man and woman who had entered the car from the opposite to that in which she and Killem arrived, after she had been served and was holding a smoking cigar. Raising her free hand in a friendly wave, she went on, 'Hey, boss-man, look who's here.'

'Do you know them?' Cavallier inquired, glancing over his shoulder at the newcomers as the man gave an almost languid-seeming gesture in response to the red head's salutation.

'Name's the Remittance Kid. He's English, but one hell of a good feller, and his latest lady-love, which he likes 'em old 'n' skinny and she's no son-of-a-bitching lady for all her airs and graces,' Calamity answered, conveying the impression that she had considerable dislike for the woman in question. 'Hey, Rem you old tinhorn, come on over and get acquainted with "Mon-sewer" here.'

'I thought we were going to sit down, Rem!' Belle Boyd protested as the Englishman strolled forward, her attitude suggesting the dislike was mutual.

'Sit down if you want to,' Captain Patrick Reeder replied, without pausing or looking back. 'Hello, Wolf, old chap. I wasn't expecting to see you on the train.'

'Hey, do you two know each other?' the red head inquired.

'We played blackjack together yesterday,' Cavallier explained, then turned his gaze to the Englishman. 'But I have a feeling we've meet somewhere before that.'

'It's possible,' the Kid admitted, although he hoped the suggestion was not prompted by a remembrance – or at least a suspicion – of where the meeting had taken place. 'I'm saunter-ing to New York from San Francisco, so we could have run across each other along the way.'

'If you was in Fort Connel a week Tuesday, you'd've seen him likely,' Calamity stated. 'Only, way he carved up that card shark with his fancy old toad-sticker, you'd not soon have forgotten him.'

'It was purely in self defence, dear girl,' the Kid protested. 'It's a rather peculiar perversion of mine, but I find myself taking the gravest exception to there being more than four aces in a – *deck*, don't you colonials call it – of cards.'

'So do I,' Cavallier seconded, having been told much the same about what had happened in Fort Connel by a sergeant and corporal who were stationed there when he had talked with them in the Fair Lady Saloon the previous evening. He indicated the hilt of the *badik*, which still protruded from beneath the Englishman's jacket and asked, 'Is that the knife you used, *m'sieur*?'

'It is,' the Kid confirmed.

'I would have thought with a hilt that shape, it would be difficult to handle in a fight,' Cavallier suggested, genuinely interested.

'One gets used to it,' the Kid pointed out truthfully, for he had always found the *badik* an exceptionally effective weapon after he had grown accustomed to its pistol-like hilt and having been taught how to hold it properly when wielding it. 'Certainly the Bugis find it to be so. They call it the "butterfly knife", because it's supposed to look like one, but it stings more like a damned deadly wasp.'

'*Mademoiselle* – No, I'm sorry, *madame*. How remiss of *me*.' Cavallier said, with well simulated contrition, as Belle drew attention to her presence by giving a sniff which was redolent of indignation at having been neglected. 'We have overlooked you.'

'Don't worry none, "Mon-sewer",' Calamity put in. '*She'll* make sure you don't do *that*. I thought you wanted to sit down, girlie?'

'I'll stand, or sit, as I choose!' answered Belle, to whom the question had been directed. Then she turned a more pleasant face to the *Metis* and continued in his paternal language, 'And it is *mademoiselle*, *m'sieur*. I'm *not* married.'

'May I congratulate you on your excellent French, *mademoiselle*?' Cavallier praised in English.

'She has to be good for *something*,' Calamity sniffed.

'At least I don't have to go around dressed like a man to get people to look at me,' Belle countered. 'I think it's disgraceful and *most* unladylike to wear such clothes.'

'Listen, skinny gal!' Calamity growled, reaching towards the

Rebel Spy with her left hand and knotting the right into a fist. 'I don't – '

'Quit it!' Killem barked, catching the red head by the upper arms and swinging her bodily away from Belle.

'Lemme go, god blast you!' Calamity yelled, struggling futilely against her employer's powerful grip. 'Damn it to hell, boss-man, turn me loose. No son-of-a-bitching calico cat's going to mean-mouth *me*!'

'You started it, you cheap, low-bred hussy!' Belle shouted, sounding just as furious and clenching her fists while acting as if contemplating attacking the incapacitated red head.

'Stop that!' the Kid thundered, swinging towards the Rebel Spy and lifting his right hand as if prepared to strike her as a means of compelling her to obey.

'Come now, ladies,' *le Loup-Garou* supplemented pacifically, although he would not have been averse to the confrontation being allowed to develop into a hair-pulling brawl. 'Why don't we all have a drink and be friends?'

'I'm all for that and so is Lavinia,' the Kid declared, scowling in a threatening fashion at Belle until she gave what appeared to be a reluctant and sulky nod and lowered her hands.

'You won't get any argument from this one, either!' Killem stated, giving the red head a reasonably gentle shake and shove which propelled her away from Belle. Meeting her apparently resentful and hostile glare, he continued in threatening tones, 'Now quit it, damn you. Don't you go forgetting what I told you afore we left Mulrooney. If there should be any more trouble on your doing, you can start looking for some other kind of work. Because, if I have to kick you out, you'll never be handling the ribbons on a freight wagon again. I'll see to that and I'm the man who can do it.'

'I'll keep what you say in mind!' Calamity promised bitterly, spitting out the words in a kind of defiant anger which suggested it was mingled with a realisation that her employer could make the threat good. Then she gave what passed as an attempt at a devil-may-care shrug. 'Oh what the hell! Come on, let me set up the drinks to show there's no hard feelings. Then how about us playing a few hands of poker. Damn it, I shouldn't hurt nobody's feelings doing that.'

CHAPTER SEVEN

YOU CAN TRUST ME

'There are two colours in a deck of cards,' Captain Patrick Reeder said to Calamity Jane. 'Reds and blacks. Which do you want?'

Night had just fallen and the lights of the club car were glowing warmly as the train continued its journey northwards. After breaking off for dinner, the players in the poker game organised by Calamity were once more gathered at their table. Before play was recommenced, a question about the Remittance Kid's *badi*? had started him reminiscing on his travels in and around the East Indies. His anecdotes were so amusing and interesting that the others had encouraged him to continue. When he had mentioned the way in which Indian *fakirs* and other holy men had the power to direct another person's thoughts to an object of their own choosing, Calamity had stated vehemently that it would not work on *her*. Claiming he had learned how to do it, he had taken and looked at the top card of the deck. Placing it face down on the table, he had gazed at her for a moment and asked the question.

'Reds,' Calamity answered.

'The reds are divided into hearts and diamonds,' the Kid went on. 'Which suit do you want?'

'The diamonds,' Calamity decided.

'Which are divided into odd and even cards,' the Kid continued, still looking into the girl's eyes. 'Which do you want?'

'The evens,' Calamity selected.

'That leaves the odds for me, dear girl. And out of the odds you've left, which would you prefer, the three high cards, nine, jack and king, or the low cards, three, five and seven.'

'I'll take the high ones.'

'Out of the high ones, there are three combinations of two, nine and jack, nine and king, or king and jack. Which combination do you want?'

'The – ' Calamity began. 'The nine and the king.'

'And which would you prefer out of the nine and the king?' the Kid inquired.

'I'll take the nine,' Calamity answered.

'And here it is,' the Kid declared, turning the card over and tossing it to land before the girl.

'Wh –!' Calamity gasped, staring at the nine of diamonds and, for once, taken aback. Frowning in puzzlement, she examined the card to make sure the king she had rejected was not behind it; although she could not imagine how the Englishman could have known what she would choose and so remove them. The king was not there and she asked, 'How the hell did you do it?'

'Controlled your thoughts and directed them the way I wanted,' the Kid drawled, as if stating the obvious, noticing that Dobe Killem, Arnaud Cavallier and Jebediah Lincoln appeared to be equally baffled.

'If that's what it is,' Calamity said pensively, 'I'll bet you can't do it again.'

'Did you say *bet*, dear girl?' the Kid asked.

'That's just what I said,' the red head confirmed. 'And I've got ten lil ole iron men's says you can't.'

'I doubt whether my aunt, the Dowager Duchess of Brockley, would approve of me taking money from a lady,' the Kid protested.

'Don't let that worry you none,' the red head replied. ''Cause I ain't no son-of-a-bitching lady and don't pretend to be –' She darted a glance to where Belle Boyd was sitting at a near by table. 'Not like some folks I could name. Anyways, *you* won't be taking it offen *me*.'

However, being just as puzzled as the others, the Rebel Spy did not respond as she would have if she had been less interested in trying to work out how the trick was done.

Throughout the afternoon, Belle had continued to play the part of the jealous woman sensing she had a rival for her man's affections. She and Calamity had bickered at intervals, with the Kid and Killem keeping the exchanges from passing beyond the verbal stage. She had noticed the two anarchists studying her and the Englishman, but neither had offered to strike up a conversation. Nor had Cavallier, although he too had subjected them to considerable scrutiny.

'Ten dollars?' the Kid inquired.

'Cash on the barrel head,' Calamity promised.

'You're on, dear girl,' the Kid accepted, retrieving the nine of diamonds and shuffling it into the deck.

'Is this a closed hand, or can anybody sit in?' Lincoln asked.

'I leave it to the lady,' the Englishman replied.

'I tell you I ain't no *lady*!' Calamity grinned. 'But anybody's wants to *win* along with me can get in on it.'

'Give me ten dollars worth,' Lincoln requested.

'You have it,' assented the Kid, extracting the four of hearts. 'Anybody else who doubts my powers can join in.'

'Not me,' Killem refused with a grin. 'I don't know how you do it, but I do know you will.'

'Your judgement is good enough for me,' Cavallier stated, remembering the bet made at the end of the blackjack game. 'So I'll decline with thanks.'

'Well, here we go,' the Kid announced, peering into Calamity's face. 'There are two colours – .'

'I'll take black,' the girl interrupted, deciding that the card would be a spade or a club as the previous one had been red.

'Which leaves me the reds,' the Kid answered. 'Which are divided into diamonds and hearts, which do you want?'

'I'll take the diamonds,' Calamity selected, on the principle that a double bluff was being pulled.

'And leave me the hearts. Out of which there are odd cards and evens – '

'I'll have the evens.'

'Which are comprised of the high ones, the eight, ten and queen, or the low ones, the two, four and six. Which do you want?'

'The low ones.'

'They make three combinations of two, deuce and four, four and six, or six and deuce. Which pair do you want?'

'The six and the deuce,' Calamity said.

'And that leaves *me* with the four of hearts,' the Kid declared, exposing the card and reaching for the money.

'Well I'll be damned!' Calamity gasped. 'You've done it again.'

'Amazing, isn't it?' the Kid smiled.

'Amazing's the word,' Killem said dryly, having noticed and drawn an accurate conclusion to how the trick was performed from listening to the way the questions had been posed in response to the previous answer.

'Come on, Kid,' Calamity pleaded. 'How do you do it?'

'Actually, dear girl, it's a case of mind over matter,' the Englishman answered so soberly he might have been speaking the truth. 'I remember well my aunt, the Dowager Duchess of Brockley explaining it to me. She said – ' his voice changed to a rich, fruity contralto, ' "Patrick, my boy, it's all a case of mind over matter. I don't mind and *you* don't matter".'

'Ugh!' the red head ejaculated, giving a shudder. 'I wish I hadn't asked. Come on. Let's play us some more poker and we'll see if you can control my thoughts at that.'

'How much longer are you going to be playing, Rem?' Belle asked in an irritable tone, glaring across the car.

'Until the game ends,' the Kid answered shortly.

'Then I'm going out on to the observation car for a breath of fresh air!' Belle stated, rising with a show of indignation.

'I think I will have to sit out for a few hands,' Cavallier remarked, doing all he could to make himself sound casual and regretful, glancing at the Rebel Spy's departing back. 'After all, "Mr and Mrs Roxby" are hiring me and I've not said a word to them all afternoon. I'd better go to their stateroom and make sure they have everything they want, then I'll be back and see if you can control my thoughts as well as Calam's, Kid.'

In spite of the excuse he had given for taking his departure, *le Loup-Garou* made no attempt to join his fellow conspirators. Remembering the surly way in which 'Matthew Devlin' had been glowering at him all afternoon and Vera Gorr-Kauphin's increasing annoyance when he continued to ignore her, he doubted that he would receive a very cordial reception if he visited them. What was more, he considered that he could spend his time more profitably elsewhere. So, although he went by the temporary quarters to which they had retired in high dudgeon after dinner, he had no intention of entering.

Serving the needs of the more wealthy passengers who required privacy on the journey, the car containing the line of staterooms was the rearmost of the train. In addition to offering separate accommodation to those who could afford it, there was a small covered-over observation platform at the back upon which the occupants could stand and view the scenery, or take the fresh air. Opening the door which gave access to it, Cavallier found the person he was seeking and was pleased to see she was alone.

'Oh!' Belle greeted, turning as *le Loup-Garou* came on to the platform. She reverted to French as she went on, 'It's *you*, *m'sieur.*'

'Did you expect it to be the Kid?' the *Metis* inquired, stepping forward after he had closed the door.

'Not when there's a chance for him to fleece suck – !' Belle commenced in bitter tones, then made a very obvious and hurried correct to her comment. 'To play cards.'

'Especially with so pretty a girl as Calamity Jane,' Cavallier supplemented.

'*Her?*' the Rebel Spy snorted. 'Huh! All she is to him is another suck – player, no matter what *she* might think. He needs somebody like me, not a common, uncouth slut like her as his assist – woman.'

'Have you and he been together for long, "Lavinia"?' Cavallier asked, using the only name by which the Englishman had referred to his "mistress". 'I hope you don't mind me being so informal, but he didn't introduce us properly.'

'He *wouldn't*, the damned British snob!' Belle declared, with well simulated asperity. 'Huh! For all his fine talk about his aunt, the Dowager Duchess of Brockley – who I bet doesn't even exist – his family can't be all that important, or he'd never have had to leave England just because he was accused of cheating at cards.'

'And was he?' Cavallier inquired, being eager to learn more about the Kid.

'He *says* he *wasn't*,' the Rebel Spy replied, in a way which implied she had doubts over his veracity. Then she continued to elaborate upon her grievance with regards to the disrespectful way he had treated her. 'Why we Saltyres of Cottonbriar Manor, Louisiana, wouldn't have allowed it to happen to any of our kin before the god-damned Yankees ruined us. And we were just as well bred and even more wealthy than his family, I bet. Why if it hadn't been for all our menfolk going and being killed in the War and the carpetbaggers taking our home from us defenceless women, I wouldn't have had to do the things I've had to do. And I for sure wouldn't have been put in pris – Oh Lord, what I just said!'

'I'm certain you were innocent and unjustly treated,' Cavallier lied, convinced by Belle's superlative acting that she had brought her words to a halt and made the alarmed ejaculation because of a belated realisation that she was telling him far more than was advisable.

'Why I for sure was!' the girl declared, contriving to give the impression that she was speaking anything but the truth. 'I didn't steal that prissy lil Nob Hill girl's necklace. But that mean old judge in San Francisco was a damned Yankee and wouldn't believe me when I told him somebody must have put it in me reticule when I wasn't looking.'

'The dirty dog!' Cavallier commiserated with passable sounding sympathy.

'He surely *was*!' Belle agreed. 'Why he sent me to prison for six months and it's terrible how they treat you-all there!' Her right hand fluttered in an angry gesture towards the togue cap. 'Do you know, they cut off my lovely hair as short as a boy's when I first went in. Then, just because I said something one of the wardresses didn't like the day before I was due to come out, she had it done again. That's why I'm having to wear this unbecoming thing.'

'You make it becoming,' Cavallier consoled. 'And your hair will grow again to be just as lovely. How long have you been out?'

'Only a couple of weeks or so,' Belle replied, deciding her hair was sufficiently long to have grown in that time. 'I met up with the Kid the next day and he asked me to team up with him.'

'Doing what – Or is that an indelicate question?'

'Nothing *wrong*.'

'I'm sure it *isn't*,' le Loup-Garou said reassuringly as a

defensive note returned to the girl's voice. 'But I heard there was some trouble at Fort Connel a few days ago.'

'Wasn't there just?' Belle confirmed. 'Some tinhorn gambler accused Rem of cheating at a poker game.'

'Was he?' Cavallier inquired.

'Nobody could *prove* he was,' Belle replied evasively. 'But I don't think I should be talking like this. Rem wouldn't take kind to it.'

'Don't worry,' Cavallier said soothingly, laying his left hand on the girl's right arm and feeling the hard firmness of its bicep. He had received a similar answer when discussing the cause of the knife fight with the sergeant in the Fair Lady Saloon. 'You can trust me not to mention *anything* you might say about him.'

Going by what he had just heard and from past experience, *le Loup-Garou* decided that 'Lavinia Saltyre' was one of those formerly wealthy Southrons who had been driven to a life of crime as an aftermath of the War Between The States. His instincts suggested she was hard, thoroughly dishonest and not overburdened with intelligence. The latter, which had been implied by the indiscreet comments she had allowed to slip out, was a quality he could turn to his advantage. He felt sure that, while she probably did not know all, she could at least satisfy his curiosity to a great extent about the Remittance Kid if she was handled correctly.

*   *   *

'My brother and I came upon a dead buffalo on our way here,' Phillipe le Boeuf said loudly and in an accusatory tone, looking at Irène Beauville and Roland Boniface, although he clearly intended that his words would be heard by everybody who was in the barroom section of Paul Goulet's general store. 'At first, as so little of the meat had been taken, we thought it must have been shot in passing by *white* so-called sportsmen.'

Tall and slender, with a distinct family resemblance in their good looking young faces, the two men who had just arrived at what was the business and social centre of the small town of Nadeauville were dressed in the same general fashion as the other male occupants. However, their faces were less dark skinned than the *bois brulé* – scorched wood – pigment of the *Metis* who were the town's sole residents and showed even less trace of Indian blood. Their hands were soft, suggesting they had done little manual work and, while travel stained, their clothing showed less signs of hard wear.

'And who *told* you it wasn't?' the girl inquired, her voice redolent of contempt, lounging with the slothful elegance as a great cat on a chair by the table in the centre of the room.

'How do you mean, who *told* us?' Leon le Boeuf demanded indignantly. 'We – !'

'I don't doubt that you both know *all* about the ways of *white* men, "so-called sportsmen" or otherwise,' Irène interrupted, before the young man could complete the explanation that he and his elder brother had drawn their conclusion without requiring assistance. 'But, from all accounts, you know much less about *hunting*.'

Having returned to the small wagon they were using to carry their belongings which had been left in the charge of its driver – Jacques Lacomb's slightly younger and almost identical twin brother, Henri – while hunting, the girl had cleaned and placed the lance inside, concealing it beneath some of the load. Then they had resumed their interrupted journey. The delay had prevented them from reaching Nadeauville as soon as they had anticipated. Although they had not expected to arrive that day, they had been compelled to make camp further away than would have been the case if they had kept moving instead of taking the time required for her to test her ability.

Spending a night without a roof over their heads was no novelty even for Irène. She and her three companions had done so at the end of each day's journey since they had set out to join Arnaud Cavallier at the pre-arranged rendezvous on the United States' side of the international border, and often enough in the past.

On reaching Nadeauville late on the afternoon of the day after the hunt, the party had gone straight to Goulet's store. They had been informed that the messenger who was to have met them had not arrived and they had made arrangements to stay until he came. There was no difficulty in doing this, due to their known association with Cavallier. While unaware of the exact nature of the scheme upon which they were engaged, Goulet was one of *le Loup-Garou*'s staunchest supporters and had offered hospitality without inquiring into their business. Being cognisant of the fact that his future was dependent upon Cavallier's continued good will, he had considered that to display curiosity would be inadvisable; but their arrival had aroused considerable interest elsewhere.

Visitors to the town, a somewhat grandiloquent title for a cluster of around a hundred one-storey wooden buildings gathered for company and mutual protection, were not so frequent that any newcomers would be overlooked as potential bearers of news. When it had become apparent that the girl and her companions intended to stay at least over night, there had been no shortage of helpers to unhitch the wagon's team and take care of the saddle horses, but the ends of the canopy were secured to prevent anybody from seeing what was inside the vehicle. The magnificent palomino gelding, which was to be used by Irène when playing her part in Cavallier's scheme – and which, reckless as she was, she had not been so irresponsible as to endanger by riding when 'running' the buffalo – had been praised for its excellence without its purpose being disclosed.

The messenger still had not put in an appearance by nightfall, but the girl's party had plenty of company. There was considerable speculation over whether the vague rumours about Cavallier's aspirations had any foundation. Practically the whole of the male members of the population had gathered at the store after the evening meal in the hope of being enlightened, but little information had been divulged. Instead, they had been treated to nothing more informative than a harangue upon the principle grievances of their people; such as laws and impositions produced by the Government in far off Ottawa and the ever growing threat of white settlers in large numbers flooding into what should be regarded as the *Metis'* domain.

All of the talking had been done by Irène and Boniface, an arrangement with which the unsociable Lacomb brothers had been in full agreement. They had been too wise to satisfy their audience's curiosity over their presence with the truth. Everybody in Nadeauville was a *Metis*, but not all of them supported

Cavallier. More important, few of those who were in favour of him would have condoned the means by which he intended to implement his scheme. Being aware of the protests against such waste which had been aroused as the effects of over-hunting of the herds – in which the *Metis* and Indians as well as the white men had participated, no matter how much latter day ethnic apologists might try to claim otherwise – had become increasingly apparent, neither had had any intention of referring to the killing of the buffalo.

From the moment Irène had seen the le Boeuf brothers enter, she had expected them to be a source of dissension. She had also wondered if they had come to Nadeauville for that purpose, being aware they were anything but in sympathy with *le Loup-Garou*'s plans for the future. Although Louis Riel Jnr.'s efforts to carry on his father's attempts to redress the *Metis*' grievances had failed and he was still exiled in the United States, they belonged to the faction who regarded him rather than Cavallier as the most suitable candidate to lead their people to independence.

As soon as it had become apparent that the brothers hoped to use the killing of the buffalo to turn the crowd against her, Irène had struck back in what she considered to be the most effective manner.

The majority of the *Metis* were content to follow the comparatively primitive and simple existence of the earlier generations and, with a few exceptions, saw no use for formal learning and remained semi- or completely illiterate. Others, however, had seen the advantages offered by adopting a more sedentary and stable way of life. Having prospered, the latter class had seen the wisdom of sending their children to be educated in the more sophisticated eastern Provinces of Canada, the United States, or even Europe. Having been given such an education did nothing to endear the recipients to their bucolic compatriots, who considered that being submitted to it robbed them of their traditional abilities and skills.

'You've got a big mouth!' Leon spat out. The memory of similar aspersions upon his lack of hunting skill and the suspicion that adopting the ways of the white man had been to the detriment of his birthright, which had been frequently levelled his way since his return from college in Montreal, rankled to such an extent he could not control his anger. 'But don't think being Cavallier's *klooch* gives you –'

The comment went unfinished.

Exhibiting a cat-like ability to change from lounging passiveness to sudden and rapid motion, Irène sent the chair skidding away with the force by which she came to her feet. Before either of the brothers realised what she intended to do, she had reached Leon and delivered a kick to the pit of his stomach which brought his words to an abrupt end. Nor had she finished her attack, although he was not the recipient of her further attentions. As he gave vent to an agonised croak and was sent stumbling backwards to sit down involuntarily on the floor, she lashed a savage backhand blow to the side of his brother's face. Impelled by all the power of her far from puny right arm, it caught Phillipe just as unawares and knocked him spinning in an almost graceful pirouette that ended with him sprawling face down across a table.

Silence fell over the room for several seconds. Every pair of eyes went from where Leon had collapsed on to his rump, via his recumbent brother, to the cause of their misfortunes. Then bellows of laughter rose, even from those older members of the crowd who would usually have disapproved of such behaviour in a woman.

'Hey, you "almost whites"!' Boniface whooped, carrying on the line taken by Irène by continuing to point out that the brothers had only a fraction of their family's original Indian blood and suggesting they were losing touch with their *Metis* heritage. 'That was something they didn't teach you at your fancy Eastern college.'

Coming almost as if it were an echo to the comment, the sound of shots and the scream of a man in mortal agony diverted everybody's attention. Realising that the disturbance had originated from the rear of the building, where their wagon had been left, Irène and Boniface exchanged alarmed glances. Then, as startled exclamations arose, they started to run towards the rear door. Sharing their apprehension and equally oblivious of the commotion in the room, the Lacomb brothers led the rush of men who set after them.

CHAPTER EIGHT

I SHOT IN SELF DEFENCE

That Jerry Potts was carrying out the difficult and potentially dangerous task of attempting to reach and search the wagon accompanying Irène Beauville's party did not imply Sandy Mackintosh had been disinclined to take the risk. While his abilities as a scout were almost equal to those of his young companion, he had conceded that he was less suitable to perform the task successfully under the prevailing conditions. So he had accepted a more passive role.

Maintaining their unsuspected surveillance after the killing of the buffalo, the two scouts had drawn accurate conclusions over why the lance had been replaced in the wagon. What was more, having guessed from the direction in which the party was travelling that the destination might be the town of Nadeauville, they had decided to take advantage of any opportunity offered to search the vehicle, and also to obtain fresh food by helping themselves to meat from the dead animal.

Having seen their quarry settled for the night, Potts and Mackintosh had bedded down in a small grove about half a mile away. They had lit a small fire upon which to grill some of the meat during the hours of darkness, ensuring it was doused long before the sun rose to prevent any chance of smoke being seen when daylight came. Continuing their quest, they had not ridden directly along the party's tracks. Instead, as they had done from the beginning, they took a parallel route and kept the others in sight from a distance. It was a precaution for which they had cause to be grateful.

Because their association with the Canadian Northwest Mounted Police was not a secret, the scouts had considered it was not advisable for them to go too close to Nadeauville in the daytime. There was too great a chance of somebody seeing them and they had no wish for Irène's party to learn of their presence. Nor had there been any need for them to approach beyond the limit of prudence. When sending them to investigate the disturbing rumours which had reached him regarding Arnaud Cavallier's activities, Colonel George A. French had supplied them with a powerful telescope. With its aid, they had been able to carry out their observation from a safe distance.

Being conversant with Paul Goulet's political affiliations, Potts and Mackintosh had expected that it would be at his general store their quarry sought accommodation. This had proved correct and the party's actions suggested a stay of at least one night was intended. The scouts had not been surprised by the interest aroused by the visit any other reaction would have puzzled them. They had wondered if the town had been selected as a rendezvous for more of Cavallier's adherents, but the only other newcomers they had seen did not fall into that category. Rather the opposite in fact, being known associates of the exiled Louis Riel. Approaching along a route which had suggested that they might have been following the other party's tracks, the new arrivals' behaviour had implied they had not been invited to participate in any meeting that might be taking place. On coming into view shortly before sundown, they had circled around to convey the impression that they had reached Nadeauville from the opposite direction.

Turning from their speculations on the newcomers' motives, Potts and Mackintosh had given their attention to another matter. Ever since they had commenced the surveillance, they had wondered what else might be in the wagon besides the lance. Having noticed the care with which the Lacomb brothers had checked that the ends of the canopy were closed and fastened together securely before reaching Nadeauville, they had deduced that the contents were such that it was considered inadvisable to give anybody an opportunity to examine them.

Not only had the scouts concluded that an investigation of the vehicle would prove informative, they had considered that they might not be granted a better opportunity to carry it out. There had been no chance of getting close enough to do so while the party were on the move and spending each night camped in the open, but it was possible – if risky – during a stay in a town. Nor had there been any argument over which of them was the more capable of performing the task. While there was little to choose between them in courage, or ability, past experience had taught them that there was one hazard which ruled out Mackintosh as a candidate.

As was the case in every *Metis* community, numerous large and powerful dogs, used for hauling sledges in winter and carrying packs during the summer months, were allowed to roam at will. Not only could they differentiate between *Metis*, Indians and white people, possibly assisted by dissimilar body odours,[1] they displayed a marked antipathy towards anybody who did not belong to their owners' ethnic group. While a grown man who did not show fear could generally prevent them from attacking by shouting ferociously, or drive them off with blows and kicks, neither could be done quietly.

Accepting that there was no chance of either of them passing through the town without coming into contact with at least some of the dogs, Mackintosh had known Potts – being of mixed blood, even though not a *Metis*, and having grown up around similar animals – was the more likely to be able to cope with them. Even should he be compelled to do no more than raise his voice in threatening manner, he spoke French fluently and in the same fashion as the citizens. So any shouts he was heard to make would be less likely to call attention to there being a stranger in the town than if the Scot was causing the commotion.

Potts had decided against waiting until the population had retired for the night before making his attempt. While a later arrival would reduce the danger of him meeting anybody on his way to the wagon, the disadvantages outweighed the

[1] *To avoid being accused of racial prejudice, the author would like to point out that during twelve and a half years' service as a dog trainer in the Royal Army Veterinary Corps, we saw numerous dogs in Kenya, the Middle and Far East which displayed an inborn ability to differentiate between members of their owners' ethnic groups and people belonging to other races. Also, as Louis L'Amour explains in Chapter Two of* HONDO *and we have seen carried out in practice, it is possible to train a dog to to distinguish between and have an antipathy for members of different races. J.T.E.*

benefits. His clothing and ability to speak French would allow him to pass as a *Metis* in the darkness, providing he avoided too close contact with whoever he chanced to come across. Of far greater importance, however, the dogs would be less likely to set up too much of a clamour when other people were moving around than they would after everybody had gone to bed. Lastly, if he should be noticed, the fact that he was going towards the general store would tend to allay suspicion. Any visitor to the town might be expected to make for Goulet's establishment in search of food and entertainment.

Although he was aware that he might require to make a hurried retreat, Potts had decided against attempting to carry out the reconnaisance on horseback. After riding to within about half a mile of the town, he left his fourteen hand, spot-rumped dark grey Appaloosa gelding in Mackintosh's care and concealed by a clump of bushes. Taking several uncooked buffalo steaks, he had continued on foot.

The latter precaution had proved worthwhile!

Three times as Potts walked between the buildings separating him from his destination, he had come into contact with one or more of the dogs. They had growled a little, slinking forward with bristling fur and stiffly held tails, but making far less noise than would have been the case if he was of pure white or Indian blood. On each occasion, his lack of fear and quietly spoken French, supplemented by the presentation of one or more steaks, had satisfied their curiosity and they had allowed him to pass without further challenge.

On coming into sight of the wagon, Potts halted beneath the spreading branches of a good sized boxelder tree which had escaped being felled so as to provide shade for the store's patrons. Possessing excellent night vision, he was able to make a careful examination of his surroundings with no more illumination than was given by a new moon and the stars.

Satisfied he was unobserved, the scout was about to advance when he saw a man walking with every appearance of stealth from beyond the corner of the store. Recognising him as the third of the Riel supporters who had arrived in the roundabout way at nightfall, Potts moved behind the boxelder's trunk and watched what he was doing. His attitude as he was approaching the vehicle suggested that he did not want his presence to be detected. Nor did the scout need to wonder why he had been selected to carry out what was clearly a clandestine scrutiny of its contents. Unlike the college-educated, 'almost white' le Boeuf brothers, David Hesdin was a backcountry *Metis* who knew far better than they would how to handle such a risky undertaking.

After glancing around and failing to discover he was under observation, Hesdin set about trying to unfasten the lashings which were holding the flaps at the rear end of the canopy closed. From all appearances, the Lacomb brothers had secured them with knots of some complexity. He became so engrossed in his task that he gave his full attention to it instead of maintaining his vigilance, which proved to be an unfortunate omission. Unlike the watching scout, he failed to notice that a man was coming from between two nearby buildings.

Dressed in much the same fashion as Potts and the would-be investigator of the wagon's contents, the newcomer was on foot. He had a Henry rifle in his right hand and was carrying a saddle with a bulky bed roll attached to its cantle over his left shoulder. At the sight of Hesdin standing by the wagon, he lowered the latter to the ground carefully so as to avoid making any unnecessary sound and betraying his presence.

Having disposed of his burden, the man moved his rifle into a position of readiness and resumed his advance with great stealth. As he had not called out a challenge, Potts deduced that he intended to capture rather than frighten the intruder away. By the time he had taken his third step, he was sufficiently close for the scout to guess why this course had been selected. He was Raoul Canche and gave his allegiance to Arnaud Cavallier. What was more, his actions implied that he knew to whom the wagon belonged even if he was not aware of what it was carrying.

Even as Potts was reaching the conclusions and trying to decide upon what action he should take, the matter was removed from his control in no uncertain fashion.

There could have been no audible warning of Canche's

arrival on the scene. He was moving with too much care for that. So it must have been instinct, or a belated realisation that he was behaving in an incautious manner by devoting all his attention to unfastening the knots, that caused Hesdin to look around. Seeing the approaching figure, he let out a startled and furious oath. He spun on his heel with his right hand grabbing for the revolver thrust through his waistband.

It was an instinctive, but futile, gesture!

Coming to a stop, Canche was already swinging the Henry rifle upwards. He nestled its butt against his right shoulder in a smooth, yet lightning fast motion and his right eye squinted along the twenty-four inches' length of the octagonal barrel. Before Hesdin could drag the revolver free, his forefinger tightened on the trigger and the cartridge in the chamber was ignited. Working the loading lever with deft rapidity, turning the weapon as he did so, he fired three more shots and sent the lead winging in an arc which encompassed the intruder. Two of the bullets ripped into Hesdin's chest and a scream of agony burst from him as they spun him around. Colliding with the wagon he had been trying to enter, he bounced from it and crashed dying to the ground.

Although Potts had drawn and cocked his Colt Artillery Model Peacemaker as Canche opened fire on Hesdin, he was aware that his situation was extremely precarious. The moment he left his hiding place, the newcomer would see and, in all probability, recognise him. Even if the latter did not happen, Canche would assume from his flight that he was not one of *le Loup-Garou*'s sympathisers and take the appropriate action. The distance separating them was more suitable to shooting with a rifle than a revolver. What was more, the shots already fired were certain to bring Goulet and his customers out to investigate.

Sure enough, even as the thought came to the scout, he heard shouts and other commotion from within the building which assured him he had been correct in the assumption. However, watching Canche walking towards the wagon with the rifle held ready to be used again if necessary, he conceded there was only one course left open to him. The boxelder was some fifty yards from the wagon and of sufficient bulk to

86

conceal him as long as he stayed behind it –

And nobody came that way!

*　　*　　*

First to reach the door, Irène Beauville fumbled with its catch in her apprehension and haste. Elbowing her aside roughly, Roland Boniface grasped and wrenched it open. Hauling out the long barrelled Colt 1860 Army revolver as quickly as he could manage and wishing, not for the first time, he had the facility which he had heard gun fighters in the United States possessed, he plunged across the threshold. Regardless of having only a knife on her belt, the girl followed him into the open air. Making a commotion more suggestive of Gallic excitability than the stoic nature of the Indians, the Lacomb brothers and all but two of the room's occupants left on their heels. In their eagerness to discover what had happened, none of them gave a thought to the le Boeuf brothers.

'Hesdin wouldn't have taken a rifle with him!' Phillipe hissed, rolling from the table as the last of the local customers were disappearing through the door. His face hurt and his head swam, but he was sufficiently in command of his faculties to appreciate his and his brother's position. 'Come on!'

An equally poignant awareness of the peril they could soon be facing acted as a restorative to Leon. Taken swiftly and landing at something less than the full power of which Irène was capable, the kick and his subsequent involuntary sitting on the hard floor had robbed him more of his wind than his wits. What was more, while speaking, his sibling sprang forward and hauled him to his feet. With that accomplished, a shove set him into motion and he scuttled towards the front door, beyond which their horses were tied to the hitching rail.

'Who is it, Raoul?' Boniface demanded, identifying the man with the rifle as he started to line the revolver.

'David Hesdin!' Canche replied, having taken a similar precaution by covering the couple in spite of expecting that the rush to investigate would be led by allies.

'*David Hesdin!*' Irène spat out, knowing where the sympathies of the man in question lay. Then she threw a worried glance at the wagon and went on, 'Did he get inside?'

'No,' the newcomer stated, returning the Henry rifle to a more relaxed position.

'But what happened?' asked the bulky, florid featured Paul Goulet worriedly, being aware that he would be called upon for an explanation if, or – more likely with so many witnesses present and not all of them in favour of Cavallier's ideas – when, news of the incident reached the Canadian Northwest Mounted Police.

'I caught him trying to break into *Mademoiselle* Beauville's wagon,' Canche explained truthfully, sharing the storekeeper's belief that the supporters of Louis Riel who were present would inform the 'Mounties' and being determined to produce an excuse for his actions which would satisfy the neutrals in the crowd. He continued, with less veracity, 'I called and asked him who said he could, knowing he's no friend of hers. He turned and when he tried to pull a gun on me, I shot in self defence.'

'Why would he be trying to get into the wagon?' challenged a man known to be an adherent of Riel.

'To steal, of course!' Boniface declared, looking defiantly at the speaker and making a slight, but noticeable gesture with the Colt he was still holding. Already the customers who had come from the store were separating into three distinct groups, with the unaligned citizens between the two factions. 'Why else?'

'I wondered how those damned "almost whites" could have managed to trail us!' Irène snapped, as the Riel supporter lapsed into silence without offering to suggest an alternative reason for Hesdin's actions. Being aware that the dead man possessed the requisite ability to follow her party's tracks even though the le Boeuf brothers might not, she swung around and scanned the crowd, going on, 'They must have been in it with him. Where are they?'

Almost as if wanting to supply the answer to the girl's question, the sound of horses moving off rapidly arose from the other side of the general store.

'That's them and you're right about them, Irène!' Boniface yelled, setting off at a run. 'Come on!'

Not only the girl, the Lacombs, Canche and the other

Cavallier adherents started to follow their compatriot as he made for the end of the building. The man who had asked the question did not know what had brought Hesdin and the le Beouf brothers to Nadeauville, but suspected their arrival had had to do with the rumours that *le Loup-Garou* was planning an uprising which would establish him and not Louis Riel as the undisputed leader of the *Metis* nation. So, wanting to prevent the brothers from sharing their companion's fate, he glanced at his colleagues and gave a commanding shake of his head. They were all armed, but he was gambling that Cavallier's supporters would not be willing to provoke an open confrontation under the circumstances. Putting his judgement to the test, although willing to fight if need be, he led the other Riel adherents on their rivals' heels towards the front of the store.

Not all of the men who had come from the barroom joined the rush away from the wagon. Those who were neither Cavallier nor Riel supporters considered that discretion was the better part of valour. They knew that they might find themselves compelled to declare for one side or the other if they went after the two factions. Having no wish to be placed in that invidious position, they adopted the wise course of remaining where they were.

Watching the way the two groups set off on hearing the le Boeuf brothers' hurried departure, Jerry Potts made an accurate guess at each faction's motives. He also realised that his own situation had been greatly improved and decided to make the most of the changed circumstances.

Lowering the hammer under the control of his thumb, the scout returned the Colt to its holster. Then, after a glance to make sure he was not observed by the men who had remained by the wagon, he stepped away from the concealment offered by the boxelder. Moving in the silent manner for which he was famous, he kept the tree between himself and the neutrals as he retreated in the direction from which he had come. His departure was made easier by the commotion from the front side of the store. In addition to the drumming of the departing horses' hooves, people were shouting for information from the doors or windows of houses and dogs raised a clamorous barking as they followed their natural instincts to pursue anything which was apparently running away from them.

Only one man saw Potts taking his departure, but made no mention of it. He did not identify the scout, but deduced incorrectly that the figure moving away with such stealth must be another of Riel's adherents. While realising that a denouncement would earn the approbation of Cavallier's supporters, he appreciated it would just as surely arouse the other faction's ire. So he decided to keep his mouth shut and retain his neutrality.

Making his way back to where Sandy Mackintosh was waiting with the horses, Potts was disappointed. Not only had his bid to search the wagon been circumvented, he felt sure that Irène Beauville and her companions would take so many precautions from now on that there would be no chance of doing it in the future. Nor, being aware that the Riel faction were interested in their doings, would continuing to follow them be as comparatively easy as it had so far. The only consolation he could draw was that, from what had happened at the wagon, it seemed unlikely Cavallier and Riel had forgotten their differences and formed an alliance.

* * *

'What do you think those damned "almost whites" will do now?' Irène inquired, as she, Boniface, the Lacomb brothers and Canche sat in the privacy of Goulet's office after having been unable to do anything to prevent the le Beoufs from making good their escape.

'Keep running,' Canche growled. 'Damn it! If I could only have laid my sights on them, I'd –'

'It's as well you didn't have a chance, or we'd have had a fight on our hands,' Boniface pointed out, having appreciated the danger and been relieved to find the fleeing brothers had already disappeared from view by the time they had reached the front of the store. 'De Bruix and his crowd didn't come after us to help stop them.'

'The Devil take de Bruix and his crowd!' Canche snarled. 'Let them look to themselves when it starts, I say!'

'We expected you to be here when we arrived, Raoul,' Irène

remarked, the comment having brought her thoughts back to the business upon which they were engaged.

'My horse went lame and I had to walk in,' Canche replied. 'But it's lucky for *you* it happened. If I hadn't come when I did, Hesdin would have been in the wagon and he'd have known what we were up to as soon as he saw the lance and those clothes.'

'There won't be a chance for it to happen again!' the girl stated, throwing a baleful look at the Lacomb brothers who had insisted that no watch need be kept on the vehicle as doing it would have fallen upon them. 'Have you and Conrad done your part?'

'We've got the six chiefs and he'll be taking them to the rendezvous by now,' Canche confirmed. 'But I don't like the idea of the le Beoufs getting away.'

'Those "half whites"!' Irène snorted disdainfully. 'What can they do?'

'Get somebody to take Hesdin's place,' Canche suggested. 'Or gather enough help to take a look into the wagon without sneaking up at night.'

'It's possible,' Boniface seconded. 'They've got to be stopped!'

'I'll get another horse and see to it,' Canche promised. 'One of you'd better come with me, so I can pass you the word if anything should go wrong.'

'I'll come!' Henri Lacomb offered, having no liking for acting as a driver.

'Good,' Canche assented. 'We'll leave in the morning.'

'Until then, we'll have a guard on the wagon,' Irène declared and this time there was no argument. At that moment, Goulet entered with a tray of drinks. Taking up one of the glasses, she said, 'Everything's going the way *le Loup-Garou* wants, my friends. So let's drink to the day when the *Jan-Dark* rides and carries out the prophecy.'

CHAPTER NINE

ROTTEN TO THE CORE

'You've got to be on pretty friendly terms with that English son-of-a-bitch and his Dixie peach blossom, haven't you?' "Matthew Devlin" challenged, with more than a slight hint of suspicion in his demeanour, as Arnaud Cavallier entered the room he and Vera Gorr-Kauphin were occupying as "Mr and Mrs Roxby" at the Palace Hotel in Stokeley.

'And what if I am?' *le Loup-Garou* challenged, making no attempt to conceal his resentment over being questioned in such a fashion.

'I should think it's obvious what's wrong,' the actress put in, showing a mistrust which equalled that of her "husband". 'As all our troubles in Chicago were caused by agents of the British and United States' Secret Service, it strikes us both as a *very* remarkable coincidence that an Englishman such as the Remittance Kid, as he calls himself, and a woman who was obviously born of upper class Southern States' parentage should decide to travel on the same train as us and go out of their way to make *your* acquaintance.'

Despite having left Mulrooney without – at least as far as they were aware – the Chicago Police Department having guessed they would be going there instead of taking the more obvious course of fleeing the country via a port on the East coast, the events during the journey to take possession of the consignment of arms and the discovery that there would be an unavoidable delay before they could resume their journey had done nothing to improve relations between the conspirators.

Rather the opposite in fact!

The events on the train which had followed the arrival of Calamity Jane and Dobe Killem, then Belle Boyd – in her guise as 'Lavinia Saltyre' – and Captain Patrick Reeder might have presented Cavallier with an opportunity to make their closer acquaintance, but doing so had aroused Vera's disapproval as she had been left with no other company than that of her 'husband'. She had made it plain that she resented not being the centre of attention. Nor had the knowledge that her place in *le Loup-Garou*'s interest was being supplanted by two women she considered as far below her social position and importance made her any better disposed towards him. 'Devlin' had been equally disenchanted by the situation, although his objections had sprung from being prevented from joining such obviously convivial company.

For his part, Cavallier had considered his time had been well spent.

On first becoming aware of the Rebel Spy's and the Kid's nationalities, *le Loup-Garou* had harboured suspicions similar to those expressed by the actress. However, he had become convinced that they were what they pretended to be; a not over scrupulous professional gambler and his mistress. Being unaware that Sergeant Magoon and the corporal were friends of Calamity and had agreed to help when told what would be wanted of them in Freddie Woods' private quarters at the Fair Lady Saloon, he had seen no reason to doubt the information he had received from them with regards to the 'incident' at Fort Connel. According to Magoon, the Kid had been suspected of cheating. However, the only one who might have been able to prove it had died as a result of a blow from the 'fancy foreign toad-sticker' before he was able to do so.

Knowing something of the strict way in which Mulrooney was policed, Cavallier had not been unduly surprised when the Kid appeared on the train. Before it arrived at Stokeley, *le Loup-Garou* had become convinced that 'Lavinia' and the Englishman might be of use to him. After his talk with her on the observation platform, neither the girl nor the Kid had done anything to arouse his suspicions. She had apparently decided not to mention the conversation and her 'protector' had shown not the slightest suggestion of being interested in him other than as a participant in a card game. Even the discovery that, on reaching Stokeley, he had booked himself and 'Lavinia' into the same hotel as the conspirators had not struck Cavallier as other than a coincidence. A successful gambling man would always select the best accommodation, knowing it would offer opportunities to make the acquaintance of wealthy potential victims.

As the messenger *le Loup-Garou* was expecting had not arrived, his party could not set off immediately on reaching Stokeley. They were going to the rendezvous with the Indian chiefs who were to be persuaded to support the *Metis'* rebellion, but he was disinclined to be in the vicinity for too long before the meeting took place. As he had pointed out, the cargo their wagons would be carrying when they set off on their 'hunting expedition' would be too attractive for any brave-heart warrior who heard it was there for them to take any chances.

However, laudable and praiseworthy as Cavallier's motives had been, the delay had done nothing to remove the rift between himself and the two anarchists. On the other hand, it had allowed him to spend the time in the company of the Rebel Spy and the Remittance Kid, without coming any closer to discovering their true identities or purpose, which had aroused the hostile comments from his fellow conspirators when he arrived to announce that the news they were awaiting had come.

'They couldn't have been in Chicago,' *le Loup-Garou* answered, 'unless they could be in two places at once, that is.'

'We don't *know* for sure they were in Fort Connel that night,' 'Devlin' pointed out, with some justification.

'Or that they *weren't*,' Cavallier countered, the objections only serving to strengthen his obstinacy on the matter. 'Unless *you* can tell me why those two soldiers should have lied about it.'

'Just what's behind all this interest you're showing in them?' 'Devlin' challenged, being unable to think up an acceptable answer.

'It's because of the *woman*, I should imagine!' Vera accused.

'She is the most beautiful, I admit,' Cavallier answered, running a far from complimentary gaze over the actress's thin features and angular figure. 'But I have little interest in a jailbird –'

'A jailbird?' 'Devlin' repeated. 'Do you mean she's been in prison?'

'She could hardly have become a jailbird unless she had, *mon cher Père Mathieu*,' *le Loup-Garou* replied, employing the mocking tone he had always used when addressing the anarchist while the other was posing as a priest. 'She has only recently served six months for the theft of a necklace in San Francisco and that may not have been the first time. However, it is the Remittance Kid I'm interested in, not her?'

'Why?' 'Devlin' challenged.

'I've watched him playing cards,' Cavallier explained. 'He's so good I'm not sure whether he is *very* lucky, or cheating – and I can usually tell when somebody is. Not that I greatly care if he does cheat. He has the kind of background which will make him of great use to me if he accepts my suggestion that he accompanies me – '

'You've told him what we're –?' "Devlin" began, rising from the table with such vehemence that he threw his chair over.

'Calm yourself, *mon cher Père Mathieu*!' Cavallier advised, his right hand going across to scratch his stomach *very* close to the hilt of the "Green River" knife. 'Do you think I have been so foolish that I would say, "*M'sieur le* Remittance Kid, I am proposing to raise the *Metis* in rebellion against the Government of Canada and wonder if you would like to join us"?'

'Then why are you –?' Vera commenced, laying a hand on her 'husband's' sleeve and darting a look of warning at him.

'For a most practical reason, *mademoiselle*,' *le Loup-Garou* replied, without duplicating "Devlin's" relaxation. 'My struggle to establish the *Metis* as an independent nation will not soon be over. Nor, grateful as I am for your help in obtaining the arms, will *you* be able to render any further assistance to me in it; particularly as the diversion which should have been provided by your Irish dupes is now unlikely to take place – .'

'They might still go through with it even though we didn't get the arms for them,' 'Devlin' protested, setting the chair on its legs and sitting down.

'They *might*, but I would say they won't,' Cavallier answered, then raised a hand as both the anarchists were on the point of speaking. 'Oh don't worry, I will honour my promise of offering you sanctuary even though *your* scheme failed. But, as I said, you are no longer able to render any further assistance.'

'And *he* can?' Vera asked disbelievingly, not caring for the realisation that she had heard the truth and their safety was in the hands of *le Loup-Garou*.

'He has qualities I can make use of,' Cavallier stated. 'There will be many advantages to having the services of a man who can mingle with British Army officers at their own level and would even be able to pose as one if the opportunity arose. And that is what the Remittance Kid would be able to do.'

'But will he do it?' "Devlin" wanted to know, appreciating how a person possessing such qualities would prove a valuable asset in the *Metis*' uprising.

'That we shan't know unless he decides to come along and help me to fleece you of your money when we go hunting tomorrow,' Cavallier replied, without mentioning he had made tentative hints which had not been accepted as eagerly as would have been the case if the Englishman was trying to join the party. Seeing the glances exchanged by the anarchists, he smiled and delivered the news which had brought him to their room. 'Yes, my messenger has come and I'm going to find Lincoln and tell him he can set off in the morning.'

'Will you be able to persuade the Englishman to come?' "Devlin" asked.

'I don't know,' Cavallier confessed. 'But I'm going to seek him out and put it to him after I've found Lincoln.'

'Do you think he'll help you when he finds it's for something a lot more risky than just cheating me?' the anarchist continued.

'Time alone will tell us *that*,' Cavallier admitted. 'But, from what "Lavinia" has said about him, he has little love for the English since he was cashiered from their Army for cheating at cards and disowned by his family. So I believe he will not be averse to causing them trouble, especially as he will be very well paid for doing it.'

'He'll do it for money all right!' Vera declared, ever eager to think the worst of anybody who did not subscribe undeviatingly to her beliefs. 'All of his kind are rotten to the core and corrupt.'

'That's as maybe,' "Devlin" conceded grudgingly. 'But only as long as he's what he seems to be and can be trusted.'

'I agree, *mon cher Père Mathieu*,' Cavallier replied. 'But that is something else for us to consider. If they are what *you* fear, it

is better that we have them where we can watch over them –
and kill them if there is the slightest suggestion they should be.'

* * *

'Dadnab it, Kid!' Jebediah Lincoln was protesting, as *le Loup-
Garou* walked towards the table at which he was one of the
participants in a game of poker. Although he was clearly trying
to sound light-hearted and avoid giving offence, he was not
entirely able to keep a note of asperity from creeping into his
voice. 'Don't you *ever* lose?'

'Only when I'm playing against my aunt, the Dowager
Duchess of Brockley, old chap,' the Englishman replied,
raking in the pot to add to an already considerable pile of money
in front of him. 'It's advisable to do so in that case.'

Despite his genuine desire to obtain the Remittance Kid's
services, combined with an antipathy to the thought of allowing
the anarchists to see him fail in something he had stated an
intention of bringing about, Cavallier was aware that achieving
his purpose would be far from easy.

The coming of the railroad had brought a growth and
prosperity to Stokeley which was in excess even of the boom
which the rest of the State of Montana was currently enjoying.
With the tracks being pushed onwards, there were numerous
construction and other workers using the town as a base.
Miners, cattle and sheep ranchers brought in their respective
means of livelihood for disposal and, along with soldiers from
nearby Fort Stokeley, their employees found relaxation or
entertainment upon which to lavish wages. Fur traders and
other businessmen in Saskatchewan and Alberta found not
only a more readily available market for their wares than
existed in their own regions, they could also come and use the
town as a staging point via which they could travel to the
Eastern Provinces more quickly by any overland route north of
the international boundary.

With so many potentially lucrative sources of wealth available
and other almost as fruitful towns throughout the State, a
professional gambler would be unlikely to accept an offer to
leave just to help fleece one wealthy businessman. Nor would

7

telling the truth make the proposition any more attractive. At the moment, Cavallier could do no more than suggest the financial benefits of enlisting in his cause for *Metis* independence. He considered it unlikely a man like he imagined the Kid to be would be influenced by vague promises. There was, however, one thing in his favour. Stokeley's town marshal had acquired a reputation for capability and ran the town with an iron hand, taking grave exception to trouble-causers, thieves and crooked gamblers. If he had a reason, he would not hesitate to order the Englishman to leave and was likely to pass warnings to other peace officers throughout the State.

Having come to the Worn Out Tie Saloon on being informed that Lincoln could be found there, *le Loup-Garou* studied the other players in the game and felt elated by what he saw. They were the freighter's four drivers and a far from prepossessing bunch. From all appearances, they had shared their employer's misfortunes and none were enamoured of the prospect of losing.

That applied particularly to Waldo Matchetto. Largest of the quartet, he had a beard-stubbled surly face which warned correctly of a brutal nature. Bare headed, with greasy shoulder long brown hair, he wore a filthy buckskin shirt, U.S. Cavalry breeches so encrusted with grease and dirt they had lost almost every trace of their original colour and heavy, flat heeled black boots. The belt around his bulging paunch carried a massive bowie knife at the left side and a Colt Cavalry Model Peacemaker on the right. While he could not claim to be one of the names which was mentioned in any discussion about experts in either's use, he felt he had no cause to complain about his ability.

Not that any of the other drivers could be considered significantly superior to Matchetto in the matter of looks or cleanliness. All were dressed in much the same fashion, the variations being in the matter of nether garments and headdress. Solly Snagge was almost as big, black bearded, with a well worn brown Stetson hat. Slightly shorter, but marginally heavier, Joe Polaski wore a red woollen knitted cap, aged Levi's pants and had a scar down his unshaven right cheek which did nothing to improve his looks. Tallest of the quartet, lean and mournful looking, sporting a Burnside campaign hat and buckskin trousers that *had* to have seen better days, Frenchie Ponthieu was slightly cleaner when compared with his associates, which was not saying much for him. Each was armed with a knife and a revolver, but none carried the coiled bull whip which usually identified members of their trade.

'*Her* again!' Ponthieu grumbled, eyeing his depleted wealth sullenly. His voice had a harsh New England timbre and no trace of a French accent. 'All I can say is, if she's any luckier than *you*, she must be *real* lucky!'

'Maybe *luck's* got nothing to do with it,' Matchetto suggested offensively.

'Damn that flea!' the Kid ejaculated, his right hand disappearing in a languid manner beneath the off side of the cutaway coat where it started to scratch his back. He had done so on two previous occasions since joining the game, excusing himself for the same reason. Without bringing the hand out so it would be able to reach for the hilt of the *badik* which emerged from the garment's left flap, he looked straight into Matchetto's scowling face and continued in a faintly mocking tone underlaid with warning, 'I hope you're not implying something other than my skilful play and a fortunate run of the cards has been responsible for your losses?'

'What if I am?' the driver challenged, starting to ease back his chair.

'I wouldn't like to think *anybody* had doubts about my honesty,' the Kid answered, still speaking almost mildly, but his right hand came into view grasping the butt of a British made Webley Royal Irish Constabulary revolver. Placing the weapon on the table alongside his winnings, without removing his hand or pointing the short barrel at anyone in particular, he went on and this time there was open menace in his voice, 'Are there *any*?'

Taken unawares, as Lincoln had spoken of the Englishman as a knife fighter who professed never to employ firearms, Matchetto gulped and subsided on to the seat he had been on the point of quitting. In spite of his bullying and aggressive nature, he had sense enough to know when the cards were stacked against him. The way in which the revolver had been brought out and was being handled suggested a greater proficiency than he had been led to expect.

'Take it easy, Kid!' Lincoln requested, equally surprised to discover that the Englishman carried a revolver and, as obtaining a replacement would be far from easy at what he deduced from Cavallier's arrival was likely to be short notice, having no desire to lose a driver. 'Waldo didn't mean anything!'

'With all due disrespect, old boy,' the Kid answered, showing no sign of being mollified. 'That's for *him* to say, not you.'

Silence began to descend upon the hitherto busy and noisy barroom as a realisation that something with dramatic possiblilities might be taking place. Beginning with those nearest to the Kid's table, more and more eyes were turned in that direction. Drinks and other activities were forgotten as the next developments were awaited with wary trepidation or vicarious interest depending upon the observer's proximity to what might become the line of fire.

The anticipated, hoped for even in some cases, clash did not materialise!

'What seems to be the trouble, gents?' asked a calmly authoritative voice.

Strolling with what might have been taken as an aura of nonchalance from where he had been talking with the owner of the Worn Out Tie Saloon, Marshal Dixon Troop was tall, handsome and in his late thirties. He wore neat and well tailored range clothes, but his boots had flat heels more suited to walking than working cattle and the ivory handled Colt Civilian Model Peacemaker hung in a holster designed to permit its rapid withdrawal when necessary. There was neither arrogance nor bombast in his bearing, only the suggestion of competence in his specialised line of work.

'We appear to have run into a slight difference of opinion, constable,' the Kid replied, without taking his attention from Matchetto.

'It looks that way,' the peace officer conceded dryly, glancing pointedly at the Webley. 'And, which being the case, you won't be needing the gun.'

'Possibly,' the Kid answered. 'However, as there appears to have been an element suggestive of bad sportsmanship developing, I thought I'd better take it out to ensure I wouldn't need it.'

'That being so,' Troop said quietly, coming to a halt and, despite his apparently relaxed posture, as tense as a compressed coil-spring. He knew that the easiest way to avert trouble was to prevent it from beginning. 'You won't need it any more and I'd be obliged if you'd put it away.'

'If you insist,' the Kid replied, but made no suggestion of complying.

'I do!' Troop confirmed, then nodded to the other players. 'These gents won't mind if you put it away.'

'As long as I have *your* word for that, I'll comply,' the Kid stated and, after the peace officer had glowered around to receive if not agreement at least no sign of refusal, returned the Webley to its holster, saying, 'As I said, it seems that I was in error. I thought I was playing with gentlemen possessed of sportsmanship, but found only poor losers.'

'Hell, marshal!' Matchetto protested, as Troop's gaze swung to him. 'I don't mind losing, unless it happens *every* god-damned hand.'

'Not *every* hand,' the Kid corrected calmly. 'And, I would also point out that I only shuffle and deal, after the deck has been cut at least once, one hand in five.'

'You got any complaints, *Mr* Lincoln?' Troop inquired, laying noticeable emphasis on the honorific.

'N – None, marshal,' Lincoln replied, realising he had no proof other than that the run of the cards and skilful playing had been responsible for the Englishman's successes since being invited to join the game. 'Nope, I reckon the Kid's just lucky and good.'

'How about the rest of you gents?' the peace officer demanded, swinging his gaze from each driver in turn. After receiving a clearly grudging concurrence with their employer's summation, he went on, 'Anyways, I reckon you'll all agree the game's over.'

'Does it need to be, constable?' the Kid objected, sounding like a hunter who was faced with the possibility of a desirable trophy slipping away.

'I'd say it does!' Troop declared, in tones of finality.

'Do you want to see me, Mr Cavallier?' Lincoln asked, wanting to give the impression to the marshal that he was looking for a way in which to bring the game to an end.

'Yes,' *le Loup-Garou* agreed, although tempted to give a negative answer in the hope of provoking a situation which would cause the marshal to order the Englishman to leave Stokeley. Being unable to guarantee such a result would not end in gun play and the loss of a potentially useful assistant, he resisted the temptation. 'My clients have asked me to tell you they'd like to leave tomorrow.'

'That's fine with me,' the freighter stated. 'Come on, boys. We've got work to do so we're ready to pull out.'

Watching Lincoln and his men leave, Cavallier next swung his gaze to the marshal. Troop was eyeing the Kid in a speculative and far from amiable fashion. Deciding that the latter was being considered as a possible trouble-maker, he considered it should not be difficult to engineer an incident which would convince the marshal of how Stokeley would be a better and more peaceable place without the Englishman's continued presence.

CHAPTER TEN

WHICH OF US'S GOING TO WIN?

'Good evening, "Miss Lavinia",' Jebediah Lincoln greeted, as Belle Boyd came across the Worn Out Tie Saloon's barroom from the direction of the door with "Ladies" painted on it. 'Happen you're looking for the Kid, he's along there talking to Calam.'

'So I notice!' the Rebel Spy answered, making it obvious that she did not approve of the company Captain Patrick Reeder was keeping.

'Can I get you something to drink?' the freighter offered.

'Why that's most generous of you-all, sir,' Belle assented, still glaring to where Calamity Jane was laughing loudly at something the Remittance Kid had said and brandishing a glass which appeared to be filled with whiskey. 'Could I have wine, please? I think anything else is so *unladylike* and unbecoming, don't you?'

'I sure do and wine it is,' Lincoln declared, watching the slender girl and deciding the situation had possibilities. Having been kept busy since the end of the poker game and being faced with a long period on the trail, he was not averse to spending the evening in such a beautiful member of the opposite sex's company, particularly if she felt the need for solace over her boy friend appearing to prefer another woman. 'Calam looks like she's in a funning mood tonight.'

'I had *noticed*!' Belle sniffed icily and, having received a glass of wine, went on, 'Shall we go and join them?'

'Sure,' Lincoln agreed and, remembering the orders given by Marshal Dixon Troop before he and his men had left earlier that afternoon, continued, 'But no poker for me tonight. We're pulling out comes morning.'

'I wish *we* were!' the Rebel Spy declared, giving no indication of knowing the real reason for the abstinence. Instead, she elaborated as she and the freighter started to walk towards the red head and the Englishman, 'I don't care for the kind of people there are in this town.'

'Whee-dogie, if it ain't good ole Jebediah Lincoln!' Calamity whooped, coming close to drowning the music of the small band which now was playing for the benefit of those customers who wished to make use of the clear place offered as a dance floor in the company of the establishment's obliging female employees. Her voice and gestures with the glass she was holding suggested she had already imbibed more ardent spirits than was wise. 'It's great to see there's one son-of-a-bitching wagon boss who's not to all-fired high-toned and fancy to come out 'n' take a drink with the hired help, damned if it's god-damned not.'

'Hey there, Calam,' Lincoln greeted, noticing that the red head was not wearing either her gunbelt or the whip and wondering whether her absent employer, who had annoyed her by refusing to come along if her comments were any guide, had insisted upon her leaving them behind.

'How soon're we going to get them pasteboards moving, Rem-boy?' Calamity inquired, favouring Belle with a mocking grin and laying her right hand on the Kid's left arm. ' 'Cause I reckon this's my night to howl.'

'You're doing plenty of *that*,' the Rebel Spy commented disdainfully.

'Well hot damn, your *mother*'s here, Rem-boy!' the red head said, loudly enough to bring the attention of the people closest to her party in her direction. 'Hey, old woman, why aren't you at home in bed with a shawl 'round your skinny shoulders, 'stead of being here putting the miseries on us young folks?'

'Why don't *you* decide whether you're a man or a woman and dress for it?' Belle countered, then swung her gaze appealingly to the Kid. 'Rem-honey, Mr Lincoln doesn't feel like playing cards tonight – and I can't say I blame him, considering some of the company.'

'How'd you like to smell my foot after I've rammed it knee deep up your butt?' Calamity demanded savagely, slamming her glass down on the counter.

'Steady on there, Calam!' Lincoln put in, although he was hoping his advice would be ignored, wanting to be able to claim he had tried to prevent any trouble that happened if he should be questioned later by the red head's employer. 'Don't you forget what Dobey Killem told you.'

'To hell with what Dobey Killem, or anybody else told me!' Calamity answered, oozing truculence. However, the memory appeared to sober her a trifle and she shrugged with exaggerated nonchalance. 'Aw hell, she's not worth it! How's about them cards?'

'It's like I told Miss "Lavinia" here,' the freighter replied, disappointed by the red head's reaction. 'I'm pulling out tomorrow morning and it's always unlucky for me to play poker the night afore I leave.'

'I wish to hell *we* were pulling out,' Calamity sighed, apparently satisfied by what was an acceptable excuse for a superstitious gambler to refuse to play. 'Hey, Rem-boy, how's about you 'n' me making the most of that fancy dancing music seeing's how there's no chance of us setting up a game?'

'Do *you* know how to dance?' Belle injected, having put down her glass in a less noticeable manner.

'Do *I* know how to *dance*?' Calamity snorted. 'Girlie, I've whomped up more god-damn fancy steps than – !'

'I don't mean doing some clodhopper chaw-bacon's hoedown,' Belle interrupted. 'I was talking about the *real* dancing done by *ladies* and gentlemen.'

'You mean like *you* can do?' the red head challenged.

'I do,' Belle confirmed.

'All right, skinny gal!' Calamity said truculently. 'Happen you're so god-damned fancy-footing, let's see how good *you* can dance.'

'Certainly,' Belle replied, raising her arms and putting her hands behind her head.

Moving with graceful dancing steps, the slender girl brought first her left and then the right elbow around sharply to land on the red head's cheeks. Letting out a yell of well simulated anger, Calamity swung her right fist to connect with Belle's jaw. Following the staggering Rebel Spy, she tore off and flung aside the togue to sink both hands into the short 'blonde' hair.

Being treated in the same fashion, she pushed Belle backwards to fall on to a table and, while its occupants vacated it hurriedly, was brought down on top of her.

Screeching, tugging at hair, scattering bottles and glasses, the girls rolled across and caused the table to tip over. Still entangled, they were deposited on the floor. Churning over and over, putting considerable vigour into a far less skilful kind of brawling than either would generally have employed, they made the customers and employees who were gathering around yelling encouragement move out of the way and they disappeared under a chuck-a-luck table.

'Well, we've got us a fight going!' Calamity said quietly, between shrieked out curses. 'There's only one thing, though.'

'What's that?' Belle inquired *sotto voce*, employing similar tactics to avoid being overheard.

'Which of us's going to *win*?' the red head wanted to know.

'I don't suppose you'd agree to it being *me*?' the Rebel Spy suggested, after gaining the upper position and screeching a description of Calamity's possible relationship with her mother which was physically impossible.

'No more'n you'd let me,' the red head stated, when she had toppled Belle over and writhed on top, interspersing her efforts with a flow of blistering profanity. There was a wistful note in her voice as, upon being displaced and straddled again, she went on just as softly, 'It's a real pity we can't find out.'

'Isn't it?' Belle agreed, sounding just as disappointed. 'Let's get out of here and see if we can persuade anybody else to join the fun.'

'Ease up a mite then!' Calamity requested, bracing her shoulders and buttocks on the hard boards of the floor. She followed a louder expletive which cast doubts on the marital status of the Rebel Spy's parents when she was born with a much quieter, 'I'll help you on your way.'

Hoisting herself upwards until resting on her hands and feet, Belle felt the other girl's moccasins come under her torso to deliver a thrust which propelled her from beneath the table. On alighting, she kept herself rolling until she had room for what she planned to do next and then came to her feet. By the time she was erect, Calamity had also emerged and was advancing with head lowered in the same manner as when delivering the butt that had sent the soldier through the window of the Fair Lady Saloon.

The red head's attack did not meet with a similar success.

Stepping aside just before the moment of impact, Belle pivoted and, as Calamity plunged by, swung a kick to the tightly stretched seat of the buckskin trousers. Yelling with what was close to genuine fury, the red head was driven onwards into the arms of a group of excited saloongirls. Having considerable antipathy for what they regarded as her intrusion of their domain, they turned and held her so that the 'blonde' – who might be a stranger, but at least was dressed like one of them – could arrive and take advantage of their co-operation.

Following Calamity, Belle hoped that she would know what was expected of her. Justifying the Rebel Spy's confidence, the red head stamped hard on the foot of the girl at her right. As the grip on that side was released, she rammed her liberated fist into the ample bosom of the woman at her left. Twisting free, she ducked her head and inclined her torso to the right. Timing the move so perfectly that it might have been rehearsed for weeks instead of extemporised on the spot, Belle's right arm shot out. Missing Calamity by a very close margin, her knuckles 'accidentally' rammed into the nose of a girl behind the red head.

Next moment, a hair yanking, clothes snatching, slapping, punching and kicking mêlée erupted as the saloongirls became embroiled with one another as well as against the pair of outsiders who had deliberately brought the conflict about. Which, for all their speculations about who would be the victress while under the table, was part of the result the intruders had hoped to produce.

Much as each would have liked to satisfy her curiosity on that point, Belle and Calamity were aware that they had something far more serious demanding their attention. So they devoted all their efforts to defending themselves, or one another when the situation called for it, against the saloongirls. Nor did they continue to employ the unscientific tactics which had characterised their own 'fight' until they had emerged from beneath the table. Instead, while Calamity punched with an almost masculine precision, Belle demonstrated her skill at *savate* to such effect – in spite of having kicked off her shoes to avoid inflicting too serious injury upon the recipients – that their assailants were soon being kicked or knocked in all directions.

With so many factions represented by employees in various local businesses and industries being present and the excitement of the spectators rising, it was not long before the end to which the Rebel Spy and the red head were working was achieved. Knocked backwards by Calamity, a girl ran into the arms of a burly railroad worker and turned upon him furiously. More amused than alarmed, he caught her by the wrists to restrain her. However, his laughter ended in a curse as her feet hacked at his shins and he began to shake her in an attempt to control her temper.

'Get your hands offen her!' yelled a soldier with whom the girl had been drinking when Belle and Calamity started their "fight" and rushed forward.

Thrusting the girl aside, the railroad worker met the charge willingly!

No further inducement was needed!

Spreading like the ripples crossing a pool when a rock is thrown in, the fight became general. Customers and saloon workers joined in, everybody picking upon the nearest person belonging to a different type of employment.

Within a few seconds, a full scale brawl of considerable gusto was in progress.

Which is what Belle, Calamity and the Kid had hoped would happen.

'This is hardly the place for two gentlemen of our calibre, old boy,' the Englishman remarked to Lincoln, having pushed him aside and dodged the chair which had been swung in their direction by a cowhand. Knocking its wielder sprawling into the nearest knot of fighters, he went on, 'Shall we adjourn to somewhere more peaceable?'

'I'm all for that,' the freighter answered with alacrity. He gave no thought to what might be happening to his employees, although he was aware that all four drivers were present. Nor did he see anything unusual in the "gambler" displaying a similar disinterest where "Lavinia" and Calamity Jane were concerned. 'Let's get the hell out of here!'

While starting to cross the room on Lincoln's heels, the Kid demonstrated that neither fear nor lack of fighting skill was responsible for his eagerness to vacate the premises. In fact, he displayed that he was exceptionally capable of protecting himself and his companion. His travels in the Far East had been of sufficient duration for him to have attained proficiency in a form of unarmed combat little known in the Western Hemisphere at that time and he put his training to good use.[1]

While throwing, avoiding and kicking, then thrusting three successive would-be assailants away as each in turn tried to attack him, the Kid employed only sufficient force to avoid injury to himself and being compelled to take a more active participation in the general fighting. All the time he was doing so, he remained alert for an opportunity to carry out his part of the scheme.

Engaged in a wild slugging mill with a group of soldiers and cowhands, Solly Snagge noticed the 'gambler' who had won almost all of his party's money that afternoon was following his employer towards the side door and clearly intended to escape involvement in the fighting. Filled with a desire to take revenge, he flung himself out of the mêlée and towards the Kid.

Seeing the driver approaching and guessing what had motivated the attack, the Englishman was slightly disappointed. He had hoped that the chance he was seeking would be presented by Waldo Matchetto. However, Snagge matched him in height and was somewhat heavier. He was also a foul mouthed bully who, according to Calamity Jane, had been fired from more than one freight outfit for cruelty and neglect of his team. Nor had anything occurred during their short acquaintance to make the Kid regret what he proposed to do. In fact, Snagge was his second choice after Matchetto.

Stepping forward as if to engage in the kind of head-down, bull-rushing fashion that was Snagge's style of fighting, the Kid once again exhibited his alien expertise. Catching the

[1] *As Captain Patrick Reeder had not visited Japan at the period of the narrative, the author concludes that the unarmed combat techniques he was employing were either some form of* pentjak-silat *system practised in the East Indies, or what had become known as* kung fu *and originated in China. J.T.E.*

driver's outstretched right arm by the wrist, he raised and pirouetted underneath it. Then, using the other's weight and impetus as an aid by applying a wrenching heave which dislocated his shoulder, the Englishman threw him over the bar.

Being concerned only with saving his own skin, Lincoln would not have raised any objections over his employee's rough handling, nor attempted to find out what injuries Snagge might have sustained. Without even looking behind to find out how his protector was faring, he was unaware that he would be one driver short in the morning. Instead, he felt only relief as he reached the side door. Pulling it open, he preceded the Kid through and they started to walk along the alley towards the front of the building.

'No you don't, you Limey son-of-a-bitch!' a voice snarled, before the Englishman and the freighter had covered half of the distance. 'You ain't getting off this easy!'

One glance over his shoulder confirmed what the Kid already knew. The speaker was the member of Lincoln's freight outfit he had hoped would offer him the opportunity to render incapable of leaving the following morning. He also realised that achieving his purpose would prove more difficult than disposing of Snagge.

Still bareheaded, with his hair in even greater disarray and a trickle of blood running from his nose, Matchetto looked a most menacing figure as he lumbered along the alley. Nor did the Kid consider his looks were deceiving. When describing his qualities shortly before they had set off for the saloon to implement their scheme, Calamity had claimed he was the most dangerous of Lincoln's drivers. Not only was he noted for his ability as a dirty fighting roughhouse brawler, he had no scruples over using either the bowie knife or the Colt Cavalry Peacemaker revolver when roused.

Knowing that the red head would not have exaggerated or sensationalised her description, the Kid felt disinclined to depend upon his unarmed combat skills. While far from a coward, he was too aware of the dangers to tackle the big driver with his bare hands. Size and bulk were in Matchetto's favour, if not skill. Even with the element of surprise on his side, the Englishman realised there was too much at stake for him to risk sustaining an incapacitating injury which would leave the Rebel Spy devoid of his assistance.

'What do you have in mind, old sport?' the Kid inquired, swinging to face the driver, but showing no suggestion of his thoughts.

'I'm going to get back that money you cheated us out of!' Matchetto declared, interspersing the explanation with language too foul to be repeated.

'I hate a poor loser,' the Kid sighed, sounding almost patiently resigned as he decided how to cope with the latest development. Glancing around quickly, he offered the freighter an opportunity to intervene and prevent injury to another of his employees. 'I'd advise you tell him to forget it, old boy.'

'He wouldn't pay any attention if I did,' Lincoln answered, harbouring similar views to those expressed by Matchetto over the way in which he had lost his money to the 'gambler' and confident that it would all be refunded in return for his support when the town marshal arrived. Which should not be long, if the sound of a fire engine's bell clanging was any guide taken with his knowledge of how the peace officer had acted when other saloon brawls erupted. 'So you'll have to tell him yourself.'

'On your head be it,' the Kid warned, speaking almost languidly and having received the response he anticipated.

Sharing the freighter's appreciation of what was meant by the evidence that a fire engine was approaching, Matchetto changed his mind on how he would deal with the 'gambler'. Although the prospect of pounding the other to a bloody pulp and reducing the handsome features to a ruin had its appeal, there would not be sufficient time to carry it out. He watched for the first suggestion that the Englishman meant to reach around to draw the revolver and increased the pace of his advance. To his delight, he saw his potential victim's right hand crossing to the hilt of what Lincoln had informed him was some kind of foreign knife. Considering there was little to fear as his opponent was only what he had described as a 'yellow-bellied Limey tinhorn', he decided it would be more satisfying to hand the other his needings via the massive bowie knife. With that in mind, he swept the selected weapon from its sheath.

Studying his attacker with what appeared to be disinterest,

the Kid was moving with a deceptive speed. While his actions seemed to be carried out in the usual leisurely fashion which characterised him, they were in reality made with great rapidity. Enfolding the pistol-like handle of the *badik* with the second, third and fourth digits of his right hand, he adopted the traditional 'pinch grip' of its Bugi makers by taking the upper end of the blade between the thumb and forefinger as it emerged from the sheath. Cumbersome as the method might appear to Occidental eyes, he soon demonstrated that it did nothing to impair the weapon's efficiency when performed by one who was well trained in the Bugis' system of wielding it.

Stepping clear of the raking thrust Matchetto directed at him with a motion as graceful and effective as a matador evading the charge of a bull, the Kid swung the *badik* in the whip-like left to right swing so favoured by the exceptionally proficient knife-fighting Bugi warriors who had learned the best way to handle their favourite close quarter's weapon. Flashing upwards at an angle, the razor sharp convex edge of the 'butterfly' blade reached the outside of the driver's extended right arm just above the elbow. It curved onwards to slice through the sleeve of the shirt and deep into the bicep. Slipping from the fingers of a hand which had suddenly become inoperative, the bowie knife clattered to the ground.

Watching horror and pain distort, then turn Matchetto's face ashen under its dirt and tan, the Kid felt little remorse. He knew the driver would not have hesitated to kill, or seriously injure him given an opportunity. As his victim stumbled on for a few more steps and collapsed, he concluded that he had fulfilled his part of the scheme more adequately than was required.

Instead of Lincoln finding himself minus one driver for the delivery of the consignment of firearms, he now had two incapable of helping him.

Everything now depended on whether Calamity Jane could carry out her specialised function.

Or was given the opportunity to do so.

CHAPTER ELEVEN

YOU COULD OFFER MY SERVICES

'God-damn it, you stupid, no good bitch!' Dobe Killem thundered, in what struck the onlookers gathered outside the open door of the town marshal's office as being a towering rage. 'Didn't I warn you to keep out of trouble?'

'It wasn't all *her* fault!' Belle Boyd put in, moving to the sullenly truculent looking Calamity Jane's side in a protective manner.

'You can keep your blasted mouth shut!' Captain Patrick Reeder ordered, exhibiting an irascibility that was as well simulated as the freighter's anger and the two girls' behaviour.

Standing side by side in the cell to which they had been escorted the previous evening, the Rebel Spy and the red head looked decidedly the worse for wear. However, although each had received bruises and their clothing had suffered damage, they had survived the brawl at the Worn Out Tie Saloon without serious injury.

Taken all in all, Belle had had not the slightest cause for complaint over the way in which Marshal Dixon Troop had carried out the request for assistance she had made to him. Accepting as genuine her identification documents and learning what had brought her to Stokeley, he had realised that the *Metis*' intended uprising could have adverse effects upon Montana as well as Canada. However, he had demurred on one point when being told what she had in mind. She had countered the objection by giving an assurance that the owner of the saloon would be reimbursed by the United States' Treasury for all damage and loss of business caused to his premises. With that matter settled, the peace officer had proved to be a willing and helpful collaborator.

Following his usual practice when dealing with such situations, Troop had used the hose pipes and close to two hundred of gallons of cold water from the tender of the fire engine to bring the fighting to an end. Then 'learning' from the irate owner who had been the cause of the disturbance, he had taken the culprits to jail. Nor had he allowed either girl to change from her sodden garments. Instead they had been placed in the same cell and informed they could do what the hell they wanted to each other and nobody would stop them. Pretending to be alarmed by a realisation of the predicament in which they had involved themselves had provided them with an excuse to refrain from further hostilities and being told that neither Killem nor the Remittance Kid could be located had supplied the means for them to 'forget' their differences and become allies in the face of adversity.

There had been an added satisfaction for Belle over the way in which the scheme had been carried through so far. Much to her relief, she had learned from Troop that nobody had been badly hurt in the brawl and the damage was not sufficiently extensive to make the saloon close down. In fact, the marshal had claimed the owner said the fight would have a salutary effect on business. Both pieces of news were useful in that they would not allow Troop to avoid holding the girls for trial, but also gave him an excuse to do what was needed to let the plan have a chance of succeeding.

At ten o'clock in the morning. the deputies had located the freighter and the Kid. Word of what had happened the previous night had spread around the town and there was a good sized crowd assembled in front of the marshal's office to see what the famous Calamity Jane looked like and find out how Troop intended to deal with her. Passing through the spectators, the two men had noticed Arnaud Cavallier and Jebediah Lincoln were present, but not standing together.

'It's all right for you to talk, Pat St John-Haythornthwaite!' Belle protested in shrill indignation. grabbing and shaking the bars of the cell. 'If you-all hadn't got us both drunk and riled at each other, Calam and I wouldn't have fought and been put in here. Where have you be – ?'

'Well I'm blowed!' the Kid ejaculated. 'I didn't tell you to start clawing like damned alley-cats and, dash it, if that's your attitude, I'm going – '

'Not so fast, *mister*!' Troop put in as the Englishman started to turn away. He was so impressed by the way in which all the participants were reacting that he was almost convinced it was true and that helped him to put the correct tone in his voice. 'Your wife and that gal caused a ruckus that near on wrecked the Worn Out Tie Saloon and the damage has to be paid for.'

'My *wife* as you call – !' the Kid commenced, swinging to face the peace officer.

'I surely hope for your sake that *you* call her your wife, seeing's how you're living together as "Mr and Mrs Whatever-She-Said" at the Palace Hotel,' Troop interrupted in a threatening fashion. 'Because, no matter what they reckon to such doings where you come from, we don't take kind to folks committing what's known as adultery here in Montana. Fact being, it's against the law and them who do it stand to be fined *real* heavy if not throwed in jail. What was you saying?'

'She's my wife,' the Kid conceded reluctantly.

'The owner of the Worn Out Tie'll be right pleased to hear it,' the marshal declared. 'Under Montana law, a man's responsible for any debts incurred by his legal wife.'

'Damn it, I'm not standing the whole lot!' the Kid objected, pointing at Calamity. 'She was just as much to blame as "Lavinia".'

'I'm not gainsaying it,' Troop answered, having to struggle to prevent himself grinning at the red head's far from lady-like comments about the Englishman's perfidious behaviour. 'How about it, Mr Killem?'

'How about *what*?' the freighter challenged. 'I've got nothing to do with this. Before she went out last night, again' my wishes, I warned her that she was on her own should she start any ruckus. So to hell with her. She's not costing *me* as much as another buffalo penny of *my* money!'

'The hell with you and your money, you dime-squeezing, tight-butted son-of-a-bitch!' the red head screeched, with all the fury of a woman scorned and to the delight of at least one member of the crowd which was eavesdropping on the sidewalk. 'I don't need *you* or *it*. With them savings of mine you're ·

holding for me, I don't want a thin red cent of your'n!'

'What money's that?' Troop inquired, hoping it did not occur to the men they were trying to mislead to wonder why he was allowing so many people to stand around outside listening to his business.

'It's my saving, like I said,' Calamity wailed, with such vehemence she might have been speaking the truth. Drawing upon her experience of various melodramatic plays she had seen and thoroughly enjoyed – although wondering why the heroine allowed any son-of-a-bitch like the villain to get away with his abuses instead of kicking him where it would do some good – she went on in a similar downtrodden fashion, 'Money I got out of working my fingers to the bone for him. He said he'd hold it safe for me. Now he's figuring on using what happened last night as an excuse to keep it and stop a poor lil orphan gal getting what's rightfully her'n.'

'God damn it!' Killem boomed in tones of exasperation, despite being as amused as the marshal by the red head's convincing histrionics and knowing she was anything but a 'poor lil orphan gal'.[1] Managing to continue in the same indignant manner, he went on, 'You can have a bank draft for every last dime of it, you caterwauling, drunken, no-account hot-butt. Then we're through and by God I'll be pleased to see the back of you.'

'No more'n I will you!' Calamity stormed back. 'I don't need you. Any outfit'll take me on.'

'Not if I've anything to do with it,' Killem warned.

'You do what you want after I'm through,' Troop interrupted, then swung his gaze to the Kid. 'Half the cost each should be a fair split, I reckon.'

'*Half* – *!*' the Englishman commenced.

'I found a feller lying in the alley by the saloon with his right arm laid open so bad he'll likely never use it again,' the marshal said menacingly. 'When he got so he could talk, he allowed you jumped him from behind and did it without giving him a chance to – '

---

[1] *Details of Miss Martha 'Calamity Jane' Canary's parents are given in:* Part One, Better Than Calamity *of* THE WILDCATS *and* WHITE STALLION, RED MARE. *J.T.E.*

'It was self defence!' the Kid protested.

'I'd say that all depends on whose story a man'd be ready to believe,' Troop countered. 'Is it *half*, or not?'

'It's half!' the Kid confirmed bitterly.

* * *

'How did it go, *mon ami*?' Arnaud Cavallier inquired, although he already knew and was delighted by the result he had overheard, as Belle and the Kid walked towards him on leaving the marshal's office.

'Badly,' the Englishman answered, scowling balefully at his companion. 'This stupid bitch has cost me almost every penny I have.'

'Don't you go blaming me!' the Rebel Spy protested indignantly. 'If you-all hadn't started leading poor Calamity along so's you could win – '

'All right, all *right*!' the Kid interrupted. 'Don't harp on it, dear girl. We've too many problems to start quarrelling between ourselves.'

'Perhaps you like to come and have a drink with me?' *le Loup-Garou* offered, seeing Lincoln was accosting a worried looking Calamity Jane as she came slowly from the marshal's office and guessing what the sight implied.

'That's jolly civil of you, old boy,' the Kid assented. 'I think we could both use one after *that* little episode.'

'You say things didn't go well for you,' Cavallier remarked, as he and the couple set off along the sidewalk.

'They couldn't be *worse*!' Belle declared, hooking her left hand through the Englishman's right arm. 'That damned Yankee marshal's made Rem pay for the damage at the saloon and, on top of that, he's told us to be out of Stokeley by sundown.'

'It never rains but it pours, as my aunt, the Dowager Duchess of Brockley, used to tell me,' the Kid went on. 'The blighter also said he means to warn all his colleagues throughout Montana to keep a watch for me.'

'Why would he want to do a thing like that?' Cavallier asked, deciding the situation had developed better than he hoped.

'Chap seems to have formed the impression that I'm not only dishonest, but dangerous,' the Kid explained. 'I considered taking legal action against it, but doubt whether there would be a chance of winning.'

'There's not a chance you would,' Cavallier confirmed, doubting that such a line of action had been contemplated seriously. 'Don't think I'm being nosey, *mon ami*, but do you have any plans for the future?'

'We *had*,' the Kid said bitterly. 'But putting them into being won't be easy unless we can get a – stake, I think you colonials call it.'

'Then perhaps I can help you,' *le Loup-Garou* hinted.

'I never borrow from friends!' the Kid protested, but not in a convincing manner.

'And I *never* lend, believing that to lend money to a friend loses you his friendship,' Cavallier answered. 'But I thought you might be interested in a proposition.'

'Such as?' the Kid asked and felt Belle's hand tighten a little on his arm.

'As I've mentioned before, although he didn't play on the train, the man "Roxby" is a gambler and not a very good one,' Cavallier answered. 'But, like most of his kind, he doesn't know how bad he is. You and I could make a lot of money from him.'

'But I thought you-all were leaving today?' Belle put in.

'So we are, *mademoiselle*, provided Lincoln can get replacements for the two drivers who were injured in the fight last night,' Cavallier replied. 'I noticed him talking to Calamity and, as her boss fired her, he might be able to get her. If not – '

'I still can't help you,' the Kid put in, sounding disappointed. ' "Lavinia" and I have to be out of Stokeley by nightfall, or we're likely to be put in jail until the constable can see us on our way personally.'

'Why not come with us?' Cavallier suggested.

'It might solve the problem,' the Kid admitted. 'Except that I don't really see the "Roxbys" allowing us to. They didn't strike me as a couple brimming with the milk of jolly old human kindness. Unless – '

'Yes?' *le Loup-Garou* prompted.

'You said you were *two* drivers short,' the Englishman

explained. 'I haven't been on one of those big Conestoga things, but I've driven a coach and four back in England often enough and the principle wouldn't be too different. So you could offer my services in that capacity.'

'That's true, I could,' Cavallier agreed, delighted the suggestion had come from the other man. 'I'll say you want to get up to the Canadian border and have offered to drive to help you get there.'

'By gad, are you going to Canada?' the Kid asked, with such sincerity in his voice he might have only learned the destination at that moment.

'We are,' Cavallier confirmed.

'Then things couldn't be better, old boy,' the Kid declared. 'Even if that "Roxby" blighter complains to the U.S. authorities that he's been fleeced, they can't do a thing about it. Canada's British territory and a man can't be extradited from the country of his birth.'

'That's true,' Cavallier admitted. 'Are you on?'

'By jove, yes!' the Kid accepted. 'I'm your man, old boy.'

'And I'm your woman!' Belle injected determinedly. 'Because there's one little thing you'd both get into your heads. I'm not being left behind. Either I go along, or I'll make sure "Roxby" knows what you're up to – and other folks, *Remhoney*.'

'We wouldn't think of leaving you behind, *mademoiselle*,' Cavallier said reassuringly, deciding from the last comment that the Englishman had other crimes which could be brought to the attention of the authorities. 'In fact, you'll be able to help us set him up for the fleecing.'

'Why I'll be pleased to do every little thing I can to help,' Belle promised and continued, not without truth. 'Well, Remhoney, it surely looks like things are going our way after all.'

* * *

'Didn't you get any more drivers?' "Matthew Devlin" demanded, turning from watching the three Chinese men who were transferring his and Vera Gorr-Kauphin's baggage off the buggy which had brought them to Jebediah Lincoln's camp and into the wagon they had selected as their accommodation during the journey.

'Only Calam here,' the freighter replied, indicating the red head at his side. 'But either me or one of the Chinks can handle the other wagon. So we'll be able to pull out as soon as Mr Cavallier gets here.'

Like *le Loup-Garou*, Lincoln had been completely taken in by the events at the marshal's office. He had managed to position himself close enough to an open window to be able to watch and hear everything that happened. Listening to the various acrimonious comments which had passed between them, he had been on tenterhooks in case Dob Killem relented at the last moment instead of carrying out the threat to fire Calamity. It had not happened. He had not only discharged her, but had stormed out reiterating his threat to pass the word about his reasons for having done so and ensure she would be unable to inflict herself upon any other wagon boss.

Waiting until the dejected and worried-looking girl had made arrangements to pay the fine which she swore would leave her almost penniless, Lincoln had offered to hire her as she emerged from the office. He had found that, although she was clearly taking Killem's threat to heart, she was not completely deflated and retained something of her usual spirit. Accepting his offer, she had made it plain that she considered she was doing him a favour and would expect to be regarded as his top driver. Believing such an arrangement would be beneficial, he had agreed. For all that, he had wondered how his two remaining drivers would consider the matter.

Instead of mentioning his concern, the freighter had accompanied Calamity to the small rooming house at which she was staying. After she had changed her badly torn shirt and collected her belongings, he had escorted her to where his camp was set up about half a mile from Stokeley. Before leaving in search of replacements for Waldo Matchetto and Solly Snagge, he had had the teams hitched up. On his return, he found that 'Mr and Mrs Roxby' had arrived, but there was no sign of Cavallier. As he expected, Frenchie Ponthieu and Joe Polaski were lounging by the camp fire and leaving the work to his trio of Chinese helpers. Dressed in the usual kind of black cotton 'coolie' clothes and sandals, with long pigtails, they were of indeterminate age, taller than the average for their race and hard looking.

'That being the case,' Calamity remarked, laying down her bulky bed roll – in which reposed the war bag holding most of her possessions – and leaning her Winchester Model of 1866 carbine against it. 'I might's well go on over and get acquainted with those two hard-working jaspers.'

'Sure,' Lincoln assented, deciding that any trouble between the girl and the pair of hard-cases had better be resolved before the journey was commenced.

Neither of the drivers offered to rise as Calamity and their employer approached the fire. A coffeepot was bubbling and steaming in the embers and each had a sizeable tin cup in his hand. However, a threequarters' full bottle of whiskey standing between them suggested that they might have been flavouring the beverage from the pot with some of its contents.

'Frenchie, Joe,' the freighter said, coming to a halt. 'I reckon you know Calamity Jane here. She's taken on with me.'

'In Waldo Matchetto's place,' the red head supplemented in challenging fashion.

'Waldo's place!' Ponthieu growled. 'He was top driver.'

'Which's why Jebediah's took *me* on in his place,' Calamity answered. 'I'll go take a look at the wagons, boss, 'n' make sure everything's ready to roll.'

'I'll say one thing, Frenchie,' Polaski commented, feasting his eyes on the well-filled seat of the red head's pants as she strode away in the direction of the wagons. 'She sure walks prettier'n any other top driver I've ever seen.'

'That's for sure,' Ponthieu admitted, also taking in the view as he reached for the bottle and drawing no more conclusions than his companion from the way in which Lincoln was moving aside hurriedly. 'But it still don't mean I cotton to the notion of having a *gal's* top driver over me.'

Having anticipated there would be some form of opposition to her appointment, Calamity had already decided upon what she considered would be the best way to counter it. As she started to turn around, her right hand flew across to the bull whip with such rapidity that it was out of the belt loop and the long lash was uncoiling by the time she was facing in the opposite direction.

In a smoothly co-ordinated continuation of the move, without the red head appearing to take aim, the lash snaked through the air as if possessing a will of its own to curl around the neck of the whiskey bottle. Snatching back his fist with a startled exclamation, Ponthieu watched the bottle plucked from its position. Although the lash fell away in mid-flight, it sailed onwards to the girl's waiting left hand.

'What the hell – !' Polaski ejaculated furiously, starting to lurch erect and reaching for his holstered revolver.

Once again Calamity sent the whip curling out. The popper gave an explosive crack which dissipated most of the force with which it was moving. Then, acting as if of its own volition, it moved sideways to wrap around the driver's right wrist and jerk his hand away before its fingers reached their destination.

Snarling in a mixture of fright and anger, Ponthieu saw what he believed to be an opportunity while the red head was dealing with his companion. He too began to thrust himself to his feet and his hand descended in the direction of his gun. Dropping the bottle and transferring the whip's handle to her left hand so deftly that its lash still remained taut around Polaski's wrist, Calamity turned the right palm outwards. Dipping, her fingers curled around the ivory butt of the Colt 1851 Model Navy revolver. Twisting it from its holster, the hammer riding back under her thumb, she aligned its seven and a half inch long octagonal barrel before Ponthieu's weapon had cleared leather.

'I can copper your bet, same as his,' the red head warned as the lanky driver froze into immobility. 'Happen you want it done, that is.'

'By cracky!' Lincoln laughed, as Ponthieu signified a refusal of the offer. 'I reckon you're top driver all right, Calam.'

'I *never* doubted that,' the girl replied, liberating her whip and twirling away the Colt. 'Now maybe I can get on with checking over the wagons.'

CHAPTER TWELVE

YOU'VE TOLD ME ALL I NEED TO KNOW

'Damned if I've *ever* sat the box of a wagon's's been as bad kept as this one,' Calamity Jane complained to Vera Gorr-Kauphin, handling the reins of the six horse team with the deft ease of long training. 'There's no wonder good ole Jebediah Lincoln was so all-fired eager to take me on after that mean son-of-a-bitch Dobe Killem kicked me out without so much's a thin dime in my pockets.'

After the red head had established her right to be considered top driver, she had conducted her examination of the wagons. She had discovered, as she had expected, they were far removed from the high standards to which she had become accustomed. There was nothing basically wrong with them and the teams appeared adequate for handling the work, but the vehicles had been neglected to a degree neither Killem nor any of his drivers would have tolerated. All of which had played into her hands, offering an excuse to conduct an investigation of each's contents without arousing suspicions over her primary purpose.

Like the other three, the wagon to which Calamity was assigned was equipped to be drawn by a team of six horses. She was used to such an arrangement and competent to attend to hitching up and controlling the animals, as well as being able to appreciate the vehicle's good points.

Somewhat smaller than the massive Conestoga 'prairie schooners' which had gained fame during the great trans-continental migrations prior to the building of a railroad from the East and to the West Coasts, the wagon's body consisted of a sturdy open box about fourteen foot long and five foot in width. Attached to the three foot high sides were half a dozen curved hickory 'half bows' over which was spread the kind of white canvas cover that had created the 'schooners'' name. Of sufficient length to extend beyond each end of the body, the canopy could be secured by drawstrings to conceal and protect the cargo in the event of inclement weather. However, the body lacked the deep undercurve and overhang which had been a feature of the kind of vehicles originally manufactured in the Conestoga Valley of Pennsylvania and had given them their great, safe carrying capacity over even the roughest terrain. The stout oak plank known as a 'lazy board' and offering a seat for casual passengers was omitted from the left side, but the staple-hinged tool box – holding a hatchet, smaller axe, hammer, nails, an augur, some rope, spare linchpins and kingbolts among other useful items – was there, even if its contents had seen little use. Nor had the powerful wagon-jack and the bucket filled with lubricants which were suspended from the rear axle.

Heavily ironed and braced for additional support, the bolsters and axles underneath the body were made of hickory and the hubs from black gum so hard as to be almost impossible to split. Mounted on the hardwood axle beds, the front and rear wheels were respectively four and five feet in diameter to offer adequate ground clearance when traversing the uneven and generally roadless terrain west of the Mississippi River. Each rear wheel's outer rim, 'capped' – or encircled – by a three inch wide iron 'tyre', had fourteen strong wooden spokes secured by tightly fitting tenon-and-mortice joints connecting it with the hub.[1] In making it, the wheelwright had 'dished' it to ensure the spoke at the bottom of each turning cycle – which would be the one currently bearing the brunt of the weight – was absolutely perpendicular to the axle and the hub.[2]

[1] *Made in the same manner, the smaller front wheels had only twelve spokes. J.T.E.*

[2] *The need to 'dish' a wheel, giving an* outwards *flare from the hub to the outer rim, was discovered in ancient times and is still regarded as being essential in the construction of modern motor vehicles. It was caused by the necessity to make the axle conical, with the outer end having a smaller diameter than the inner. To support the load evenly, the under-bearing surface of the axle and the matching inside bearing of the hub must both be horizontal. As the wheel turns, each spoke in succession assumes a position perpendicular to the hub and the axle. Because all the strain is placed upon*

For all her happy-go-lucky way of life in general, Calamity took pride in her work and had been trained by men who were arguably the pick of the freight hauling business. Experience told her there was nothing structurally wrong with the wagons and she was willing to concede that whoever had built them was competent and fully conversant with all the important aspects of their construction. However, she had discovered that most of the essential maintenance had been neglected and she had insisted that it must be carried out before the journey was commenced.

Neither Frenchie Ponthieu nor Joe Polaski had been enamoured of the prospect when they were told what was expected of them. Although Lincoln had realised that to do so would prevent the outfit from setting off that day, he had seen the wisdom of the red head's suggestions and had given her his support. The drivers had drawn some slight consolation from the arrival of Belle Boyd, Captain Patrick Reeder and Arnaud Cavallier. Learning that the Remittance Kid was to drive the fourth wagon, Calamity had put him and *le Loup-Garou* to work along with them.

While the maintenance tasks were in progress, Calamity had been able to examine the contents of all four wagons. Each had a small load of assorted goods, but there had been no sign of the consignment of firearms and ammunition she and her companions had expected to find. Certainly none of the boxes and bundles were of sufficient dimensions or shape to have rifles, nor even carbines, concealed in them. However, as yet, she had not been able to pass on the negative information verbally to her fellow conspirators. Nor had doing so been necessary. Although the Kid had purchased suitable clothing for travelling and two saddles and a pack horse to transport themselves when they left the 'hunting party', they would have taken action if she had announced the consignment was present.

On their arrival at the camp, before the men were put to work by Calamity, Belle and the Kid had ostensibly had their

the lower part of the wheel, the resulting tendency is to push inwards *and actually adds strength to it. If the pressure were* outwards *against the wheel-nut and linchpin, as would occur without the 'dishing', the effect would weaken and eventually cause the wheel to collapse. J.T.E.*

presence explained to 'Matthew Devlin' and Vera Gorr-Kauphin. They were aware that this was done by Cavallier to prevent them from suspecting there might be a motive other than the supposed fleecing of 'Mr Roxby' behind their being allowed to accompany the 'hunting expedition'. It had soon become apparent, however, that the anarchists and *le Loup-Garou* were not entirely willing to trust them. At no time were they allowed to be alone with the red head.

Completing the maintenance to Calamity's satisfaction had precluded any chance of moving off that day. So the party had set up camp for the night. When preparing to move off the following morning, Belle was seated alongside the Kid on the wagon which had been assigned to him. The Chinese, the eldest of them proving to be an excellent cook, occupied the vehicle driven by Lincoln. As her 'husband' was riding on horseback with Cavallier, the actress had been placed in Calamity's charge.

In spite of Vera having displayed a desire to talk on moving off, the afternoon was well advanced before she was given an opportunity to do so. Until then, the red head had been too occupied with getting the feel of the wagon – which had different handling characteristics to the one she usually drove for Dobe Killem – to engage in conversation. She had also had to concentrate upon gaining the confidence and teaching the six horses of her team who was boss. This had been accomplished by skilled manipulation of the reins, judicious use of the long lashed bull whip to ensure there was no slacking and a liberal flow of choice bad language. At last, with everything going satisfactorily – although she still considered the vehicle did not feel exactly right – she had found herself able to relax somewhat.

'I thought the way Killem treated you was scandalous,' Vera consoled, forcing herself to speak in a pleasant tone. 'However, that is only what one can expect from an *employer*. But it was that English "gambler's" trollop who is really to blame for you being dismissed. What do you think of her?'

The actress would have expressed similar sentiments to any employee who was dismissed as a way of exhibiting her deep sympathy for the down-trodden working classes, no matter how justified the dismissal had been, but she had another reason for asking the question. Nothing she and 'Devlin' had seen or heard of the Remittance Kid and 'Lavinia Saltyre' suggested they were other than they appeared to be. For all that, despite having become practically convinced they were not agents of the British or United States' Secret Services, the anarchists were still doubtful of them. Neither the actress nor 'Devlin' trusted *le Loup-Garou* and, remembering his eagerness to have the Englishman accompany them, they wondered if some form of treachery was contemplated. So Vera was wondering whether Calamity might be a source of information.

'Oh she's not such a bad sort of gal when you get to know her,' the red head replied, with the air of one willing to be charitable to another less favoured. 'But she's sure lucky to have a god-damned hair left on her head. Happen those other calico-cats hadn't took her side and grabbed me, I'd've hand-scalped and whupped her so quick she'd've thought the hawgs'd jumped her.'

'So she didn't put up much of a fight then?' Vera asked.

'*Much* of a fight?' Calamity repeated and, guessing what had provoked the question, she contrived to adopt what appeared to be a mixture of contempt and amusement over the suggestion. 'Hell, happen my momma 'n' poppa'd put up such a puny donnybrook[3] when they come home drunk on a Saturday night, us Canary kids'd've been "shamed to show our faces outside come Sunday morning".'

After Cavallier had aroused their suspicions with respect to Belle's possible identity in Chicago, 'Devlin' had contacted an anarchist colleague who was living in the city and had served in the United States' Secret Service during the War Between The States. While the information he had received did not include an accurate description, one of the items mentioned had been the Rebel Spy's ability to defend herself with bare hands if weapons were unavailable. He had claimed that, according to a report which was received, on one occasion

[3] '*Donnybrook*': *colloquial name for a fight. The term originated from an annual fair at the town of Donnybrook, Ireland, which was abolished in 1855 because of the civic disorders which always occurred when it was taking place. J.T.E.*

she had fought and beaten three women who were trying to kill her.[4]

'How long have you known those two?' Vera inquired, satisfied by the red head's comment that they could not be harbouring Belle Boyd in their midst and seeking further information.

'Only since I met up with them at Fort Connel a few days back,' Calamity lied, convincingly. 'Mind you, though, I've *heard* a few things about the Kid – '

'What kind of things?' the actress asked, having heard similar tones when other women had a desire to receive a request for details of information which should have been treated as confidential.

'Well now, I wouldn't want to go spreading gossip, mind,' Calamity answered, her whole attitude suggesting that she wished for nothing more. 'But I did hear's how he got his-self run out of England 'cause some important folks reckoned he was way too *lucky* when he was gambling with 'em.'

'Good heavens!' Vera gasped, sounding worried and remembering that Cavallier had suggested a similar reason for the Englishman having had to leave the land of his birth. 'Do you mean he *cheats* at cards?'

'Well now, I couldn't come right out and say "yes" to *that*,' the red head replied, although her demeanour implied she wished for nothing more than to be able to do so. Still in the manner of one who was passing on a tasty titbit of information, despite wondering if skilful manipulation of the cards had been responsible for the Kid's consistent successes since the games had commenced on the train from Mulrooney, she continued, 'But I'd sooner be curled up all warm 'n' comfy in bed with him than sitting in on any pot he's dealing. Because, happen he *don't* cheat, he's the luckiest son-of-a-bitch I've ever come across. And he sure's hell knows some right sneaky ways of setting up 'n' winning bets from – ' Snapping her head around as she stopped speaking, she gave a perfect impersonation of having been struck by a thought and went on, 'Hey now! It's none of my never-mind, but I'm getting a sneaky notion that your loving "husband" could be a gambling man!'

[4] *Told in :* THE COLT AND THE SABRE. *J.T.E.*

'Well – Yes, he is,' Vera confirmed hesitantly, as if reluctant to make the admission. 'That's why I wasn't more sociable on the train, I didn't want to let him get involved in the card game. I'm afraid he is a gambler – and not a very successful one. Which is why I'm so worried over *M'sieur* Cavallier being so insistent that we bring those two with us.'

'So you reckon that fancy talking Canucker's brought the Kid along to help trim your loving "husband", huh?' Calamity hinted.

'It's possible,' Vera pointed out, delighted by the way she had guided the red head into the required line of thought and too arrogant to imagine it could be otherwise. 'But I can't think of any way of finding out if that's what is intended.'

'Asking 'em straight out won't get you nowhere,' Calamity warned.

'I know *that*,' the actress admitted.

'There's one way you could find out, though,' Calamity remarked, with an all too obvious false casualness. 'Or *I* for sure could.'

'From *him*?' Vera suggested rather than asked.

'The first question's how much's doing it worth?'

'*Worth*?'

'Why sure. How much do I get paid for finding out what they're up to?'

'Could you do it?' Vera challenged.

'I reckon I can,' the red head declared confidently.

'From *him*?' the actress repeated.

'I'd surely like to give that a whirl,' Calamity answered, grinning lecherously. 'Only it'll be easier, if not near's much fun, getting it out of good ole "Lavinia". We got on real good 'n' friendly while we were sharing a cell in the pokey, 'specially after the Kid didn't show to try 'n' get her out. So I conclude that, was it made worth my while, she'd tell me what's going on was we to be put together.'

'You mean ride together on this wagon?' the actress asked.

'Not so much *ride* 's *sleep* together,' Calamity corrected.

'I don't follow you,' Vera confessed reluctantly.

'I dunno about *you*, but for the life of me, I can't think up one good reason for stopping her riding along with him all day,' the red head explained, exuding thinly veiled disdain over her passenger's lack of comprehension. 'And she's not over likely to tell me much while we're all sat 'round the camp fire at night, now is she?'

'I suppose not!' Vera conceded, barely able to conceal her resentment at such a lack of respect from a social inferior.

'You *know* not,' Calamity corrected. 'Is it worth fifty dollars?'

'*Fifty* dollars?' the actress almost yelped.

'I figure they're counting on taking your loving "husband" for a whole lot more'n that,' Calamity elaborated, then shrugged. 'Hell, if it's not worth my while, I'd's soon leave it be.'

'I'll give you the fifty,' Vera promised without enthusiasm, being parsimonious by nature. 'But how can we arrange to have you put together?'

'Easy enough,' Calamity replied. 'You being such a well brought up, God-fearing lady 'n' all, you'd not take kind to having folks's aren't married sleeping together like they was. Put that way, you could set your foot down and insist's they don't and the only other place they can let her bed down's with me. Once we've got that fixed, you'll soon enough get to know what's going on.'

Which, Calamity told herself virtuously, was the truth; except that it would not be done in the way the woman at her side imagined she meant.

*   *   *

'Why the nerve of that old woman, Calamity!' Belle Boyd said, in tones of righteous indignation, watching the red head standing in a tense and slightly crouching posture at the rear end of the wagon and clearly listening to something other than her words. 'It's none of her business if Rem and I aren't married, is it?'

Never suspecting that she was playing into their hands, Vera Gorr-Kauphin had done as Calamity suggested and made it possible for the two girls to be able to exchange confidences.

At the end of the day's journey, after an excellent meal produced by the Chinese cook, Big Chew, the men had settled down to play poker and the women turned in for the night. Refusing an invitation to 'come and sit a spell', the actress had retired to the wagon she and 'Devlin' were using so that the red head could – as she imagined – start earning the fifty dollars she had been compelled to hand over.

However, on boarding her wagon, the red head and Belle had not launched into an immediate discussion of the day's events. Instead, they had talked about the things which might have been expected of them if they were what they pretended to be. Having heard the Kid calling for Cavallier to hurry back as he was holding up the game, both had realised it was meant as a warning to them and they were preparing to deal with it.

Grasping the left side rear 'half bow', Calamity swung herself over the tailgate and dropped to the ground. On landing, her right hand liberated the bull whip and, stepping around the end of the wagon, she sent its lash opening out behind her ready for use.

'All right, you sneaky son-of-a-bi – !' the red head began, glaring through the partial darkness at the man whose stealthy approach she had detected. Then her attitude changed and her voice became less hostile as she went on, 'Oh! It's *you*, "mon-sewer". I figured it was one of the Chinks, or them two butt-dragging, mouth-jerking hoss-spoilers good ole Jebediah Lincoln calls drivers 'n', no matter which, figured to teach him better manners to come trying to peak at us gals undressing.'

'I'm sorry if I disturbed you, Calamity,' *le Loup-Garou* apologised, deciding the girl had exceptionally sharp ears to have heard him approaching as silently as he had been. He also concluded from the explanation she had given, she was used to having male fellow travellers behave in the manner she had stated and he considered any attempt to eavesdrop would be fraught with danger of discovery. 'But I have just been to – *been* – and thought I would come to make sure you were both comfortable on my way back.'

'Now that was *real* considerate of you, "mon-sewer",' Calamity declared, with such a friendly spirit she might have believed he was telling the truth. 'We're fine. Only, was I you, I'd shout was you to come 'round again when "Lavinia" 'n' me're likely to be getting undressed ready for bed. Which I'm kind of jumpy when I'm doing that. Last time it happened, I cut an eye out of the jasper's outside the wagon with this ole bull whip. Way he squawled and took on, I'd sooner not do it again 'less I had to.'

'I will remember and warn the others,' Cavallier promised and, walking by the red head and crossed to where the rest of the men were seated around the two camp fires.

'I'll just bet you god-damned will!' Calamity mused, coiling the whip's lash and returning the handle to her belt's loop.

Strolling back from the dark side of the wagon, the red head saw Vera closing the rear flaps of her vehicle. Having been on the point of trying to eavesdrop on the two girls' conversation, the actress had seen *le Loup-Garou* detected while making a similar attempt. Hearing Calamity's remarks, she had decided against taking the risk and was withdrawing as the girl returned.

On the point of climbing into the wagon, a frown came to Calamity's face. She stared at the tailgate and the hinges which attached it to the bed. After a few seconds, she gave a nod and, swinging aboard, she closed the flaps.

'I don't reckon anybody else'll try it tonight,' the red head remarked, unbuckling her gunbelt.

'Or me,' Belle replied, having watched and listened to all that had taken place. Returning to sit on her opened out bed roll, she continued, 'So they don't have the arms and ammunition with them yet?'

'Not *in* the wagons,' Calamity admitted, placing the gunbelt and whip by her bed.

'Then I wonder where they'll pick it up?' Belle inquired, the possibility having been envisaged.

'I said it's not *in* the wagons,' the red head pointed out. 'Right from the start, I *knew* there was something's didn't feel right about this son-of-a-bitching rig; but I reckoned that was only 'cause it was new to me. Now I know different. We're carrying the guns and shells all right.'

'Where are they?' Belle asked.

'We're *sitting* on some of them,' the red head replied.

*   *   *

'Peddling guns to *Indians*?' Jebediah Lincoln gasped, staring at his newest employee with the kind of indignantly injured innocence which had fooled more than one lawman or Army

132

officer who had made a similar accusation. '*Me?*'

'*You,*' Calamity agreed, speaking just as quietly as she had when raising the point. She had asked the freighter to come and check on a wheel at the side of her wagon away from the two camp fires around which the rest of the 'hunting party' were gathered at the end of the second day's journey. 'Come on, boss-man, don't try to shit a lil ole shitter like me.'

'Aw now, Calam!' Lincoln protested, without raising his voice, but his expression was wary and his right hand started to rub at the centre of his chest. 'You saw inside all the wagons before we left Stokeley – '

'But not *under* the beds,' the red head countered. 'Or I should say *inside* 'em.'

'*Inside?*' Lincoln repeated, growing even more tense and the hand moved nearer to the left side flap of his jacket. 'I don't – '

'You just stop scratching like you've got a flea afore doing it gets you hurt for no good reason Jebediah!' Calamity commanded, her right hand turning palm outwards as she thumb-hooked it on to the gunbelt close to the butt of the Navy Colt. 'God damn it, I'm not like those stock-spoiling, wagon-ruining son-of-bitches you usually have to hire. I can tell from its feel that that damned rig of mine's handling too heavy for the load she's toting and, on top of that, the bed's way too thick.'

'So you reckon there could be guns hidden in it, huh?' the freighter challenged, but his right hand dropped away from the proximity of the Merwin & Hulbert Army Pocket revolver and there was a suggestion of admiration in his tone.

'If there ain't, I'll take up living with your "Chinees",' Calamity stated, then grinned and waved her right hand in a placatory gesture. 'Aw hell, Jebediah, don't go getting into a tizz. It don't mean spit to me what we're toting, just so long's I'm paid good enough for the chances I'm taking. Which means I'll be wanting more'n I was getting offen that tight-butted old bastard, Dobe Killem.'

'You'll get it,' Lincoln promised, considering the retention of the red head's services would be worth the extra wages. Not only had she proved far more capable than any man he had been able to hire, she was sufficiently well known to help divert suspicion from him. He had already decided that provided she satisfied him that she was willing to participate in gun-running, he would notify *die Fliescher* she would be well worth whatever it cost to retain her. 'We're toting two hundred and fifty Henrys and "old yellowboys", with twenty-five thousand bullets for them, in special trays let into the beds of the wagons. They're not for *our* Indians, though.'

'I don't give a damn whose son-of-a-bitching Injuns they're for,' Calamity declared, wanting to convey the impression that she was unaware the weapons were to be delivered to Arnaud Cavallier's *Metis*. 'What's worrying me is how do we make sure they don't blow our fool heads off with 'em as soon's they're handed over.'

'There's *no* danger of *that*!' Lincoln said emphatically. 'Apart from one of each I'll shoot off for them, all the rest've had their toggle links took off. Those're kept separate and won't be handed over until we're well away.' Pleased by the girl's air of puzzlement, he elaborated, 'The links're in a box in my wagon and I'll hide it some place at least a day before we meet up with them. Then I'll bring one, or maybe two of them back to collect it.'

'Whee-doggie!' Calamity enthused, with what appeared to be genuine admiration. 'That's right smart figuring on *your* part.'

'It pays to be smart,' the freighter replied, delighted by the response. 'Now are you satisfied?'

'Near on,' the red head affirmed. ' 'Cepting for one thing, you've told me all I need to know.'

'What else do you want to know?' Lincoln asked.

'How much extra pay'm I going to get?' Calamity explained, although she doubted whether she would remain in her new employment for long enough to receive the money. She also wondered what action the Rebel Spy and the Remittance Kid would take when she told them where the arms and ammunition were hidden. 'Anyways, you'll have plenty of time to tell me that. Right now, we'd best be getting back to the fire else "Mrs Roxby" 'll be getting bad notions about *us*.'

CHAPTER THIRTEEN

TOMORROW'S THE DAY

'Poor blighter,' Captain Patrick Reeder thought, standing concealed behind the trunk of a balsam poplar tree. He was peering through the darkness of the woodland to where, in the centre of a triangle formed by a patch of common juniper shrubs and two fair sized pussy willows, Jebediah Lincoln was watching the youngest of the three Chinamen digging a hole in which to bury the box they had brought from the camp. 'I hate to see so much effort being expended for nothing.'

Having realised that the attire of a professional gambler would be unsuitable for wearing if Belle Boyd, Calamity Jane and he were compelled to accompany the wagons, the Remittance Kid had made purchases of more acceptable raiment before leaving Stokeley. He had retained only the hat and boots, replacing the other garments with a waist length brown leather jacket, an open necked dark blue and green plaid shirt of heavy-napped woollen Mackinaw cloth and Levi's pants. The *badik* and his Webley Royal Irish Constabulary revolver were still carried in their usual fashion. However, for the work upon which he was engaged at that moment, he had left the Stetson behind and exchanged his footwear for a pair of moccasins which had allowed him to move far more quietly.

Under the prevailing conditions, such silence was imperative!

Ten days of uneventful travel had elapsed since Calamity Jane's discussion with Lincoln. While the four wagons were on the move, Arnaud Cavallier and 'Matthew Devlin' had ridden ahead ostensibly to select the route, find camping grounds in which to spend the night and hunt to provide the party with fresh meat. Employing the latter as an excuse when they had returned empty handed on the fourth evening, the Kid had gone out alone and found evidence suggesting they were primarily concerned in following a trail blazed by the two *Metis* whose arrival at Stokeley had caused the conspirators to set off. He had already deduced they had brought the news that all was going according to plan on the Canadian side of the border and, having delivered it, returned to rejoin the rest of *le Loup-Garou*'s adherents at some pre-arranged rendezvous.

Although Calamity had informed the Rebel Spy and the Englishman that her suppositions over the consignment of arms and ammunition were correct, they had not yet taken any steps to prevent it from being delivered.

In the course of a discussion prior to setting off, the red head had stated that the most obvious solution if the consignment was not on the wagons at Stokeley would be to go along until it was collected, then compel the conspirators to return and be handed over to the authorities. Belle and the Kid had pointed out the objections to carrying out her advice.

In the first place, there was no law which said Lincoln could not transport the arms and ammunition. If challenged, he would undoubtedly be able to produce documents establishing he had a legal right to do so. He could claim they were picked up secretly and carried concealed as a precaution against anybody discovering he was carrying such a valuable cargo. Nor would he be breaking any law as – so the trio believed – his customers were to be *Metis* and not Indians.

Furthermore, the reasons Belle and the Kid had given earlier for not having Vera Gorr-Kauphin, Cavallier and 'Devlin' arrested and sent to stand trial for their crimes in Chicago were still applicable.

When the Kid had commented upon the possible difficulties involved in attempting to enforce the compulsion to return upon the 'hunting party', Calamity had suggested – although not in the exact words – that these would not be insurmountable. She had said that, as long as they had the element of surprise on their side, they ought to be able to get the drop on the opposition. Nor, she had declared, were the odds too greatly against them. She had estimated that there would only be *le Loup-Garou*, 'Devlin', Lincoln and whatever drivers survived the brawl in the Worn Out Tie Saloon to worry about and felt certain neither the actress nor the three Chinamen would cause any trouble.

Being aware that they might find the need to act upon the red head's suggestions, the Kid had studied the composition of the 'hunting party' since joining it. While inclined to agree with most of her summations, having had a far greater experience with Orientals had caused him to warn her via Belle that the trio could prove a far greater hazard than she had anticipated.

Impetuous as the red head might be on occasion, she had accepted her companion's judgement upon the way the affair should be conducted. However, as the days went by without anything happening, she had asked when something was going to be done. Finally, the answer had come.

There had been no difficulty in arranging for Belle and the Kid to be able to converse in private, so she could pass on the latest news gathered by Calamity, after the day's journey despite Vera's efforts to the contrary. Pretending that the couple had bribed her to let them sleep together in her wagon at nights, the red head had asked her employer's permission and offered to cut him in for a share of the money she received. Wanting to keep her in a co-operative frame of mind, he had agreed she could do so and declined the offer. Furthermore, he had instructed his other employees not to mention what was happening to 'Mr and Mrs Roxby'. Having done so, he had assured Calamity there was no danger of the Chinamen talking out of turn. Nor he had considered would Frenchie Ponthieu and Joe Polaski be inclined to after the display of whip and gun handling she had given on their first day together.

Although *le Loup-Garou* had discovered the arrangement, he too had not seen fit to inform the anarchists. Lechery rather than discretion, or natural reticence, had been his motivation. His silence had been ensured by Calamity allowing him to become much more closely acquainted. As the Kid had made comments which warned him that taking an interest in 'Lavinia Saltyre' would be regarded unfavourably, he had been pleased to have another alternative and was willing to accept the red head as a substitute. For her part, she had ensured he was kept too occupied each night to be able to approach her wagon and eavesdrop on her friends.

It had been decided that Calamity should 'earn' the fee she had received from Vera in a way which made it appear 'Lavinia' believed the Kid's sole purpose in travelling was to help fleece 'Mr Roxby'. She had claimed that the actual 'fleecing' was not to take place until the party were almost in Canada. By delaying until then, the conspirators could avoid any repercussions by crossing the international border if their victim was to lodge a complaint with the authorities in the United States. As this corresponded with the reason Cavallier had said he would use for hiring the Kid, the story was accepted.

In addition, the red head had hinted that Vera and 'Devlin' were wise not to trust *le Loup-Garou*, but had insisted she could not supply specific details to support her suppositions. She had been asked to see if she could obtain corroboration and this had left the way open for her to act as a decoy with Cavallier.

On the morning of the tenth day, there had been convincing proof of how successfully Calamity had hoodwinked Lincoln. At noon, while the party had been allowing the horses to rest and feed, he had taken an opportunity to speak with her beyond anybody else's hearing and asked if she would make sure that she held *le Loup-Garou*'s attention all night. When she had promised to do so, without asking why the request was being made, the freighter had informed her that the time had come for him to hide the box of toggle-links removed from the firearms. Admitting she had suspected this must be the reason, she had guaranteed to prevent Cavallier from having an opportunity to interfere.

While Lincoln would have had no cause for complaint over the way in which the red head was carrying out her duties where *le Loup-Garou* was concerned, he would have been less pleased if he had known she was not entertaining the *Metis* solely for his benefit. Slipping away from the wagons after he had believed everybody else had retired for the night, he and the youngest of the Chinamen, who was to do all the actual work, had made their way to the hiding place he had selected during a reconnaisance he had carried out while the camp was being set up. As he – or rather his helper – had set about taking the precaution he had outlined to Calamity, neither of them suspected that they were being kept under observation.

Demonstrating a capability for silent movement which was yet another of the talents which made him so competent at his duties, the Kid had been able to follow the freighter and the Chinaman without his presence being detected. As neither had appeared to be taking any particular precautions against such an eventuality, his work had been easier in spite of being encumbered by the shovel he had borrowed from Calamity's wagon. Safely ensconced behind the balsam poplar, he was now waiting for them to finish their work and leave so that he could carry out the purpose for which he had come.

Watching everything that was done, the Kid had been impressed by the thoroughness with which Lincoln was intending to avoid allowing the cache to be discovered. Before the digging was commenced, he and the Chinaman had carefully removed the coating of fallen leaves at the point he selected and put them on one side. After the box had been buried, the surplus excavated earth was scattered in the juniper shrubs and the leaves replaced.

'There's a good little chap,' the Kid breathed approvingly, as the freighter signified that the work had been completed to his satisfaction. 'Off you go to your little bed and dream about all the good times you're going to have with Calamity after the trip's over. She's somewhat put out that she won't be able to take that visit to Chicago with you and meet *die Fleischer*, particularly as you haven't been gentleman enough to tell her his real name and where to find him. It's a pity you've been so bally inconsiderate, but Belle has at least a start when she goes after him and we'll see if we can find some way to make it up to Calamity for her disappointment.'

In addition to finding out where the consignment was being carried and learning of the precautions to ensure a safe departure after its delivery, the red head had been gathering all the information she could with respect to the organisation to which Lincoln belonged. She had acquired details without arousing his suspicions by pretending to be disinterested, or giving an unquestioning acquiescence to anything he told her, both of which had produced which might not have been forthcoming in any other way. Although she had ascertained that Ernst '*die Fliescher*' Kramer lived in Chicago, the freighter had not yet confided in her to the extent of supplying his name and address. In fact, Lincoln's attitude when he had realised how much he had told her had been a warning against any attempt to pry further. She had felt sure that to have done so would ruin all that had been achieved up to then and might even cause doubts to be raised about herself and her companions. With the approval of Belle and the Englishman, she had refrained from pressing the matter any further.

Allowing something over half an hour to elapse after Lincoln and the Chinaman had taken their departure, so they would be out of hearing and visual distance, the Kid crossed to the triangle formed by the pussy willows and juniper shrubs. He struck a match, shielding its flame even though confident the pair he had been spying on would be too far away to see the glow. Then he found the spot at which the cache was buried. Showing as much care as they had, he cleared the area and disinterred the box. As he did not have sufficient soil to replace it, he took the time to gather leaves and twigs well clear of it to supply the deficit and removed all traces of the removal.

Satisfied that there would be little or no trace of his meddling if Lincoln should return to check on the cache before leaving in the morning, the Kid turned his attention to the box. To his relief, as he had expected it to be secured in some fashion, he found that the lid was nailed on instead of a lock being fitted. Using the blade of the shovel, he prised it open. Having done so, he took the shovel and concealed it in another clump of common juniper shrubs. The reason for his action became apparent on his return. Picking up the box and carrying it on the crook of his left arm, he started to make his way back to the wagons by a circuitous route. As he walked along, he removed and scattered handfuls of the toggle-links over as wide an area as he could manage, trying to spray them into the most inaccessible places. By the time they were all gone and the empty box was disposed of, he felt confident that even a prolonged search would be unlikely to recover many of them. Satisfied that he had at least delayed Cavallier's attempt to arm the *Metis*, he completed his perambulations without anybody other than Belle knowing he had left to carry out the task.

* * *

Irène Beauville was not normally an exceptionally light sleeper. However, with only a couple of blankets separating her from the wagon's hard wooden floor, it was far from as soothingly comfortable as the bed to which she was accustomed when at home. Nor had being required to sleep in the vehicle for a number of nights caused her to grow accustomed to it. So the sound of a rider approaching through the darkness woke her and brought her from beneath the covers to investigate.

After leaving Nadeauville, the girl had continued to move at a leisurely pace towards the United States' border accompanied by Roland Boniface and Jacques Lacomb. Although they were not hurrying, four days had elapsed before Raoul Canche rejoined them and he had arrived alone. He had explained that there was a fight when he and Henri Lacomb caught up with the le Boeuf brothers. Both had been killed, but Lacomb received a wound which, while not too serious, had prevented him from continuing the journey. In spite of the reduction in the size of their party, they had considered that the danger of being spied upon was over. While they had begun to keep a more careful watch than prior to learning they had been followed by Louis Riel's adherents, Canche's news had caused them to relax their vigilance considerably and the nearer they came to the international border, the less they expected any further contretemps.

Without knowing it, throughout the journey they had adopted similar means of avoiding detection to those carried out by Jerry Potts and Sandy Mackintosh. They had not lit a fire until night had fallen and made sure it was neither burning nor even smouldering when daylight returned.

Irène had been bored and irritable as the time passed uneventfully. Although she had practised handling the lance from the back of the palomino gelding when opportunity permitted, her efforts were directed against a straw filled man-shaped and life sized dummy instead of living creatures. In spite of her complaints, she was growing ever more confident that she could carry out the task for which she had been selected when the time came.

Having delivered his news, Canche had set off to find his elder brother, Conrad, who was responsible for guiding the six Indian chiefs to the rendezvous. He had promised he would return when everything was arranged and accompany Irène's party there.

In spite of being clad only in her shirt and a pair of more scanty underpants than the average *Metis* girl would have dared to wear, Irène did not hesitate over going to the end of the wagon and opening its flaps without donning her trousers. Looking out, she found that Boniface and Jacques Lacomb were already awake. They were standing near the fire holding their rifles, but were lowering the barrels as they recognised the rider who had come into the light of the fire.

'Tomorrow's the day!' Canche greeted without preliminaries, sliding his lathered and hard-ridden mount to a halt.

Letting out a hiss of satisfaction, Irène looked behind her. There was sufficient illumination from the fire for her to see the lance, the special garments and two other equally important items which were essential for her to carry out her part in the following day's, or rather evening's, events.

* * *

'Going be tomorrow after sundown,' Jerry Potts announced to Sandy Mackintosh, who had woke up as he returned to the place in which they were spending the night.

Not only the Remittance Kid had been displaying, or rather avoiding exhibiting a superlative skill at stalking and carrying out an undetected surveillance that night. If anything, as the scout's quarry was camped in open country instead of woodland, he had performed an even more difficult feat by completing his task with equally successful results.

In spite of the added difficulties after the incident at Nadeauville, Potts and Mackintosh had contrived to carry on performing their duty. Instead of keeping the party in sight, albeit from a distance, they had improved upon the tactics employed by David Hesdin and the le Boeuf brothers. While following the tracks, they had taken the precaution of remaining sufficiently far behind to prevent their own sign being located when Boniface had made searches for evidence that anybody was taking an interest in *le Loup-Garou*'s affairs.

Not only had the relaxation of Boniface's precautions following the visit by Canche made the scouts' task simpler, they had extended their efforts. For the past three nights, knowing they were approaching the border with the United States, they had taken it in turn to move closer on foot and keep watch sufficiently near to the other party's camps to be able to hear any conversations that took place.

'Tomorrow, you say?' Mackintosh answered, sitting up with his blankets around him.

'Canche say so,' Potts confirmed. 'Reckon brother's got chiefs waiting 'n' *le Loup-Garou* be there.'

'I know my old mother always used to say, "If wishes were horses, beggars would ride",' the Scot remarked. 'So I don't hold much faith in doing it. But I wish we knew what they've got in mind. It can't be they're planning to bamboozle the chiefs into thinking yon Beauville *klooch* is the *Jan-Dark*. One close look at her would show she couldn't be, with them grey eyes and her hair cut so short.'

'Learn tomorrow,' Potts stated, as if the matter required no further discussion, picking up his blankets.

'Aye, we'll do our wee best to, laddie,' Mackintosh agreed, conceding that his young companion had once again said all that mattered on the subject with the two words. 'Thing is, though. We've got to do more than just learn what's happening. We'll have to do what we can to stop it.'

CHAPTER FOURTEEN

SHE'S THE REBEL SPY?

'Don't bother to get up, *mon ami*,' Arnaud Cavallier requested, as the two *Metis* who had accompanied him when he and 'Matthew Devlin' had returned to the wagons earlier than usual that afternoon covered Belle Boyd and Captain Patrick Reeder with their weapons to emphasise what was clearly a command for all the friendly manner in which it was being uttered. 'Just lift your knife and revolver *very* slowly, please, and hand them to me.'

'I hope this isn't your idea of a *joke*,' the Remittance Kid said calmly, remaining seated on the folding chair by the larger of the two camp fires and avoiding anything that might be construed as a hostile gesture. 'If it *is*, old chap, I can't say I find it *terribly* amusing.'

Having witnessed and countered Jebediah Lincoln's precautions the previous night, the Englishman had realised they must be nearing the rendezvous. However, he had not anticipated that they were so close. His first intimation had come when Cavallier and 'Devlin' arrived from ranging ahead. They were accompanied by – although no introductions had been made – Roland Boniface and Raoul Canche. Knowing that the newcomers were not the pair who had delivered the message to Stokeley, the Kid had guessed what had brought them to meet their leader. It was not, he had felt certain, as *le Loup-Garou* had claimed, that they were two of his countrymen who had been met by chance and invited to take a meal before they resumed their journey.

Having been convinced that they were accepted for what they were pretending to be, Belle, the Kid and Calamity Jane had allowed Cavallier's story to go unchallenged. None of them had envisaged the development which was arising at the conclusion of the meal. There had not been the slightest indication of what he was planning.

As had happened every night, the Occidental members of the 'hunting party' and their *Metis* guests had gathered at the larger of the fires which were lit on making camp while the three Chinamen prepared the evening meal for everybody on the smaller. Having eaten more rapidly than the others, Boniface had announced that he and his companion would be moving on. Picking up the Winchester Model of 1866 carbine and the Henry rifle, they had turned the barrels in the direction of Belle and the Kid. Then *le Loup-Garou*, who had risen on the pretext of seeing his countrymen off, had delivered his politely worded order.

'It isn't intended as a joke, *mon ami*, and I regret deeply that I am *compelled* to ask you to do so,' Cavallier answered, then indicated Vera Gorr-Kauphin and 'Devlin' as they came to their feet. 'But I am afraid my – partners – insist upon taking what *they* consider to be a necessary precaution.'

'Your *partners*?' the Kid queried, wanting to avoid letting it be apparent that he already knew of the connection.

'Regrettably, they are,' *le Loup-Garou* confirmed, either oblivious of or uncaring about the way in which the anarchists were scowling and clearly disapproved of his far from complimentary references to them.

'I can understand why you say regrettably,' the Kid declared. A glance at Calamity informed him that she was ready to render assistance but was waiting for a hint as to what form he wanted it to take. Giving a slight prohibitive shake of his head as a warning that it would be inadvisable for her true status to be made known at that point, he went on, 'It would appear that "Lavinia" and I have been led upon what I believe you colonial chappies refer to as a wildgoose chase.'

'Hardly that, *mon ami*, although I admit that I did invite you on false pretences,' Cavallier corrected. 'But I assure you that the journey will prove more profitable than you imagined and will tell you why before midnight tonight. Until then, I must ask you to do as I said.'

'Whatever you will, old boy,' the Kid assented. Carefully,

using his left thumb and forefinger only, he extracted first the *badik* and, having surrendered it to *le Loup-Garou* took out and passed over the Webley Royal Irish Constabulary revolver. 'Although I can't say I'm in favour of your way of doing it, I find you've aroused my curiosity and am eager to have it satisfied.'

'I'm pleased to hear it,' Cavallier declared. 'And, as I told you, my partners *insisted* that we did it this way.'

'Partners do tend to make one do what one would rather not and may even suspect is inadvisable,' the Kid admitted, noticing that neither the actress nor her 'husband' cared for the way in which *le Loup-Garou* continued to place the responsibility for his actions upon them. Wanting to convince them all that he was accepting the situation, he continued, 'Anyway, you'd better have "Lavinia" hand over her little Derringer-thing to keep *them* happy. Give it to them, dear girl.'

'Whatever you-all want, Rem-honey,' Belle answered, following the Englishman's line of reasoning and taking the Remington Double Derringer from the right side pocket of the jacket of the brown two piece travelling costume – which had been tailored to meet certain specialised needs of her profession – she was wearing. 'But I think it's a sin we should be treated this way.'

'It is only with the deepest reluctance that I do it, *mademoiselle*,' Cavallier declared, then swung his gaze to Lincoln and held out the weapons. 'Take care of these, *m'sieur*, and make sure my friends are made comfortable until we return. Remember, too, that they are *my* friends and treat them with *every* courtesy.'

'Sure thing, Mr Cavallier,' the freighter replied, drawing the required conclusions from the way his orders had been expressed. 'I'll tend to it for you.'

'See you do, *m'sieur*,' Cavallier commanded. 'And now, "Mr and Mrs Roxby", it is time we let my compatriots take us to the meeting.'

'*You* go, "Mr Dev – Roxby",' the actress suggested, throwing a pointed look at Belle and the Kid. 'There's nothing I can do if I come and I don't feel like doing any more travelling today.'

'All right,' "Devlin" agreed, sharing the woman's disinclination to trust any of the people with whom they were involved out of one or the other's sight. 'I'm ready to go when you are, Mr Cavallier.'

*　　*　　*

'You know something, "Mrs Roxby"?' Calamity Jane remarked, strolling towards where the actress was sitting on the folding chair she had taken from the fire to the side of the wagon in which she and her "husband" were travelling and was nursing a shotgun across her knees. 'I get the feeling that you don't trust *somebody* around here.'

About half an hour had elapsed since 'Devlin' and the three *Metis* had taken their departure. While they were saddling the horses, Vera had called Lincoln aside and spoken with him. She had pointed out that she and her 'husband' were aware of his employer's identity and could make life very unpleasant for both of them in the future if there was any cause for complaint. She had also warned him that there were other anarchists to take revenge in case anything happened to them. Then she had insisted that the weapons taken from 'Lavinia Saltyre' and the Remittance Kid were handed over to her, promising to save him from any repercussions if Cavallier objected later.

Ever ready to run with the hare and hunt with the hounds, the freighter had not hesitated to comply with the actress's wishes. What was more, appreciating how he would be affected if there should prove to be cause for her suspicions, he had ordered Frenchie Ponthieu and Joe Polaski to keep a close watch on the couple. Sharing his apprehension, the drivers had positioned themselves so they could carry out their instructions effectively and refused the Kid's suggestion that they played poker to help pass the time until *le Loup-Garou* returned.

'I've got such good cause to trust *you* haven't I?' Vera challenged, coming to her feet with the shotgun held before her in both hands.

'Lordy Lord!' the red head said, grinning disarmingly. 'Don't tell me you've got to know I've been letting good ole "Lavinia" 'n' Rem bed down together in my wagon some nights?'

'I have!' Vera admitted, without either raising the weapon to a position of greater readiness or showing any sign of relaxing. 'What was the idea?'

'They paid me to and doing it let me get to bed down all warm 'n' cosey with the "mon-sewer",' Calamity explained, coming to a halt just beyond arms' length and placing her hands on her hips. 'Which it's surely true what I've always heard about Frenchmen. And, anyways, they promised me true 'n' faithful's they'd be bundling.'

'*Bundling?*' Vera queried, showing a lack of comprehension. 'What's *that*?'

'It's what folks out here say when a young feller comes a-courting in the wintertime and can't make it home at night,' the red head informed, satisfied that her real reason for starting the conversation might be understood by her companions, but had not aroused anybody else's suspicions. 'It's too cold for them to sit out on the porch to do their spooning and, even if there's a room to spare, they'd not be wanting to have to keep getting up to feed the fire was they on their own. So, 'though they haven't been married off all churched 'n' proper, they can get into the same bed all warm 'n' cosey just so long's there a plank put between 'em so they're kept apart. Don't you do that in England?'

'I've never heard of it,' Vera admitted, then glanced past the girl to where Belle and the Kid were sitting on similar chairs to the one she had just vacated. 'Are you telling me that is what *they* were doing in your wagon?'

'Hot damn!' Calamity ejaculated, with such vehemence that she brought the actress's attention back to her. Restraining a desire to glance over her shoulder, she could only gamble upon her companions having deduced what she was contemplating and would be ready to back her play when she made it. 'Are you saying's they might not've bundled? And here's lil ole me, knowing who *she* is, figuring's her for sure could be trusted not to do nothing's wouldn't be right 'n' proper for a *lady*.'

'You trusted *her* to behave like a *lady*?' Vera scoffed and, although she indicated the slender "blonde" with a brief gesture from the shotgun, there was nothing in her attitude to suggest she suspected the truth or that anything was amiss.

'I sure's hell's for sinners *did*!' Calamity declared, after thinking. 'Here goes and, happen you 'n' Rem haven't read the signs right, Belle-gal, there's going to be hot times "round here *real* soon!"' Tensing a little, she elaborated further, 'That's not just some cat-house "hello dearie" you're selling so short, damn it. She's the Rebel Spy!'

'*She's* the Rebel Spy?' Vera repeated, almost instinctively. Then a realisation of what the red head had said struck her as if she had been slapped across the face. However, such was the effect of the belated comprehension that all she could think of doing was to continue speaking and her voice ascended in volume to such an extent that it brought the attention of Lincoln and his employees to her. 'Did you say she's the REBEL SPY?'

'That's just who she is!' Calamity whooped, praying that her purpose had not only been understood by her friends, but they would be able to make the most of the diversion she was creating.

'Lincoln!' Vera shrieked, panic mingling with the rage and mortification which were assailing her over the discovery of how thoroughly she had been taken in, as she started to raise the shotgun. 'Kill them!'

Hearing the startled exclamations from the freighter and his drivers, but still not daring to look anywhere except at the actress, Calamity was aware that she would *very* soon find out what was happening by the larger camp fire.

Although the red head had not supplied them with any definite indication of her intentions before going to speak with Vera, Belle and the Kid had drawn the conclusions she required. They were also fully conversant with the difficulties they would be facing when she presented them with an opportunity to benefit from whatever she was planning. Frenchie Ponthieu and Joe Polaski, each cradling a Winchester Model of 1866 carbine on his lap, were squatting in front of them. Both were beyond reaching distance, but not too far away and their posture was less conducive to rapid movement than that of a person who, like the Kid, was sitting on a chair, or Belle, as she had stood on the pretext of going to answer the call of nature beyond the firelight. The awkwardness would be particularly applicable if the drivers' attention should be distracted when the need to respond with alacrity arose.

The Rebel Spy and the Englishman knew, however, that there were two jokers in the deck!

While Lincoln was not holding a weapon, being seated on another of the folding chairs at the opposite side of the fire, he posed a greater threat than either Ponthieu or Polaski.

So did the three Chinamen who were gathered at the smaller fire, if the Kid's estimation of them was not at fault.

Deducing correctly that something was radically wrong from the name they had heard, the freighter and the drivers realised they must take action even before the actress yelled her instructions. Having looked towards the wagons, they also became aware that they were allowing their attention to wander at a most inopportune moment and started to rectify the situation.

Knotting her work-hardened right fist, Calamity stepped forward. Rotating her torso and dropping the right shoulder to put the full weight of her powerful young body behind it, she drove forward her right arm as she had been taught by Dobe Killem was most effective when throwing a punch. Rising rapidly, her knuckles made contact beneath Vera's jaw with a click such as two billiard balls made when kissing. With the shotgun dropping from her grasp, and her body being tilted rearwards at the hips, the actress was knocked from her feet by the force of the blow. In going down, the back of her head struck the side of the wagon with a wicked crack. Already stunned, she did not feel the impact even though it fractured her skull and was to send her into a deep coma from which she would not recover.

Shaking her throbbing hand, Calamity bent to grab for the shotgun. She did not know how serious an injury she might have inflicted. Nor, remembering what she had been told and seen of Vera, did she particularly care. Already she could hear a commotion behind her. Even without looking to find out what the various sounds might portend, she realised that gaining possession of it could be of vital importance. While she had not been disarmed along with her friends, she was aware of the need for a weapon with a greater effective range than either the bull whip or her Navy Colt.

A sense of alarm assailed the red head as her hands were closing upon the shotgun's foregrip and the wrist of the butt!

Although the actress had been nursing the weapon for some time, she had *not* drawn the hammers to fully cocked!

On rising and making her excuse for having done so, Belle had started to run her thumbs around the waistband of the brown skirt. It had been an innocuous appearing gesture and neither Ponthieu, who was in front of her, nor the other two men had seen anything wrong with it.

However, the moment Vera had raised her voice, the Rebel Spy demonstrated that her action was far from harmless. Without glancing at the Kid, knowing he was aware of what she intended to do, she tugged at the garment's restraining strap. Designed for just such a purpose, it came apart and the waist of the skirt expanded so it was able to fall away without impediment. As had happened on other occasions when she had taken similar measures, she watched the three men's eyes following the skirt's descent with lascivious interest and knew they were doomed to disappointment. While they were undoubtedly expecting to have some form of feminine under garment to be revealed, having anticipated that the need might arise, she was wearing form-fitting black riding breeches and matching Hessian boots beneath the skirt.

Making an accurate guess at how the Rebel Spy would handle her end of the affair, the Kid had not needed to look at her. Instead, on hearing the actress's yell, he launched himself from the chair like a disturbed pheasant taking wing. Swiftly as he moved, he saw Polaski's gaze swinging hurriedly back to him from where it had been diverted by watching the descent of the skirt.

On discovering that the Englishman was taking advantage of his inattention, the driver began to thrust himself erect and turn the barrel of the carbine so it could be used. Equally appreciative of the danger, his employer and Ponthieu were also rising and preparing to take action. So were the three Chinamen at the other fire, although he did not notice them. A small throwing axe slid from its place of concealment up each man's wide black sleeve.

Jumping clear of the skirt as it fell away. Belle alighted in range and her right leg rose swiftly to miss its intended mark. She had meant to catch Ponthieu under the chin, but instead took him into the centre of the chest. Flung over backwards, he neither fired nor dropped the carbine. Springing forward, she delivered a stamp to his stomach which winded him and, kicking the weapon from his grasp, dived after it.

Showing surprising agility considering his thickset bulk, Polaski was rising and trying to align the Winchester rapidly. Out thrust the Kid's hands, the left caught the barrel and turned the muzzle aside, while the right clamped over the brass frame. Twisting down with the former and lifting the latter until he felt the driver resisting, he suddenly reversed the directions. Snatching the carbine from its confused owner's grip, he swung and drove the metal butt plate against the side of the knitted woollen cap.

Even as Polaski was going down unconscious, the Englishman saw that Lincoln was posing a very serious threat to himself and the girls.

Like the driver felled by the Kid, the freighter was capable of rapid movement when the circumstances called for it. He had been taken just as unprepared as any of his employees by the developments which followed Calamity engaging Vera in conversation. For all that, coming to his feet with alacrity, he commenced his draw as soon as he had perceived there was a real and urgent need to arm himself. Even as he was starting to liberate the Merwin & Holbert Army Pocket revolver from the 'half breed' shoulder holster, he became aware that having it in his hand was anything but a guarantee that he would be in control of the situation. Not only were his male drivers being rendered helpless, the red head's actions suggested she was far from being the loyal employee he had imagined.

Swivelling around with the shotgun snapping to her shoulder, Calamity had not waited to draw the hammers to fully cocked before raising it. She saw the freighter was bringing out the revolver and guessed from the way he was holding it that the Kid was the object of his attention. There was, she concluded, only one thing she could do. Run the best god-damned bluff she had ever produced and hope it would pay off.

'It's him or me, Jebediah!' the red head yelled. 'You can't take us both!'

Even though Lincoln had the weapon out, he was cognizant of the precarious position he was in. Being unable to discern that Calamity could not fire the shotgun immediately, he felt sure she would have no hesitation over using it. While he might shoot the Englishman, she was just as certain to get him. Or would be, if it was not for one thing. Already his Chinese employees held their deadly throwing axes and were starting to move forward to a range at which the weapons could be launched with the certainty of hitting. He was confident that neither Calamity, 'Lavinia', nor the Kid were aware of the danger.

'Drop the axes!' the Kid snapped, suffering from no such delusion as the freighter anticipated, twisting around until he was directing the carbine at the leader of the trio and speaking in the Cantonese dialect he had picked up in the Far East, knowing they would understand. 'Quickly!'

'Your "Chinees" are out of it, Jebediah!' Calamity warned.

'But *I'm* not!' Belle went on, completing her rolling dive on her knees and with the butt of the carbine she had collected in passing nestled against her right shoulder. 'You can't get more than one of us. Which is it to be, give up – or *die*?'

Taking in everything that was happening, Lincoln found his hole card had failed to produce a winning hand.

No cowards, the three Chinese were far from fools. They were still too far away to be sure of hitting with their axes. What was more, their leader knew he would be the first to die if they should try to attack. He had not overlooked the way in which the Englishman had addressed him and knew he could not hope to pass as the harmless 'Chinee' most Occidentals he had met in the United States considered him. There was, he concluded, only one thing to do.

'All right!' Lincoln yelled, seeing the three throwing axes drop to the ground at their owners' feet and realising all was lost. The sound of shooting might be heard by Cavallier's party and bring them back to investigate, but they would be too late to save him from being killed. Tossing his revolver aside, he raised his hands, continuing, 'I'm through.'

Although the freighter did not know it, one of Cavallier's party was in the vicinity.

In spite of having been convinced that the Kid was a potential assistant, *le Loup-Garou* was not the man to leave anything to chance. So he had sent Raoul Canche back with orders to remain concealed in the woodland near the camp and watch everything that happened.

Concluding that Cavallier's faith in the Englishman was misplaced, the *Metis* brought up and started to aim his Henry rifle.

CHAPTER FIFTEEN

WHAT IS THE '*JAN-DARK*'?

'Congratulations, old chap,' Captain Patrick Reeder said approvingly, as Jebediah Lincoln signified his surrender. 'You've made a wi – !'

Before the comment could be completed, there was a soft thud – the cause of which was obvious to anybody who had heard a knife being driven into human flesh – from the darkness. It was followed instantly by a grasping cry of pain and the crack of a rifle being discharged to send a bullet not too far above the Remittance Kid's head. Dropping his smoking Henry, Raoul Canche advanced with staggering steps into the light of the camp fires. Agony distorted his swarthy features and his hands were reaching behind his arched back. They returned to the front, covered with something red and wet, as his knees buckled and he collapsed face down.

Startled exclamations burst from Belle Boyd, Calamity Jane, the Kid and Lincoln. However, although his captors' attention was diverted from him, the freighter realised that the situation was not being improved as far as he was concerned. The long knife in the right hand of the tall, dour-faced man who followed the dying *Metis* from the darkness was red with blood, which meant he was unlikely to be an ally. What was more, the Winchester Model of 1866 rifle in his left fist could be brought into use too quickly for there to be any hope of turning the tables on him or the trio.

'Good evening, folks,' the newcomer greeted, with the accent of a Highland Scot, glancing at Canche's feebly moving body in passing. 'The name's Sandy Mackintosh and I'd be obliged if you'd tell me who you are.'

'I see that my letter reached Colonel French,' the Englishman replied, having sent details of Arnaud Cavallier's scheme to the commanding officer of the Canadian Northwest Mounted Police before leaving Chicago and being aware of the Scot's connection with that force. 'So you may have heard of me as "the Remittance Kid".'

'The Colonel didn't say anything about it when he sent Jerry Potts and me to keep an eye on *le Loup-Garou*'s crowd,' Mackintosh stated, bending to thrust the blade of his dirk into the ground. Having cleaned off the blood, he returned the weapon to its sheath. 'And I can't say I've heard of you.'

'I'm Captain Patrick Reeder, Rifle Brigade, seconded to the British Secret Service,' the Kid introduced. 'These ladies are Belle Boyd and Calamity Jane.'

'I heard of you when I rode under Jeb Stuart in the War, Miss Boyd,' Mackintosh declared and his tone showed he approved. 'Are you still working for Dobe Killem, Miss Calamity?'

'I sure am, Sandy,' the red head agreed, then put down the shotgun and pointed to Vera Gorr-Kauphin. 'I'd best take a look at her. She hit the wagon a hell of a crack with her head as she went down.'

'And we'd better disarm those blighters, dear girl,' the Kid suggested, indicating the two drivers. 'Then Mr Mackintosh can tell us how he came on the scene at such an opportune moment.'

'It's going to be more than the *Metis le Loup-Garou*'s trying to get on the war path,' the Scot explained, after the precautions had been taken and he had exchanged information with the Rebel Spy and the Englishman. 'They've brought a young war chief from each of six Indian tribes down here for a *powwow*.'

'Where is it to be held?' Belle asked.

'In a valley about three miles from here,' the Scot replied. 'I left Jerry keeping watch and followed Raoul there, *Vieux Malhuereux* Lacomb and Roland Boniface until they met *le Loup-Garou*. He sent Lacomb off and brought the other two here. I was going to keep after him, but thought I'd better stay for a while longer when Raoul came sneaking back. So I stayed until I knew who was who among you and stopped him shooting.'

'It's fortunate for us that you did,' the Kid stated, glancing to where Calamity was keeping Lincoln and his employees covered with the now cocked shotgun, having decided she could do nothing for the unconscious actress. 'What are the chances of Cavallier persuading the Indians to join his uprising, old chap? After all, you say they are from different tribes.'

'Aye,' Mackintosh confirmed. 'There's one each from the Crow, Bannock, Blood, Cree, Assiniboine and Blackfoot. They're all young hot heads and trouble-causers who are known as itching to go to war with *anybody* just for the hell of it.'

'Aren't some of them traditional enemies?' the Kid asked.

'They are,' the Scot confirmed. 'But they'd be willing to come together if the *Jan-Dark* made an appearance.'

'What is the "*Jan-Dark*"?' Belle put in.

'Not so much "what" as "who", ma'am,' Mackintosh corrected. 'It's an old Indian legend that all the tribes have. The *Jan-Dark*'s a warrior maid armed with a war lance who'll come from nowhere and unite the tribes in an uprising that'll see all the white folks, British and French alike, driven out of Canada.'[1]

'And you think this *Jan-Dark* girl is due to make her appearance?' the Kid guessed.

'It could be what *le Loup-Garou* has in mind, or something like it,' Mackintosh admitted. 'Although, good as she is with a lance, that grey-eyed *klooch* of his will need to change her appearance before she'll get them to believe she's the *Jan-Dark*. Her hair's too short and the wrong colour and her skin's a touch too light for her to get by.'

'Making the necessary changes wouldn't be difficult,' Belle pointed out, thinking of the selection of wigs and other items in her trunk which allowed her to make realistic alterations to her appearance. 'But will the chiefs really believe she is the *Jan-Dark* arrived at last?'

'They'll be ready to pretend to believe it, even if they don't, to get a share of the repeaters in the wagons.' Mackintosh declared. 'Taken both together, *Jan-Dark* and the arms,

---

[1] *In* ON REMITTANCE, *Major General Reeder says he believed that the legend of the warrior maid with the war lance could have had its origins from the Indians having heard French Canadians telling stories about Joan of Arc (Jeanne d' Arc). J.T.E.*

they'll each be able to get up a following to go on the war trail. When they do the Government's going to start hitting back. Once that happens, it'll grow and no matter who wins, only I can't see it being the Indians and *Metis*, blood's going to flow like water from one end of Canada to the other.'

* * *

'Your presence is disturbing the chiefs, "*M'sieur* Devlin",' Arnaud Cavallier announced, his voice seeming friendly and almost apologetic. He was also employing English for the first time since he, the anarchist and Roland Boniface had arrived by the fire in the large clearing at the bottom of an otherwise wood covered valley which had been selected as the site for the *powwow* with their intended allies. 'Although I have assured them that you whole-heartedly support our great cause, they consider it would be bad medicine for a white man to be here.'

Aided by the fire's glow, which illuminated the whole of the clearing, 'Matthew Devlin' looked at the Indians. Swinging his gaze from Many Horses of the Crow tribe to *Bois D'Arc* of the Bannocks, via Red Arrow of the Crees, Loud Thunder of the Bloods, Swift Water of the Assiniboines and Wolverine of the Blackfoots, he could sense the hostility in their cold eyed return scrutiny. All were young, clad in the ceremonial attire of their respective nations, with eagle feather war bonnets, bear claw necklaces, dyed horse-hair shirts, fringed buckskin trousers and fancy moccasins. Knives and, or, tomahawks swung from every belt. While each had either a rifle or carbine to supplement his close range armament, not one of the firearms was a repeater and only three were chambered for metal-case cartridges.

'You mean they want me to leave?' the anarchist asked, bringing his eyes back to *le Loup-Garou*.

'They do,' Cavallier confirmed, still in the same amiable fashion. 'And so you *must* go. It is the only way I can win them over.'

'All right,' 'Devlin' assented, coming to his feet. 'Shall I wait by the horses?'

'That won't satisfy them,' Cavallier answered. 'You'll have

to go back to the wagons. I'll have Roland take you.'

'There's no need for that,' the anarchist stated, not averse to having an opportunity to speak with the *Metis* who had been left to keep watch on the rest of the party without his countrymen being able to hear them. 'I'll be able to find my own way.'

'As you wish,' *le Loup-Garou* replied.

Walking towards the horses, which had been left at the fringe of a particularly dense clump of common juniper shrubs at the edge of the clearing, 'Devlin' felt vaguely uneasy. He could not help wondering if Cavallier rather than the chiefs had been responsible for his dismissal from the *powwow*. As all of the somewhat lengthy conversation had been carried out in the *lingua franca* evolved over the years by *voyageurs* and others to allow communication with members of the various Indian nations and neither of the *Metis* had offered to translate for him, he could not understand anything of what was being said. He had noticed that the assembled chiefs, who all were much younger and less impressive than he had been led to expect, had not regarded him in a friendly fashion.

On the other hand, 'Devlin' remembered there had been few occasions during their association when Cavallier had treated him with such polite friendliness and he found it disturbing. In the past, such an attitude had only been in evidence when the person at whom it was directed would soon be in some kind of difficulty. With that thought in mind, he unbuttoned his jacket to give access to the Colt Storekeeper Model Peacemaker tucked into the waistband of his trousers.

All in all, though, the anarchist was not entirely sorry to be told to leave. He had decided he was not going to learn anything of use to his primary purpose of attending the *powwow*, which had been in the hope of meeting a more suitable candidate with whom to supplant *le Loup-Garou* as the leader of the *Metis'* rebellion. However, there was only Boniface there and, not only was he lacking in qualities of leadership, he seemed completely devoted to Cavallier's interests. Nor had the elderly, miserable looking man who had been with Boniface and Canche, but did not accompany them to the wagons, strike 'Devlin' as being more acceptable.

The anarchist wondered whether Raoul Canche had the

qualities he was seeking. Or, if not, whether he should tell Lincoln to turn back with the firearms instead of handing them over to Cavallier. Should he decide on the latter alternative, he reminded himself, he would not only have to kill Canche, but either win over, or dispose of the Remittance Kid. While he would prefer to get rid of the Englishman, he had to concede the former choice would be more advantageous. *Le Loup-Garou* and the Indians would give chase as soon as the desertion was discovered, so the support of an extra gun could prove most useful.

Before 'Devlin' could decide which line of action to follow, his thoughts were diverted from their treacherous course. He was still some yards from the tethered mounts when the silence of the night was shattered by a savage yell, feminine in timbre yet menacing for all of that, followed by the snort and other sounds of a horse being set into sudden and rapid motion. Snapping his gaze towards the source of the commotion, the sight which met his eyes stilled him with open mouthed amazement and brought him to a halt.

Sitting astride a large and powerful palomino gelding's high-horned Indian saddle with the easy grace of one well versed in equestrian matters, a rider emerged from the darkness. Passing swiftly through a gap between two clumps of juniper shrubs to the anarchist's left, the newcomer made straight for him. He needed only a single glance to know why this should be, but he was so taken aback that he momentarily gave no thought to reaching for his revolver. Cradled between the rider's right forearm and side, a long lance was pointing in his direction. For all the savage demeanour being displayed, its wielder was *not* a man.

Coal black hair was held back by a brightly coloured cloth band decorated with medicine symbols and taken into a plait on either side of the head. They framed a coppery bronze face with similar, if more beautiful, features to those of the Indians at the fire and which were distorted by a savage elation enhanced with the bands of red and white war paint running diagonally across the cheeks and vertically down the nose and chin. As if to prevent there being any doubt about the newcomer's sex, all she wore was a knee length buckskin skirt, an Indian-made belt supporting a bone handled hunting knife on its left side and moccasins. The scanty attire displayed a magnificently curvaceous figure 'Devlin' would have appreciated under different circumstances. Nor did the hard and well developed muscles playing under her smooth skin detract from her sensual and primeval-seeming pulchritude.

'It's the *Jan-Dark!*' *le Loup-Garou* yelled, rising from his heel-squatting position. 'She's come to bring death to the palefaces!'

The name was repeated in tones of awe by the six young chiefs as, snatching up their firearms ready to defend themselves against any intended treachery, they too were bounding to their feet. Seeing the newcomer and accepting her as what she was pretending to be, each of them felt sure she meant him no harm.

Hearing Cavallier's shout and recognising the name even though unable to understand the rest of the words, 'Devlin' could not prevent himself from starting to turn in the speaker's direction. He had heard the legend of the *Jan-Dark* from *le Loup-Garou* and had been told she was to make an appearance at the *powwow* to persuade the assembled chiefs to join the uprising. However, he had not suspected how the 'warrior maid with the war lance' was to be brought into view. It was now clear that, wanting to make her arrival as spectacular and dramatic as possible, Cavallier was intent on sacrificing him.

Unfortunately for the anarchist, his appreciation of the situation came an instant too late for him to halt the ill-advised if involuntary action of turning around. By taking it, he was making Irène Beauville's task considerably easier and less dangerous. Even as he was trying to swing back to face her and started grabbing at the Colt Storekeeper's butt, she was within striking distance.

Giving another ringing screech which expressed the sensation of bloodthirsty elation filling her, the girl thrust with the lance as she had when running the buffalo. Powered by the impulsion of the swiftly moving palomino gelding, the weapon's diamond section head could have sliced through 'Devlin's' rib cage if necessary. Instead, it entered his back and, penetrating his heart, flung him from his feet.

Turning the lance as she had been taught in passing, Irène drew it free. Without as much as a backwards glance at the man she had killed in cold blood and feeling no more remorse than when she had brought down the buffalo, she galloped by the group around the fire. A feeling of exultation and delight filled her at the sight of the expressions on the faces of the young chiefs. If the way in which they were staring at her was any guide, every one of them believed her to be the genuine *Jan-Dark*. That this should be was a tribute to her ability in bringing the palomino through the darkness of the woodland to the vicinity of the clearing without making sufficient noise for them to be aware of her presence.

Approaching the bushes at the other side of the clearing and some fifty yards from her audience, the girl brought the palomino around in a rearing spin which caused it to paw the air with its front legs. However, when its hooves returned to the ground, she made no attempt to join the men. Although her features would let her pass as an Indian even in daylight since she had stained them and her body to an appropriate coppery bronze and had a wig covering her short-cropped tawny blonde hair, at close quarters her grey eyes would betray her *Metis* birth. So, signalling her mount to remain motionless, she swung the bloody-bladed lance above her head in both hands. Shaking it triumphantly, she lowered it to rest across her knees and awaited the next development.

Having kept the chiefs under observation, Cavallier was duplicating Irène's summations regarding the effect of her unexpected and dramatic appearance was having on them. Until she had burst from the juniper shrubs and he called her name, there had been no mention of the *Jan-Dark* during the *powwow*. So, due to the silence in which she had approached and waited until the opportune moment, the arrival of a girl who could be her had been as much of a surprise to them as it was to 'Devlin'. Although they were almost certain to discover that they had been tricked later, at present they were all convinced that the 'warrior maid with the war lance' had finally materialised to unite the Indian nations and drive the white people out of Canada. Knowing the kind of men with whom he was dealing, he was confident that each would see the wisdom of continuing to pretend she was the *Jan-Dar*? even after they learned of the deception. Admitting they had been tricked would cause them such a grave loss of face that none would be willing to announce it had happened.

Being aware that he was not the kind of dupe desired by the anarchists, *le Loup-Garou* had felt sure 'Devlin' and Vera Gorr-Kauphin hoped to replace him with a more compliant leader of the rebellion. So he had intended to terminate their acquaintance as soon as the arms and ammunition were within reach of his supporters. It had been Irène's suggestion, passed to him by Jacques Lacomb – who had remained to guard the wagon after notifying her that the *powwow* would go ahead as planned – that the disposal of 'Devlin' could be carried out in a fashion which would create a powerful impression when she made her first appearance as the *Jan-Dark*. While conceding the point, knowing nothing of the hunting of the buffalo, Cavallier's only reservation had been that she might lack the ability in wielding the war lance and fail to kill her victim outright. For this to have happened would have ruined everything. However, on hearing how she had already proved her skill in no uncertain fashion, he had yielded to Lacomb's and Boniface's assurance that she could carry out the task and their confidence had not been misplaced. He had done his part by contriving to have the anarchist accompany him alone and sending 'Devlin' away so she could launch the attack. Now he must press home the advantage she had gained for him.

'Well, my brothers!' *le Loup-Garou* said, bringing the attention of the chiefs to him. 'Now *everybody* will know who is destined to lead your nations' warriors against the white people. It is to *you* the *Jan-Dark* has appeared. She knows who have the courage and spirit to carry out the prophecy. That is why she has waited until she could appear before *you*. When you carry the word of her coming back to your villages, so many will flock to ride with you that *nobody* will dare oppose your *right* to lead them.'

There was a rumble of concurrence from the Indians. Each was a chief, but of a subordinate status and with little authority when it came to dictating matters of policy. With the generally beneficient and fair manner in which the British governed

Canada, the leaders of the respective nations had tended to restrict hostilities and keep the peace. So they had lacked the opportunities for personal aggrandisement which accrued to successes gained on the war path. Being mutually ambitious, all appreciated how being present when the *Jan-Dark* had at last made her long awaited appearance could do much to bring about the situation and conditions each desired.

Listening to the response elicited by his speech, Cavallier found it most satisfying. No longer were the assembled chiefs watching each other with wary suspicion, as they had been so far. Convinced that the purpose of the *powwow* had been achieved and the potential leaders of the six nations were united in their willingness to create an uprising against the white people, he decided Irène could depart. She was waiting in case her exhortation was required. As it was not, she could retire to the wagon. When Boniface and Canche joined her, she would return to Canada and make ready for her subsequent appearances as the *Jan-Dark*.

CHAPTER SIXTEEN

LET'S SEE IF YOU CAN KILL *ME!*

Just as Arnaud Cavallier was on the point of signalling for Irène Beauville to leave, startled exclamations burst from the chiefs and they started to raise their weapons. Looking around, he spat out a furious curse as he recognised the two young women and the three men who were emerging from the bushes on the opposite side but almost level with the point from which the girl had burst into view.

For all his awareness of the official status enjoyed by Jerry Potts and Sandy Mackintosh, *le Loup-Garou* found the fact that they were accompanied by 'Lavinia Saltyre', Calamity Jane and the Remittance Kid just as disconcerting as discovering they were in the vicinity.

Everything about the trio from the wagons implied Vera Gorr-Kauphin and 'Matthew Devlin' had been justified in mistrusting them. Also that the precautions taken to render them innocuous had failed.

Cavallier could see the pistol-like hilt of the *badik* protruding from beneath the left flap of Captain Patrick Reeder's waist-length leather jacket and did not doubt the Webley Royal Irish Constabulary revolver was in its holster behind his back instead of being watched over by Jebediah Lincoln. Studying Irène in a speculative manner, Calamity Jane was still wearing her gunbelt and whip as she had been when *le Loup-Garou* had last seen her and he did not care for the implications he was drawing from that.

The most significant change, Cavallier told himself, was in the blonde's appearance. It went beyond her brown two piece travelling costume having been replaced by a masculine open necked black shirt, with matching breeches and Hessian boots. Nor was it entirely attributable to the gunbelt of the same colour, carrying an ivory handled revolver in its low cavalry twist holster, strapped so it hung correctly for a fast draw about her slender waist. There was an expression of confidence, command and determination on her beautiful face. Tapping her leg with the handle of the parasol in her left hand, its head having been removed for some reason which was not apparent, she walked in a purposeful manner yet still retained her feminine grace. Everything about her carriage, bearing and deportment was far removed from that of the jailbird-turned-gambler's woman she was purported to be.

Contemplating the metamorphosis, Cavallier's memory stirred and he felt as if a cold hand was touching his spine. According to the information received from 'Devlin's' anarchist colleague, such attire was frequently worn by Belle Boyd. Despite her nickname, the Rebel Spy was now a member of the United States' Secret Service. So, if that should be 'Lavinia's' true identity, her organisation must be trying to prevent an uprising in Canada being launched from their country.

What was more, even if the slender 'blonde' was not Belle Boyd, the fact that she and the Englishman were armed proved they had not been brought from the wagons as the two scouts' prisoners. As Calamity Jane was also still in possession of her weapons, she had clearly been working in cahoots with them from the beginning.

Although none of the newcomers were Indians, the chiefs did not start shooting at them in spite of knowing Potts and Mackintosh were scouts for the Canadian Northwest Mounted Police. Between them, the party were displaying prominently six belts made from black, white and dark purple beads interwoven with a variety of different medicine symbols. Each chief identified the sacred emblem of his nation emblazoned on one of the belts and recognised the insignia of the others who were present. They also knew what the sight portended.

Known as *wampum*, the belts signified that the bearers were the emissaries of the senior chiefs and medicine men of the tribe whose symbols formed the decoration. Backed by such authority, the intruders must be allowed to attend the *powwow* and could neither be harmed nor ordered to go away until they had had their say.

In spite of realising that his plans were being put at risk by the arrival of the quintet, Cavallier halted the movement of his right hand towards his holstered Colt Civilian Model Peacemaker. Not only did he share the chiefs' understanding of the status conferred upon the bearers by the *wampum*, he considered that an attempt to complete the draw would be a serious error in tactics. In fact, it was almost certain to prove fatal. Each of the scouts was carrying a Winchester more accessibly than his revolver and would not hesitate to use it.

A quick glance informed *le Loup-Garou* that Roland Boniface had duplicated his estimation of the situation and was standing passively. Another quick look let him know that Irène was watching and waiting for some sign of how he wanted her to act. Then he returned his gaze to the newcomers.

'What do you want here, Mackintosh, Potts?' Cavallier demanded, forcing himself to try to regain control of the situation. He spoke in the *lingua franca* so the Indians would be able to follow the conversation. 'This is United States' territory and the red coats have no authority outside Canada.'

'We're not here on behalf of the red coats,' the taller scout answered, making a gesture with the Assiniboine *wampum* draped over his rifle's barrel. 'When the councils of the six nations heard you were calling a *powwow* of chiefs, but had not been invited and could not come in person, they gave Jerry Potts and me their *wampum* so we could speak for them.'

'And what of these others?' Cavallier challenged, being aware that such delegation of authority was permissible, indicating Belle, Calamity and the Kid.

'We were told that we could invite anybody who we thought should be allowed to attend,' Mackintosh explained, such authority also being proscribed by convention. 'Captain Reeder here's speaking on the behalf of the Brit – '

'*Captain* Reeder?' Cavallier repeated, before he could stop himself and reverting to English as he glared at the Kid. Controlling his rising fury with a visible effort, knowing he would almost certainly be the first to die if he provoked hostilities, he went on bitterly, 'So you *are* a lousy British spy?'

'On the contrary, old thing,' the Englishman corrected and waved his left hand, the right holding the Cree *wampum*, in an almost languid fashion at the slender 'blonde'. 'Almost as good, even if I say it who *should*, as Colonel Boyd of the jolly old United States' Secret Service.'

'*Almost*, Captain Reeder, *toujours la politesse* I suppose,' the Rebel Spy acknowledged with a smile. The rank was correct and had been granted to give her authority when dealing with members of the Army or Navy in the line of duty. Her amiability disappeared as she swung her gaze to *le Loup-Garou*, but she did not address him. 'Apologise to the chiefs for my inability to speak their language, please, Mr Mackintosh. And be so good as to act as my interpreter.'

'I will, ma'am,' the Scot promised and did so.

'Unlike Captain Reeder, Mr Mackintosh and Mr Potts, *M'sieur* Cavallier,' Belle announced, her words being relayed to the chiefs by the taller scout. 'I *do* have authority here.'

'And in what way do you intend to assert this authority, *Mademoiselle la Colonel?*' *le Loup-Garou* inquired, more to buy time than from a desire for confirmation of what he already knew. He also wished that circumstances had not compelled him to restrict his *Metis*' contingent to just three men – one of whom he suspected was already dead, or had been taken prisoner and the second guarding their wagon – and Irène Beauville.

'I'm here to prevent you from provoking an uprising against the Government of Canada from what you have *admitted* is United States' territory,' Belle replied, speaking with quiet authority. 'To which effect, I have sent back the arms and ammunition which had been purchased to bring this about and, if you wish to have the money reimbursed, you will have to contact whoever sold them to you.'

'The wagons can't travel as fast as ridden horses, *Mademoiselle la Colonel*,' Cavallier pointed out, scowling as he noticed the way in which the Indians were responding to Mackintosh's translation. They were looking disturbed and far from pleased to learn the weapons which they had been promised might not be available. 'My friends, the chiefs, can easily overtake them before morning and make the contact for me.'

'The chiefs can follow the wagons if they wish, but I wouldn't advise it,' Belle replied, after Mackintosh had translated *le Loup-Garou's* comment for her benefit. 'Jebediah Lincoln took the precaution of removing the toggle-links from each weapon and hid them. Captain Reeder was watching him and, after he came back to the wagons, retrieved and scattered them so that you would have to search for a very long time before you recovered more than a handful of them.'

'And while you're searching for the bally things, old chap,' the Kid supplemented, 'the soldiers Colonel Boyd has arranged to follow us will have arrived. Which could prove more than embarrassing for all of you.'

'I *see*!' Cavallier purred, but the tone was indicative of the rage seething inside him. Then he gave what he hoped would be taken for a shrug of submission. 'It seems that, having no wish for harm to come to my friends, the best thing we can do is go back across the border without delay.'

'I'm pleased to hear the chiefs will be leaving,' Belle replied. 'But neither Miss Beauville nor you will be going with them.'

'Why not?' Cavallier demanded, although he knew what the answer would be, darting a glance at the bogus *Jan-Dark* and knowing she spoke sufficient English to follow the conversation even without Mackintosh continuing to carry out the duty of interpreter.

'She will have to stand trial for the premeditated murder of "Mr Roxby",' Belle elaborated, being informed by the *Metis* girl's restless movements she could hear all that was being said and pointing to the anarchist's body. 'And you are an accessory.'

'You will have to arrest us first,' *le Loup-Garou* warned, without waiting for Mackintosh to pass on the comment to the Indians. 'And I doubt whether the chiefs will allow you to take the *Jan-Dark* from them now she has appeared.'

'Probably not,' Belle conceded, pausing until the scout had informed the Indians of what had just been said. While he was speaking, she dropped the parasol's handle and the Blackfoot *wampum* she was carrying. 'But we know she isn't the *Jan-Dark*.'

'The chiefs *believe* she is,' Cavallier pointed out, watching the slender 'blonde' unbuckling the gunbelt and sensing he was being led into a trap.

'They're going to learn different,' the Rebel Spy declared, lowering the belt and its revolver to her feet.

Before setting off to attend the *powwow* with Mackintosh, Belle, Calamity and the Kid had removed all their belongings from the wagon. Telling Lincoln how the Englishman had disposed of the toggle-links, the Rebel Spy had ordered him to return to Stokeley and deliver Vera Gorr-Kauphin into the town marshal's custody. While she had not been enamoured of taking such an action, there had been no other way to deal with him which would ensure the arms were removed beyond the Indians' reach. Hoping that he would be apprehended by the troops who should be following them, she had made no mention of the assistance she had requested – via Sergeant Magoon – from Fort Connel before setting off.[1]

Having rid themselves of that problem, Mackintosh had led his unexpected allies to where Jerry Potts was waiting and they had held a brief council of war. Learning of the *wampum* before joining the younger scout, Belle had suggested she and the Kid should be invited to attend the *powwow* as representatives of their respective Governments. Pointing out that they might need an extra gun in case things went wrong, Calamity had suggested she should go along instead of, as had been suggested, remaining to look after their horses and belongings.

When Belle had explained how she meant to cope with the anticipated appearance of the bogus *Jan-Dark*, Mackintosh and Potts had agreed that it would produce the desired results; but warned her of the dangers entailed. There had not been time for a lengthy debate, nor could anybody come up with a better method for dealing with the situation. They had been approaching the clearing when Irène burst into view and the manner in which she had done so took them all by surprise. In spite of realising that the task could be even more perilous than she had envisaged, the Rebel Spy still considered there was no other course open to her party.

[1] *The hope did not materialise. Declining to accept Sergeant Magoon's word, the commanding officer of Fort Connel delayed sending the troops until he had telegraphed Washington, D.C. for verification of Belle Boyd's bona fides and Jebediah Lincoln evaded them. They did, however, find Vera Gorr-Kauphin's body where he left it. J.T.E.*

Sharing the Kid's confidence in the slender 'blonde', Calamity had been willing to go along with the scheme until she saw Irène kill 'Devlin'. Then she had decided that she was better qualified than Belle to expose the false *Jan-Dark*. Instead of taking part in the discussion, she had halted slightly to the side and rear of her companions. While everybody else was preoccupied with one another, she made preparations for carrying out her intentions. First she had laid her kepi at her feet, coiling the Bannock *wampum* and the bandana she removed in its brim. Then she had drawn off and discarded the shirt to leave her naked at the waist. Having unbuckled and laid aside her gunbelt, she waited unnoticed for the moment when she must implement her amendment to the Rebel Spy's plan.

Startled comments rose from the men as Belle began to turn away. Even as she realised what was being said by the Kid and the scouts, a hand grasped the rear of her riding breeches waistband and she was jerked backwards with some force. Looking around, she received a wink and a cheerful grin from the person responsible.

'Why should *you* have all the fun?' Calamity inquired, striding by the 'blonde'. Coming to a halt some fifty yards from where Irène sat the palomino gelding, she stood with feet apart, arms akimbo and hands on hips in a posture redolent of defiance. Raising her voice, she yelled, 'All right, you god-damned, fat-butted, cock-sucking *Metis klooch*. If you're the *Jan-Dark*, let's see if you can kill *me*!'

Almost before the red head finished speaking, Irène responded to the challenge!

Even without realising she had no other choice, the way in which she was being addressed would have caused the *Metis* girl to attack. She had a temper as quick as Calamity's, but without the saving grace of humour. What was more, she had noticed the red head disrobing and, although she could hardly believe it could be, had anticipated what was being contemplated. So she had been giving her well-trained mount heel signals and it was moving restlessly on the spot, but ready to advance on her command.

Letting out a shrieking war whoop and swinging the head of

the lance forward, Irène set the palomino into motion. As she did so, she studied the red head and was puzzled. As far as she could see, the other was unarmed. One thing was certain, the challenger could not be hoping for help from her friends. Either Jerry Potts or Sandy Mackintosh would have warned her that such would not be permissible. Having made the challenge, she must stand or fall on her own merits.

With the horse picking up speed, Irène concluded that the other girl was meaning to spring aside at the last moment and try to grab the lance as it went by. If so, she was going to be disappointed. It was one tactic Irène had already learned to counter.

Such a possibility had never entered Calamity's head!

Measuring the rapidly decreasing distance between herself and her assailant with a practised gaze, the red head sent her right hand across to pull free the bull whip. A deft flick caused its lash to open out behind her. When her instincts told her the moment had come, she swung and sent it forward almost faster than the eye could follow. Showing how well she had learned to wield the whip, the length of rawhide 'popper' at the tip of the plaited lash gave an explosive crack and caught the palomino on the nose.

The sound and sudden pain caused the animal to squeal in agonised terror. Arching its back, it tried to both stop and turn away. In doing so, it lost its footing and began to go down. Aided by the skill gained through a lifetime of riding, Irène not only contrived to throw herself clear, but alighted without falling or losing her hold on the lance. Staggering a few steps until she regained her equilibrium, she prepared to continue the attack on foot.

Having withdrawn the whip's lash after delivering the blow, Calamity sent it out again. She could have ripped the other girl's flesh to the bone, but did not aim in such a manner. Instead, she ensnared Irène's left nakle as it raised for a step and, giving a jerk, dumped the *Metis* over backwards.

In spite of being caught unawares, Irène's riding skill once again saved her from injury. Breaking her fall caused her to let go of the lance and it fell so the head stuck into the ground, but the handle tilted up at an angle. That she was not harmed showed in the way she almost immediately lurched into a sitting position and grabbed in an attempt to retrieve the weapon.

On the point of liberating the lash, Calamity changed her mind and pulled on the handle to drag Irène along the ground. Squealing in fury as she failed to regain possession of the lance, she jerked up her trapped leg and caught hold of the lash in both hands. Having done so, she freed her ankle and clung on to the plaited leather with all her strength. Using it to brace herself, she started to haul herself erect. Waiting until she was half way up, Calamity released the handle and dashed forward.

Feeling herself going down again and seeing her antagonist approaching, Irène once again broke her fall. As the red head bent with the intention of diving on her, she let go of the lash. Her hands dug into Calamity's hair, hauling forward, while she brought up her feet until they could thrust against the other's stomach. Sailing over in a half somersault, it was the red head's turn to come down and demonstrate an ability to reduce the impact. Forcing herself to continue rolling, she writhed around and, looking back, saw there was an urgent need to regain her feet without delay.

Having brought off a neat stomach throw, Irène was already rising. As she did so, her right hand went to the hilt of her knife. Bringing the weapon from its sheath, she held it Indian fashion with the blade protruding from below the heel of the fist. While not as effective as when the blade extended ahead of the thumb and forefinger, permitting hardly more than two kinds of blows, such a grip was still dangerous.

Oblivious of the rapt attention with which the group about the fire were watching what went on, Irène dashed into the attack. Up swung her right arm, with the intention of delivering a powerful downwards chop aimed at the back of the red head's shoulder. Still rising, Calamity shot out her right hand. She did not attempt to catch the descending wrist. Instead, she interposed the forearm so the knife just passed over it and was halted. Bringing up her left hand with the intention of helping the right, she received a savage punch in the right side from Irène's left fist. Gasping in pain, she only just managed to thrust the knife away as she was sent staggering.

Hissing more like an enraged bobcat than a human being, Irène followed the red head and essayed a backhand horizontal slash. A desperate bound carried Calamity not only clear of the blow but in the direction of the lance. Snatching it up in both hands, she swivelled and jabbed at her approaching opponent. Now it was the *Metis'* turn to be on the defensive, but she showed no sign of being frightened by the prospect. Jumping away from the needle sharp diamond section head as it lunged in her direction, her lips were drawn back in a snarl of hatred made even more hideous by the effect of the war paint.

The girls circled each other for several seconds, with Calamity jabbing and swinging the lance and Irène unable to do anything more than use her agility to evade it. Soon their breath was hissing in short pants and perspiration flowed freely. Too freely as far as the *Metis* was concerned. While her wig remained in place in spite of all that had happened so far, streaks appeared as the walnut juice stain used to darken her skin began to be washed away.

While it appeared on the surface that the red head had the advantage, she was unaccustomed to handling the lance and its length, ideal when mounted as it was intended to be used, made it cumbersome to wield when on foot. Realising her difficulties, she took a desperate chance. Making what appeared to be another jab, she threw the weapon at the *Metis*. As Irène's right hand knocked it aside, Calamity plunged forward in a dive to tackle her around the knees and toppled her on to her back. Losing her hold of the knife as her shoulders thudded on to the ground, her reaction to being in such close contact with her opponent was purely feminine. Almost of their own volition, her fingers sank into the sweat-soddened red curls. Tugging with all her might, she put such vigour into the effort that she hauled Calamity along her own recumbent body.

Feeling as if the top of her skull was bursting into flames and on the point of being torn away, the red head's response was just as instinctive. Her own hands went for hair, but what she grabbed was a well made wig. It came away in her grasp. As she was flinging it aside to snatch at the genuine article, she heard startled and furious yells from the Indians.

As if in echo to the chiefs' shouts, Calamity heard Cavallier yelling something in his native tongue. Being unable to speak French, she did not know what the words were:

'Die, you English bastard!'

CHAPTER SEVENTEEN

THE *JAN-DARK* HASN'T COME

Noticing how Irène Beauville's body stain was beginning to wash away as a result of her exertions, Arnaud Cavallier was aware of the danger arising from its removal. He knew that if she should be exposed as a fake, his own life would be placed in jeopardy. Those six arrogant young Indian war chiefs would show no mercy to a man who had tried to mislead them and, by doing so, would make them a laughing-stock among the members of their respective nations when – as he did not doubt Jerry Potts and Sandy Mackintosh would see it did – the news was passed around.

When *le Loup-Garou* saw Calamity Jane and the bogus *Jan-Dark* crashing to the ground and how the latter acted on landing, he guessed what would happen. So his right hand was reaching for the hilt of the J. Russell & Co. 'Green River' knife, a weapon with which he was more proficient than his Colt Civilian Model Peacemaker. If he had doubted his summations, they were verified by the Indians' response to the sight of Irène's wig being torn away to expose her short tawny coloured hair. Furiously indignant yells burst from them and they turned their angry faces in his direction.

To give Cavallier his due, cowardice could not be listed among his many faults. Faced with not only the ruination of all his dreams, but also death – or at least arrest, which was almost certain to end in his execution – he did not hesitate in deciding how he wished to meet his end. There was also, he considered, a slight possibility that he might yet salvage something from the deteriorated situation. If not, he preferred to go out fighting and his savage nature demanded that he was avenged upon the man who had done most to bring about his downfall.

'Die, you English bastard!' *le Loup-Garou* roared in French, snatching the knife from its sheath and springing towards Captain Patrick Reeder.

Having drawn similar conclusions to those of his leader, Roland Boniface arrived at a different solution to his dilemma. He had no desire to die. Wanting to escape and being cognisant of the difficulties doing so entailed, he decided his best chance lay in using the slender 'blonde' as a hostage. Once he had a grip on her and his knife at her throat, he could compel Jerry Potts and Sandy Mackintosh to protect him from the Indians. In doing so, they would also be too occupied to oppose his departure themselves.

With that in mind, the *Metis* sent his right hand to his knife and lunged in Belle Boyd's direction with the left stretching out to catch hold of her.

Although Calamity heard the commotion, she paid no attention to it. Already she was aware that the bogus *Jan-Dark* was as strong an antagonist as she had ever encountered. What was more, unlike almost every other brawl in which she had participated, this would be a fight to the death as far as her opponent was concerned. She could not spare as much as a glance to try to find out how her friends were faring. Instead, as she just managed to move her face far enough to avoid the bite aimed at it and was rolled from the upper position, she gave thought to doing something more effective than trying to make Irène's hair suffer the same fate as the wig.

During their association, the Remittance Kid had studied and formed an accurate assessment of Cavallier's character. From what he had learned, he had been able to make an accurate guess at how the *Metis* would react in the kind of situation that was developing. Aware that he would be the target, he had not allowed himself to become engrossed in watching the fight to the exclusion of everything else. Keeping *le Loup-Garou* under observation from the corner of the eye, he had seen the 'green River' knife leave its sheath and was already drawing his *badik* when the attack was launched.

As Irène had done, Cavallier was handling his knife in the Indian fashion. Hoping to take his intended victim unawares, he swung it above his right shoulder for the powerful downwards slash which could prove so effective. Or, depending upon the circumstances, so dangerous to the one making it. Just an instant too late, he discovered that he was not achieving the surprise he wanted. Swinging around and stepping to meet him, the Kid was producing the *badik* in the manner of a gun fighter performing a cross draw. Unable to halt the impetuous rush, or even try to turn aside, *le Loup-Garou* began to bring the knife over and down in a desperate bid to sink home its blade.

Startled exclamations broke from the two scouts as they realised what Boniface had in mind. Before either could begin to bring his rifle into a position where it could be used to deter the *Metis*, Belle took the matter out of their hands. Seeing her start to turn her back on him, Boniface assumed – as he had anticipated might happen – she intended to escape his attentions by running away.

Such, however, was not the case.

Looking over her left shoulder, Belle bent forward and dropped her hands to the ground. Although Boniface believed that, instead of flight, she was trying to pick up the revolver she had laid aside when meaning to challenge Irène, he discovered he was once again in error with regards to her intentions. Taking her weight on the hands, she propelled both legs into the air and thrust them backwards. The soles of her Hessian boots rammed into the centre of his chest. Such was the strength of her slender, wiry frame that he was sent staggering backwards and the knife flew from his hand. He did not go down and, snarling with rage as he managed to halt the involuntary retreat, he snatched at the Colt 1860 Army revolver in his open topped cavalry pattern holster.

Sharing Calamity's awareness of the risks involved in trying to catch the descending arm with one hand, the Kid also employed his left forearm to block the blow. While doing so, he directed the *badik* in the manner to which its design was ideally suited. Held horizontally, the 'butterfly' blade shot forward to pass between Cavallier's left ribs. Combined with its recipient's impetus, the force of the 'pinch grip' thrust caused the knife to penetrate the chest cavity to the depth of thumb and forefinger. Killed as the razor sharp steel ripped open his heart, *le Loup-Garou* went down. With him died his dream of establishing an independent *Metis* nation over which he would have made himself a dictatorial ruler.

Still watching Boniface as she was dropping her feet to the ground, Belle threw herself sideways in a rolling dive. Her right hand closed on the ivory handle of the revolver which had been presented to her during the War Between The States by the Confederate arms' manufacturers, Dance & Bros., of Columbia, Texas. Jerking it from its contoured holster in passing, she ended her roll on her back. Sitting up, she grasped the smooth butt – modelled on that of the Colt 1851 Navy and, arguably, the finest pointing grip ever fitted to a revolver – in both hands for greater steadiness and, drawing back the hammer with her thumbs, sighted along the seven and a half inches round barrel.

With Boniface's Army Colt clearing leather and starting to turn in her direction, the Rebel Spy squeezed the Dance's trigger. Flying to the point at which it was aimed, the .36 calibre round soft head bullet made its entry in the centre of his forehead to kill him instantly and burst out at the back of his skull. Although his last effort before death took him was to fire a shot, it flew harmlessly into the woodland beyond the edge of the clearing.

Cocking the Dance as she came to her feet, Belle looked around and decided she had had no need to do so. To her relief, she discovered that the Kid was unharmed. The blade of his *badik* was smothered in blood along its entire length and Cavallier sprawled motionless at his feet. None of the Indians was displaying hostility. Having looked around when the two *Metis* had launched the attacks upon herself and the Englishmen, they were returning their attention to where Calamity and Irène were continuing to fight without a thought for anything except one another.

'Let's stop them, Rem!' Belle suggested, coming to her feet.

'Leave them be, Colonel Boyd!' Mackintosh ordered and Jerry Potts nodded vehement agreement. 'Yon lassie of your's called the play and she's got to see it through – And she'd better win, so the Indians will know for sure the *Jan-Dark* hasn't come.'

Much as doing so went against the grain, the Rebel Spy and the Kid accepted the scout's assessment of the situation. Standing side by side, they watched as savage and vicious a fight as either had ever witnessed.

For the next fifteen minutes without a pause, Calamity and Irène went at each other with complete and unabated fury. Rolling over and over locked in each other's grasp, kneeling to trade punches and slaps indiscriminately at faces, shoulders, breasts and stomachs, coming to their feet to punch, kick, or wrestle, they went across the clearing from side to side and back in the direction of the fire. Neither could gain more than a brief ascendancy throughout the whole period, being so evenly matched in size, strength, weight and skill.

If Irène had expected her not inconsiderable knowledge of *savate* would give her an advantage, she was soon dissuaded. During the visit to New Orleans Calamity had mentioned to Cavallier, she had been embroiled in conflict with a girl who employed such methods and was able to cope with it. Nor did the red head's training in using her fists stand her in as good stead as it had against her opponents during the brawl at the Worn Out Tie Saloon. She landed some good punches on the *Metis*, but received almost as many equally well thrown in return.

Attaining the upper position after a vigorous period of thrashing over and over on the ground in a wild mill of flailing or intertwining arms and legs, Irène managed to press her left knee into the supine Calamity's stomach and her right fist clawed up her knife. Writhing desperately to try to break the pin, the red head grabbed for and caught the *Metis*' wrist in both hands before she could bring the retrieved weapon into use. Grinding with the knee, Irène sank her left fingers and thumb like the talons of an eagle into Calamity's right breast, crushing and twisting the mound of flesh savagely.

In spite of the terrible torment being inflicted upon her, the red head retained some semblance of conscious thought. While she put her left hand to trying to drag the fingers from her bosom, the right continued to cling to the wrist and hold the knife away. Shaking her head from side to side in agony, something familiar nearby caught her eye and caused her to remove the left hand from its abortive task. Clawing wildly, her fingers found and enfolded the plaited leather of the bull whip.

Grasping it where the two foot long handle joined the lash, she raised and swung it to catch her assailant at the side of the head with the counterweight knob on the end.

Although the blow was not delivered with Calamity's full strength, it arrived hard enough when combined with a surging, back arching heave, to dislodge Irène. Thrown clear of the red head, she did not drop the knife. They came to their feet almost simultaneously. Swaying in exhaustion, croaking in their desperate attempts to replenish tormented lungs with air, they stood on spread apart legs for a few seconds. Then, as the whip slipped from Calamity's grasp, Irène gave what should have been a shriek of rage – but which emerged as a whistling gasp – and, raising the knife, staggered forward.

Instinct rather than thoughtful planning caused Calamity's response, but it proved nonetheless effective for that. Placing the thumb of her left hand along the back of the right and forming a hollow U-shape with her fingers, she threw them up. As Irène's wrist descended into them, they closed about it and, twisting her body aside, she jerked downwards. Missing its intended target, the *Metis* could do nothing to halt the now undesirable descent and it curved around to bury the blade deep into her own stomach. Giving as near a scream of agony as her depleted lungs could utter, she tore herself free from the red head's grasp. With her hands trying to withdraw the weapon, she staggered onwards for a few steps. Then her legs buckled and she fell forward to drive it in again.

Turning and swaying, Calamity stared at Irène for a moment. Raising her eyes, she saw Belle, the Kid and the two scouts running towards her. Her last thought as she collapsed, fainting with exhaustion, was that the Indians now knew the *Jan-Dark* was an impostor and the threat of a mass uprising of Indians and *Metis* was at an end.

THE END

APPENDIX ONE

Wanting a son and learning that his wife, Electra, could not have any more children, Vincent Charles Boyd had given his only daughter, Belle,[1] a thorough training in several subjects not normally regarded as being necessary for a wealthy Southron girl's upbringing. At seventeen, she could ride – astride or side-saddle – as well as any of her male neighbours, men who were to help provide the Confederate States with its superlative cavalry. In addition, she was a skilled performer with an *épée de combat* or a sabre,[2] an excellent shot with any kind of firearm and an expert at *savate*, the French form of foot and fist boxing. All of which were soon to be very useful accomplishments for her.

Shortly before the commencement of the War Between The States, a mob of pro-Union supporters had stormed the Boyd plantation. Before they were driven off by the family's Negro servants, they had murdered Belle's parents and set fire to her home. She was wounded in the fighting and, on recovering, joined her cousin, Rose Greenhow,[3] who was operating a successful spy ring. Wanting to find the leaders of the mob, Belle had not been content to remain in one place. Instead, she had undertaken the dangerous task of delivering other agents' information to the Confederate authorities. Adding an ability

[1] *According to the researches of fictionist genealogist Philip José Farmer, q.v., Belle Boyd was the grand aunt of Jane, Lady Greystoke, née Porter, whose biography is recorded in the* TARZAN OF THE APES *series of biographies by Edgar Rice Burroughs. J.T.E.*

[2] *An* épée de combat *is used mainly for thrusting when on foot and the sabre primarily for slashing from the back of a horse. J.T.E.*

[3] *Some details of Rose Greenhow's career are given in :* KILL DUSTY FOG! *J.T.E.*

at disguise and dialects to her accomplishments, she had gained such proficiency that she won the sobriquet, the Rebel Spy. She had also graduated to handling more important and risky assignments. On two, she had worked with Captain Dustine Edward Marsden 'Dusty' Fog, *q.v.*,[4] and a third had brought her first contact with the Ysabel Kid.[5] However, she had not concluded her quest for vengeance upon the murderers of her parents until shortly after the War had ended.[6]

While the 'Yankees' might have had reason to hate the Rebel Spy when she was engaged upon her duties against them, the majority had had no cause to feel other than gratitude towards her after peace was reached at the meeting in the Appomattox Court House. On signing the oath of allegiance to the Union, she had been enrolled in the United States' Secret Service. Despite all the trouble she had given that organisation during the hostilities, she served it loyally and with efficiency. Her participation in thwarting a plot to assassinate President Ulysses Simpson Grant had prevented friction, possibly another war, between the Northern and Southern States.[7] Assisted by Martha 'Calamity Jane' Canary, *q.v.*, and the lady outlaw, Belle Starr, she had brought an end to the reign of terror created by a murderous gang of female outlaws.[8] With the aid of General Jackson Baines 'Ole Devil' Hardin, C.S.A.'s[9] floating outfit, she had broken up the Brotherhood For Southern Freedom.[10] After having helped avert diplomatic difficulties with the Republic of Haiti in the same company,[11] and wrecking two

[4] *Told in :* THE COLT AND THE SABRE *and* THE REBEL SPY. *J.T.E.*

[5] *Told in :* THE BLOODY BORDER. *J.T.E.*

[6] *Told in :* BACK TO THE BLOODY BORDER. *J.T.E. Details of Captain Dustine Edward Marsden 'Dusty' Fog's and the Ysabel Kid's careers are given in the author's* CIVIL WAR *and* FLOATING OUT-FIT *series. J.T.E.*

[7] *Told in :* THE HOODED RIDERS. *J.T.E.*

[8] *Told in :* THE BAD BUNCH. *J.T.E.*

[9] *Details of General Jackson Baines 'Ole Devil' Hardin, C.S.A.'s younger days are given in the author's* OLE DEVIL HARDIN *series. He also appears in the* CIVIL WAR *and* FLOATING OUTFIT *series. J.T.E.*

[10] *Told in :* TO ARMS! TO ARMS! IN DIXIE!

[11] *Told in :* SET A-FOOT. *J.T.E.*

attempts by European anarchists to create hostility between the U.S.A. and Great Britain,[12] she had joined forces once more with Belle Starr and the Ysabel Kid when involved in the efforts of the international master criminal Octavius Xavier 'the Ox' Guillemot to gain possession of James Bowie's knife.[13]

[12] *How the first plot was foiled is told in :* THE REMITTANCE KID. *J.T.E.*
[13] *Told in :* THE QUEST FOR BOWIE BLADE. *J.T.E.*

APPENDIX TWO

Deserted by her husband, Charlotte Canary decided the best way she could assure a future for her children was to leave them in a St Louis convent and head west to seek her fortune. However, there had been too much of her lively, reckless spirit in her eldest daughter, Martha Jane. Rebelling against the strict life being imposed by the nuns, the girl had celebrated her sixteenth birthday by running away. Hiding in one of Cecil 'Dobe' Killem's freight wagons, she had been twelve miles from the city before she was discovered. She might have been sent back to the convent if the outfit's cook had not been too drunk to work. One of the things the girl had learned from the nuns was cooking. The meal she had prepared was so good that Killem had yielded to her request to be taken to Wichita, Kansas, where she claimed to have an aunt who would give her a home.

Before the outfit had reached its destination, raiding Sioux warriors who had wiped out two other trains failed to locate them. What was more, the goods they were carrying had been sold so profitably that the whole crew received a bonus. Regarding the girl as a good luck charm, they had prevailed upon their employer to let her stay with them when the aunt proved to be a figment of her imagination. Not that Killem, having taken a liking to the spunky youngster, had taken much persuading.

At first, Martha had helped the cook and carried out other menial duties. She graduated to driving and soon there was nothing she could not do in that line of work. Not only could she drive the six-horse team of a Conestoga wagon, she had learned to use a long lashed bull whip as an inducement to activity or a weapon, to handle firearms with skill and generally take care of herself on the open ranges of the West. Nor did her self-reliance end there. Visiting saloons with the rest of the outfit, she had frequently been called upon to defend herself against the objections of the female denizens who resented her trespassing on their domain. Leading a much more active and healthy life than the saloongirls, as well as having been taught the rudiments of unarmed combat, she had only once been beaten in a fight;[1] although the lady outlaw, Belle Starr, *q.v.*, had held her to a hard fought draw when they first met.[2]

Courageous, loyal to her friends, happy-go-lucky and generous to such an extent that she had deliberately lost a saloon she inherited jointly with a professional gambler, Frank Derringer,[3] the girl had a penchant for becoming involved in dangerous and precarious situations. Visiting New Orleans, she had acted as a decoy to lure the Strangler, a notorious mass murderer, to his doom.[4] While helping deliver supplies to an Army post, she had fought with a female professional pugilist and rescued an officer captured by Indians.[5] In Texas, she had helped with a wave of cattle stealing which was threatening to cause a range war.[6] What started out as a peaceful journey on a stagecoach ended with her helping to capture the criminals who robbed it.[7] Going to visit a ranch left to her by her father in the company of the Ysabel Kid, *q.v.*, she had nearly been killed when a rival claimant had had her fastened to a log which was to be sent through a circular saw.[8] Among her friends, she counted the members of General Jackson Baines 'Ole Devil' Hardin C.S.A.'s legendary floating outfit, *q.v.*; being on exceptionally intimate terms with the handsome blond giant, Mark Counter.[9]

[1] *The story of how the defeat came about is told in the* 'Better Than Calamity' *episode of* THE WILDCATS.
[2] *Told in the* 'Bounty On Belle Starr's Scalp' *episode of* TROUBLED RANGE. *J.T.E.*
[3] *Told in :* COLD DECK, HOT LEAD. *J.T.E.*
[4] *Told in :* THE BULL WHIP BREED. *J.T.E.*
[5] *Told in :* TROUBLE TRAIL. *J.T.E.*
[6] *Told in :* THE COW THIEVES. *J.T.E.*
[7] *Told in :* CALAMITY SPELLS TROUBLE. *J.T.E.*
[8] *Told in :* WHITE STALLION, RED MARE. *J.T.E.*
[9] *Calamity Jane's meeting with Mark Counter, other than those referred to in Footnotes One, Two and Eleven are told in,* THE BAD BUNCH, THE FORTUNE HUNTERS, TERROR VALLEY *and* GUNS IN THE NIGHT. *J.T.E.*

She had also, on one memorable occasion, posed as the wife of its leader, Captain Dustine Edward Marsden 'Dusty' Fog, *q.v.*, and assisted him to deal with a band of land grabbers.[10] Later, she participated in a big game hunt during which she was kidnapped.[11]

Because of her penchant for finding trouble and becoming involved in brawls, the girl had acquired the sobriquet by which she was soon known throughout the west and beyond.

People called her 'Calamity Jane'.

[10] *Told in the* 'A Wife For Dusty Fog' *episode of* THE SMALL TEXAN. *J.T.E.*
[11] *Told in :* THE BIG HUNT. *J.T.E.*

APPENDIX THREE

As in the British game of pontoon, the object of the game of blackjack is to get a higher count – the total value of cards in hand – than the 'banker', who also deals, up to but not exceeding twenty-one. The jack, king and queen each score ten and the ace, at the player's discretion, one or eleven. Should the player draw cards taking his total over twenty-one, he sacrifices any chance to beat, or tie with, the banker. The main differences between pontoon and blackjack are:

(1) In pontoon the first and second cards are dealt face down. In blackjack, the banker deals each of the players' first card face down, but turns his first face up. Then he deals the second card to each player face up, but leaves his second face down.

(2) In pontoon, after receiving the second card, the player can either 'stick' with what he has, 'twist' and obtain another card or more to bring his total closer to twenty-one without any increase on the amount wagered upon the first two, wherein he receives the additional cards face up; or he can 'buy', increase the wager, and is dealt the additional cards face down. In blackjack, one can only 'buy' extra cards and these are dealt face up.

In a private game, unless the rules stipulate otherwise, any player dealt a 'natural' – an ace and any card valued at ten – is entitled to take over the 'bank' and becomes the dealer. If allowed by the rules, the following alternative bets are allowed:

(a) 'Insurance': made when the dealer's up-faced card is an ace. A player may elect to wager up to one half of his original stake that the 'banker's' next card will be a ten, jack, queen, or king. If a 'natural' eventuates, the bank collects the player's original bet, but pays out 'insurance' at two to one.

(b) 'Double down': if a player's count for two cards is nine, ten, or eleven, he may double his bet, but must turn all his cards face up and can only draw one more card face down, unless he has a count of nine and draws a deuce. In this case, he may double the doubled bet and draw again.

(c) Splitting pairs: when the player is dealt two cards of the same value – it can only be two jacks, queens, or kings, not two of different denominations which score ten – on the initial round, he may 'split' them and play each as an individual hand. If he does, he has to duplicate his original bet on the second hand. Should he make another pair with the cards he receives, he is entitled to split again.

In any game, the 'bank' always plays last. If no players have survived, he merely takes in all the bets without continuing himself. If players are left, he must face his 'hole' card and, should his count be less than sixteen, he must take another. Then he can decide, as he must if the original count was seventeen or over, whether to try to get closer to twenty-one. He wins from all those whose score is lower than that upon which he stands, loses to those who are higher, up to twenty-one, but any which tie 'stand off', no one collects, no one loses. In the event of the banker being dealt a 'natural', he takes all stake monies without further action, the exception being any player who had also been dealt a 'natural' and whose bet stands off.

In casino games, where the house is also the 'bank' regardless of players' 'naturals', 'propositions' on the following lines are offered:

(1) Two nines and three aces in one hand pays a bonus of twenty-five dollars on any bet larger than the limit's minimum, the latter stipulation applying in all cases.

(2) Ace–jack of spades pays a five dollar bonus.

(3) 6–7–8 of the same suit pays five dollars extra.

(4) A seven-card score of twenty-one or less pays a fifty dollar bonus, but the bet *must* be doubled on the last card drawn.

The above are only a few examples. Others and bonuses of different values are provided and stipulated in every casino.

DOC LEROY, M.D. by J. T. EDSON

Marvin Eldridge Leroy had been on the point of leaving home to attend medical college when bushwack lead cut down his parents. Although he was forced to abandon his plans and take a job as a cowhand, he never forgot his ambition of following in his father's footsteps and becoming a qualified doctor. Working on ranches, or driving cattle over the northbound trails to the Kansas railheads, he took every opportunity to continue his medical studies – and gradually he earned a reputation as a doctor . . . people even called him 'Doc'. There were men, women and children alive who would have been dead without his assistance. There were also men who had died at his hands – experience had made him lightning fast with a Colt . . .

0 552 10406 x   50p

OLE DEVIL AT SAN JACINTO by J. T. EDSON

In 1835, the oppressions of Presidente Antonio Lopez de Santa Anna had driven the colonists in Texas to rebellion. Major General Sam Houston, realizing that his small force could only hope to face the vast Mexican army when conditions were favourable, had ordered a tactical withdrawal to the east.

At last, on Thursday, April 21st, 1836, Houston decided that the time had come to make a stand. The Mexican Army, fifteen hundred strong, was on the banks of the San Jacinto river: Houston, with half that number, launched the attack that would decide the future of Texas.

0 552 10505 8   60p

SET A-FOOT by J. T. EDSON

In the days of the open range, a cowhand's most vital possesion was his horse. When a cowhand left a spread with no mount of his own, the rancher would usually allow him to borrow one from the remuda, but sometimes, if they parted on bad terms, this loan would not be made . . . There was no greater disgrace for a cowhand than to be set a-foot. It meant he was untrustworthy, and once the news got around, he would find it almost impossible to get another job. So when a cowhand was set a-foot, there was usually trouble – and often gun play.

Dusty Fog knew this, but he still set a-foot the man he blamed for the loss of an OD Connected trail herd and the injuries to some of the crew. He knew too that the cowhand he was disgracing was real fast with a gun – and knew that gun might be turned against him. The cowhand's only name was Waco . . .

0 552 10660 7   65p

CHANCY by LOUIS L'AMOUR

When Otis Chancy started out he had nothing. Then fate dealt him four of a kind – all bullets. The young drifter played his hand for keeps, taking his chances against crooked sheriffs, deadly gunmen, and renegade Indians. He fought his way along back trails and through wide-open cow towns, learning the bitter rules as he went along. And when the smoke cleared away he stood alone, boss of his own cattle outfit – but the game was far from over . . .

0 552 08007 1   65p